DISCRETION

SCATTERED STARS: EVASION BOOK 2

DISCRETION

SCATTERED STARS: EVASION BOOK 2

GLYNN STEWART

FAOLAN'S PEN
PUBLISHING

faolanspen.com

This edition published in 2022 by:

Faolan's Pen Publishing Inc.

22 King St. S, Suite 300

Waterloo, Ontario

N2J 1N8 Canada

ISBN-13: 978-1-989674-27-7 (print)

A record of this book is available from Library and Archives Canada.

Printed in the United States of America

1 2 3 4 5 6 7 8 9 10

First edition

First printing: July 2022

Illustration by Elias Stern

Faolan's Pen Publishing logo is a registered trademark of Faolan's Pen Publishing Inc.

Read more books from Glynn Stewart at faolanspen.com

1

SHOPPING HAD NEVER BEEN a major part of EB's life. Then he'd acquired a teenaged daughter, and every trip aboard a space station ended up either going shopping *with* Trace or *for* Trace.

Today's trip aboard Nigahog's primary orbital station was primarily business. Captain Evridiki "EB" Bardacki, shareholder and commander of the armed merchant ship *Evasion*, was scheduled to meet with a potential client on the station.

At that moment, however, the solidly built fifty-five-year-old captain was watching his chief engineer and his adoptive daughter poke through the sample holograms for educational artificial stupids— the semi-sentient programs that they would need to help Trace keep up her education aboard ship.

He trusted his engineer, Ginerva "Ginny" Anderson, to make sure that the software they picked up served their needs. Trace would *pick* it —the student needed to be able to tolerate the teacher, after all—but Ginny would make sure the blonde thirteen-year-old picked one that would work.

EB was spending most of *his* energy and time watching the crowds around them. It hadn't been that long since Trace, now Tracy *Bardacki* according to the paperwork he'd filed, had been sought by every bounty hunter in this civilization-forsaken chunk of space in the Beyond.

The person who'd set that bounty was now rotting in a Nigahog high-security prison, but Nigahog was the center of operations for the local Trackers' Guild. In a region with limited maps and interstellar communication or cooperation, the only means of law enforcement between star systems was the bounty hunter—a situation with definite flaws, in EB's now-educated opinion.

His headware pinged with a message from his engineer as he surveyed the mall.

I've got this, you know. There's a jewelry store over there you should check out.

Ginny's message came with a localized highlight that marked the store in question in EB's vision. The computer in his brain, his headware, was well integrated with his vision and optic nerves.

It couldn't, however, explain hints to particularly obtuse starship captains.

And why would I be checking out a jewelry store?

The store looked less gaudy than many he'd seen. It was the kind of sedate-looking place he *would* go if he was searching for jewelry, but so far as EB knew, he *wasn't*.

Are you planning on being a single space dad forever?

EB was quite sure that his engineer was making a specific point, but he sighed and shook his head at her as she looked back over her shoulder at him.

I'm not. His silent message flicked across the space between him as he arched an eyebrow at Ginny. The spiky-haired engineer was closer to his age than to Trace's—barely—but was of a height with the teenager.

And not because Trace was overly tall for her age, either.

That's my point, yes. You and Vexer are her dads. Might want to lock him down before someone gets twitchy.

Now EB got her point, and his arched eyebrow turned into a cautionary headshake.

Vena "Vexer" Dolezal was *Evasion*'s navigator, a not-quite-refugee from a feudal system where even highly trained technical professionals were still mostly serfs, bound to the nobles who'd paid for their training.

He was also EB's long-standing on-again, off-again, boyfriend, a relationship that had solidified with the involvement of Trace. But *boyfriend* was enough for everyone involved, so far as EB knew.

They were gay space dads together and that was plenty. Even if *Ginny* didn't think so.

He walked over to join his daughter and engineer as his headware produced a soft chime only he could hear.

"Time, ladies," he told them. "Are you two good to keep poking around while I go to my meeting?"

"Unless you've seen any dangerous bounty hunters lurking in the shadows to whisk us away, the only risk is Trace spending all of your money."

Ginny's comment drew a sharp glance from the teenager.

"I have *some* discipline," she observed.

"When you choose to."

EB sighed at them both.

"We're here for a teaching stupid. Nothing else."

"You're loosing a teenager on a station mall and expecting her to buy one thing? Brave man."

Trace ignored the engineer and grinned at her dad.

"I mean, *some* kind of allowance or budget would be nice," she told him.

After everything Trace had been through to end up with them, it was good to see her being an ordinary teenager. EB was *well* aware she was using that against him...but she was doing that because it *worked*.

"Fine!"

THE FIRST TIME EB had met Lear Naumov, they'd been trying to pretend that the older Nigahog man was a normal civil bureaucrat. EB had *suspected*, even before the "cargo" had turned out to be a smuggling mission, but they'd met in a quiet coffee shop on a private corporate station.

This time…this time, Naumov was making no pretenses. One of the reasons EB was comfortable leaving Ginny and Trace to their own devices was that they were on Nigahog's main orbital *fortress*.

While the hollowed-out armed asteroid paled in comparison to the defenses EB would expect in more-civilized space, it stood head and shoulders above many defenses he'd seen out there in the Beyond.

Nigahog was well outside the roughly three-thousand-light-year sphere considered *civilized space*, the region mapped and cataloged by the interstellar megacorporations. Out there, the only maps were the ones people sold you—and without maps and the nova points they contained, a ship couldn't jump between the stars.

But these worlds still had resources. The Nigahog System, with some hundred and fifty million souls, was one of the more prosperous in the region—as shown in its orbital defenses, its complex mix of elected government and control by trade guilds, and, EB suspected, an *extremely* capable intelligence service.

He'd guessed that Lear Naumov was an important member of that service when they'd met before. Now, as EB good-humoredly tolerated the trained glares of Nigahog Orbital Security Command troopers and approached the entrance to one of the battle station's many secured areas, he was quite certain of it.

"This area is off-limits, ser," the NOSC sergeant in front of the door told him. The woman had a hand on her stunner, in case he underestimated the sincerity of her message.

"I know that, Sergeant," EB confirmed. "I have an appointment."

He flicked her the data card with the information and directions he'd received. The digital file contained multiple layers of verification and authorization he could barely tell were in it, let alone access.

The stony-faced commander of the four armed guards outside the door—overkill, unless NOSC's automation and artificial stupid security were far worse than EB thought they were—hopefully could access those authorizations.

"Ah. Captain Bardacki," she greeted him, with absolutely no warmth or enthusiasm in her voice. "Your authorization checks out."

She considered him like he'd grown approximately ninety extra legs.

"Your weapon, Captain," she snapped.

EB considered arguing, but from the sergeant's body language, he was lucky she was letting him through at all. Whatever this section was, it wasn't the regular no-civilians-allowed section of the station like, say, the plasma-cannon turrets.

He unbelted his stunner and blaster and proffered the weapon to the noncommissioned officer. She briskly slung it over her left shoulder, then gestured for him to follow her.

Whatever commands she'd given her fire team and the door were silently transmitted from her headware, but the three other NOSC troopers remained outside and the door slid open ahead of her.

"I didn't catch your name, Sergeant."

Normally, the woman's headware would have been transmitting a beacon that told him her name, rank, serial number, preferred pronouns and any other pertinent information she wanted. A soldier on duty wouldn't usually have much in the last category, but all her beacon was currently transmitting was a confirmation that she was a E-5 Sergeant in the Nigahog Orbital Security Command.

"I didn't give it," she replied. "Follow. Don't talk."

EB obeyed, glancing around him as he did. Despite the excessive security at the door, this section of the station looked like nothing so much as a law firm's office. The hallway was well lit and lined with evenly spaced doors.

Presumably, if he had the correct authorization, the local beacons he could sense but not access would tell him who was in each of the offices—but there were no visible nameplates, no publicly accessible beacons, and no windows into the offices themselves.

The whole quiet section of the station *screamed* Intelligence Operations to him, but he suspected that the locals thought they were being subtle.

2

LEAR NAUMOV'S office was at the far end of the hallway, past at least three dozen other identical doors. EB was given no warning, either. The nameless NOSC sergeant stopped and gestured him to a door before leaning against the wall opposite it.

"Go in."

EB arched an eyebrow at her, but she said nothing else, just settling against the wall like she was planning on being there awhile.

Trying not to let her get to him, he approached the door and received a verification request in his headware. He replied with the same file that he'd sent the guards and waited.

Even a door should have had enough processing power to make validating his identity a matter of moments, and he began to worry after he'd been standing there for easily ten seconds. Only the fact that the sergeant didn't seem to be preparing to shoot him seemed positive.

Eventually, with no notification or other response, the door slid open.

"Come in, Captain," a familiar voice told him. "I'm glad you could make it."

"You said you needed to meet somewhere more secure than my

ship," EB replied, stepping through the door into an office that failed to live down to his expectations.

He'd been expecting a utilitarian box, with plain metal walls and maybe some filing cabinets for actual paperwork. Instead, he stepped into what appeared to be a sailing ship in the middle of a green-tinged ocean.

Of course, the deck under his feet was still metal roughened for anti-slip, and there was no wind or even moisture. The illusion was shallow at best, but it was more than he'd expected.

The only thing that looked like it belonged on that sailing ship was the desk, carved from some raw wood with a similar deep green tinge to the water and then sealed with varnish. Sitting *on* said desk was the man EB had come to meet, a small older gentleman wearing an amused smile.

"You have a very nice ship, Captain Bardacki; that's why we're having these conversations at all," Naumov pointed out. "Please, take a seat."

EB obeyed and an artificial stupid delivery bot rolled over to him with a coffee. The robot made no attempt to disguise its emergence from a door in the wall.

"And my presence was easier to conceal than other methods of contact might have been, but there was information and details I can't provide outside a location we control the security of."

"*We* being…"

At no point in either of their previous two meetings—aboard the corp station where Naumov had first tried to hire EB or aboard *Evasion* when Naumov had arranged *this* meeting—had the spy admitted who he worked for.

"Nigahog's government," Naumov replied drily.

"The one the Guilds own."

"The one that cooperates heavily with the institutions that are fundamental to the economic and cultural structure of our society. The one that runs the military and foreign relations."

"And you're not going to ever tell me more than that, are you?" EB asked.

"I owe you my life, Captain, but I'm not going to betray the confidences entrusted to me by the nature of my service. You can guess enough to serve the needs of the moment…and you can validate our money when the time comes.

"What more do you need?"

EB chuckled.

"Need, perhaps not," he conceded. "Curiosity is always difficult to sate. I don't like *no questions asked*, Em Naumov."

"And I will answer any and all question with regards to the job I want you to do. And you know who is behind the task. You don't need to know exact details of departments and job titles. Does it matter to you if I work for the Department of Agriculture or the Guild of Agronomists, after all?"

"I presume you wouldn't present yourself as from the Nigahog government if you were from one of the Guilds."

EB found the structure of Nigahog's government, where the Guilds acted as regulatory agencies, corporate alliances *and* an effectively coequal branch of the government, odd. But then, he came from Apollo, a world that was explicitly an oligarchy where only those in the highest tax bracket got to vote in planetary elections.

He was a long way from home and he had no grounds to throw stones.

"I would not," Naumov conceded. "But we are rather off-topic. How is the coffee?"

EB took a sip of the beverage. It was about what he expected for coffee in the Beyond: absolutely *terrible*. Any planet's varieties of the standard beverages—coffee, tea, wine, cola, et cetera—were heavily shaped by both the local soil and the strains imported.

Something about the region of the Beyond he'd traveled through had rendered their coffee uniformly atrocious—and EB was *not* a coffee connoisseur.

"It's fine," he told the spy. "You visited me on my ship, told me to meet you here and made all of the arrangements for us to have this absolutely secure meeting that is pretending to be on a sailing ship.

"It wasn't to thank me for saving your life, you're not the type for that, so what do you want to hire me for?"

Naumov waved a hand in concession. The same gesture conjured a holographic map of Nigahog and the handful of settled systems surrounding them.

"We spoke about the Estutmost System when we first met."

"I remember. Ongoing civil war, blockade by a third faction." EB studied the map and picked out the star. "Central government fighting communist farmers, while the space-habitating faction is trying to keep the neighbors from interfering."

"Speaking as one of said neighbors, I'm a bit offended by the Estutmost Spacers' assumption that we are an enemy," Naumov observed. "Speaking as a student of history, the Guilds' structure is surprisingly nonaggressive in terms of hostile mercantile colonialism.

"Mostly, in all honesty, because the Guilds don't want to pay the taxes to maintain the Extraterritorial Enforcement Agency at a level that could support colonialism on their part. We are quite isolationist, in truth."

"You're over a hundred light-years into the Beyond. Isolationism is assumed, isn't it?"

"You have a point." Naumov waved his hand and the Estutmost System expanded to show its six planets and its outer asteroid belt.

"Frankly, there are four times as many people in Nigahog as there are in Estutmost. None of our neighbors have more than forty or fifty million people. Humanity is sparse out here, and we really don't need to look past our own star system for resources of any kind."

"But you are paying attention to the neighbors."

"Of course. Hence this meeting." Naumov now zoomed in on the planet Estutmost, technically Estutmost III, and its four moons.

"The internal divisions of the Estutmost System have made them vulnerable to economic pressure from us, from Icem, from Blowry... Their division has cost them over the years, but overall, no one here is trying to impose on others. We all have too much going on in our space."

"But you want to get involved in their civil war anyway."

"Yes." Naumov took a sip of his own coffee and studied the planet now hovering above his desk. "The Board controls the northern half of the settled continent, and the Cinnead—the Clan—controls the southern half. While there are farms and agriculture north of this mountain range"—he indicated an east-west line of mountains—"the vast majority of the cultivated terraformed land is south of the Snowdens."

EB had information on most of the planets around Nigahog in his headware now. They'd acquired maps by various means over the last month—none of them technically illegal, given the existence of salvage rights—and maps were more than just pictures of star lanes.

Estutmost was a rarity out in the Beyond: a habitable world that resisted human crops more than humans themselves. EB wouldn't have taken on the challenge of eking agriculture from soil fundamentally lacking in key nutrients himself, but Estutmost's people had.

It helped that the native animal life *was* edible, that the planet was otherwise gorgeous, and the system was generally rich in the resources needed for human civilization. But it limited where humans could grow crops they could eat.

"So, the rebels control the food supply," EB concluded.

"Exactly. The area south of the Snowdens is the Dachaigh a Deas —*Southern Home*, in English. The northern half of the continent is the Dachaigh a Tuath."

"That lends itself to some…mythologically charged demonyms," EB murmured. He was familiar with old earth Greek myth, due to Apollo's own aspirations and imitations, and he'd studied a broad variety in his youth.

"Tuatha and Deasa," Naumov confirmed. "The Dachaigh a Deas farmers mostly use *Cinnead, Clan,* to identify themselves. The northerners lean heavily into *Tuatha*, yes."

Now icons were populating the globe in the room. Cities, known military positions, orbital stations—the paraphernalia of modern civilization at war.

"None of this answers *why* Nigahog wants to get involved," EB pointed out.

"We have many reasons, Captain Bardacki. A humanitarian desire to reduce suffering and death. A mercantilist desire to open the Estutmost System to wider trade in a way the Board has historically refused. And…we want access to Cinnead terraforming tech."

EB considered the globe.

"If they just had SCD tech, Estutmost III would be useless, wouldn't it?" he murmured.

The standard colonial database was a set of technologies that *every* world had access to. It included the standard thousand-cubic-meter class one nova drive, the reactionless-drive Harrington coils, the anti-gravity generators, the plasma-containment systems needed for fusion reactors and plasma cannon…and a billion other technologies irrelevant to a starship captain.

But to his knowledge, the SCD's base level of terraforming technology was bulky and inefficient at best.

"Out in the Beyond, we know significantly less about even our neighbors than you are used to in the Rim," Naumov noted. "We don't know who founded Estutmost, to be clear. What we *do* know is that they have access to a suite of low-intensity, high-efficiency, regional terraforming technologies that significantly exceeds the capabilities of any we are aware of.

"Our understanding is that the Cinnead have near-complete control over that technology, which is part of why the Dachaigh a Deas contains most of the land that was terraformed to be arable."

The spy shrugged.

"The same technology could be used for revitalization of damaged soil and a thousand other purposes. The Cinnead has traditionally refused to even admit it exists, let alone trade it. We want to…calm the Board's protectionist impulses and earn the Cinnead's goodwill."

"They do know you're sending them arms, right?"

Naumov chuckled.

"The blockade is preventing physical landings, but the Spacers and their allies are hardly at the level of being able to blanket the orbitals with multiphasic jamming. Not without shutting down the planet's entire infrastructure, anyway."

EB nodded, mentally tracing the icons on the holographic world.

"They're basically in a stalemate at this point, aren't they?" he asked.

"Exactly. The Board and the Tuatha have the vast majority of the modern factories and all of the factories that were producing arms, munitions and combat vehicles prior to the revolt. But the Cinnead had enough arms acquired over the years to stop them in the Snowdens. Both sides reached out to purchase weapons from the surrounding systems…and then the Spacers imposed their blockade."

"You didn't spend the last month-plus waiting for me to come back so you could hire me," EB noted. "What happened?"

The spy grimaced.

"We found a ship," he admitted. "Fast ship. Smaller than yours, inevitably, but it should have been enough. Twenty-kilocubic fast packet."

Evasion had been built in the Outer Rim, by a shipyard beholden to a monarch who owed an old comrade of EB's a favor. She was as good as the Outer Rim could build…but that meant she was small and slow by the standards of EB's Inner Rim homeworld and a century or more behind anything built at Sol.

Compared to ships built in the *Beyond*, though… Most ships out there were built with little more than the standard colonial database, which meant they were the ten-thousand-cubic cheap tramp ships ubiquitous throughout human space.

Except there, what were bottom-tier tramps in more civilized stars were the absolute mainstay of shipping, with only a handful of larger ships. *Evasion*'s forty kilocubics and limited weaponry put her head and shoulders above EB's competition.

"Not a fast-enough fast packet, I guess?" EB asked.

"Too stubborn a captain. He was intercepted by the blockaders and tried to make a fight of it with his pair of sparkplugs."

A holographic sequence took shape over the planet was EB watched. Clearly accelerated at least ten times in speed, it showed the icon of a freighter erupting from nova in low orbit. They weren't low *enough*, he judged, and he was swiftly proven right as the icons of a pair of sub-fighters appeared above the transport.

To a former nova fighter pilot, the sublight interceptors were a near-pointless joke. Against a transport with a still-cooling nova drive, they were swift death. Even with *Evasion*, EB would have tried to talk and dissuade, not fight.

He winced as the two sub-fighter icons flickered and vanished. Managing that would have taken clever timing and good shooting—but doing it at *all* had been stupid.

Two of the orbiting monitors, only ten thousand kilometers away, flashed on the display as they opened fire. They used barely a tenth of their weaponry, clearly more focused on *not* hitting the planet than on hitting their target.

Given that the monitors were four hundred meters long with a dozen turrets apiece and the transport was seventy meters long with a pair of glorified pop guns, their restraint was irrelevant to the survival of the freighter.

"*Andean Rocket* went down off the coast of Dachaigh a Tuath shortly after novaing in," Naumov summarized. "Lost with all hands—and forty TMUs of tanks and artillery meant for the Cinnead."

A TMU was a ten-meter unit—or ten-meter-equivalent unit—the standard unitized cargo shipping container of the galaxy. Ten meters long and five meters wide and high, it held two hundred and fifty cubic meters of cargo.

Forty of them was ten thousand cubic meters, which meant that the fast packet hadn't been particularly efficiently designed. EB couldn't say that *too* loudly since *Evasion*'s forty-kilocubic total volume only carried twenty-five kilocubics of cargo.

The rest of her volume was engines and guns unmatched in the Beyond by anything but a warship.

"So, your last attempt failed, the blockade is on alert and you want me to try again?"

"Exactly. We recognize the increased difficulty and importance, but your activities suggest a level of competence and discretion we feel is absolutely essential for this mission," Naumov told him. "Not many people can take down the concealed leadership of an interstellar crime syndicate."

"She didn't leave me much choice."

If the Lady Breanna had just let Trace *go*, EB would never have gone after her. But since the bounties on both Trace and EB had been high enough to make travel actively dangerous, he'd been forced to move against her Siya U Hestî Cartel to protect himself and his new adoptive daughter.

"Your reasons are irrelevant. What is relevant is that *Evasion* is fully resupplied and currently lacking a cargo—and that Breanna Tolliver is in a Nigahog jail cell that she will not leave in this lifetime."

"Running a blockade is not cheap," EB finally pointed out.

"Of course not. Five kilograms Guild-stamped lanthanum. Plus two million marks digicash to cover any further costs you incur on Nigahog."

That was two-thirds of what EB and his crew's share of the bounties for taking down the leadership of the Siya U Hestî had totaled in the end. Naumov was definitely aware of the value of what he was asking for.

Of course, if that was what Naumov was *offering*…

"The last ship to attempt this run went down in flames," EB said. "And I now have a kid aboard my ship."

"We both know *Andean Rocket* should have surrendered the moment the Spacers had her lined up," Naumov told him. "I regard the presence of your daughter as additional motivation to make that call—which, while entirely reasonable, actually counts *against* your likelihood of making the delivery."

EB snorted.

"And the delivery is?"

"The same as it was before. Seventy-five specialist TMUs carrying heavy tanks and mobile artillery, plus fifteen TMU equivalents worth of non-containerized equipment and supplies."

"I hate to get myself in *more* trouble," EB said, "but *Evasion* can haul a hundred TMUs total, though only five thousand cubics of non-containerized gear."

His ship had four unpressurized and one pressurized cargo hold, each sized for twenty TMUs. The pressurized hold was the only one he'd be comfortable storing non-containerized cargo in, since that cargo might require additional care and inspection in transit.

"And if I could get the funding for those extra containers, we'd be shipping them." The spy shook his head. "Replacing what was shot down was difficult enough. There is a limited supply of political will for this operation, Captain, which translates into a limited supply of *money*."

EB sighed.

"Payment in advance, Naumov."

"We can pay the digicash now and half the lanthanum," the spy said after a few moments. "The rest will be paid by the Cinnead on delivery."

"You expect me to rely on half of my payment to be made by a revolutionary organization in the middle of a war they appear to be *losing*. No."

Naumov chuckled grimly as he waved away the illusions of Estutmost, leaving the desk the only break in the idyllic waterborne illusion of his office.

"That's what they're supposed to be paying *us*. If they don't follow through with the payment, they will have a problem with Nigahog."

"That doesn't get me paid," EB replied. "In advance."

"We paid *Andean Rocket*'s captain in advance. Those stamped elementals are now at the bottom of the Sea of Skye on Estutmost."

Out in the Beyond, there were few ways to exchange currency between systems. Nigahog's mark was unspendable outside of the Nigahog System. Digital currency relied far too much on secured mailboxes, regular data transfers and trust to be reliable for intersystem transactions out there.

So there, where there were no reliable regular flights, no mapping corporations and few truly interstellar banks, precious metals and rare earths were the currency of choice—stamped by third-party verification agencies to confirm weight and purity.

"Not my problem," EB said. "Getting in and out of Estutmost and getting paid for it, those are my problems. If you want my ship and my crew, Em Naumov, we need to be paid."

Naumov sighed. He made a nondescript hand gesture that suggested he was flipping through data on his headware.

"We can do three million marks of digicash on contracting and two point five kilograms of lanthanum on loading of the cargo." He held up a hand before EB could say more. A million marks was worth about half a kilo of lanthanum—*if* you found someone willing to convert it. "I know; converting digicash to elementals isn't the favorite task of nova ship captains.

"Still, two-point-five kilos of lanthanum on delivery, that's actually locked in with the Cinnead. And…" The spy made a circling gesture with his hand and then paused for what EB suspected was a silent conversation. `

"There's no more budget for this project," he finally said aloud. "But we have discretionary funds. I can throw in a two-hundred-and-fifty-gram ingot of samarium."

EB had a solid idea of what gold, platinum, stabilized cesium and lanthanum were worth off the top of his head. He had to look up what samarium was worth. Over five times rarer than the already-expensive lanthanum, that was easily a twenty percent bump in the total compensation.

"Before we leave."

"Obviously." The spy sounded disgruntled and opened a drawer of his desk. "Updated contract is in your headware now."

The notification arrived as Naumov finished speaking, and EB ran through it swiftly. Fortunately, the contract was straightforward and the reading speed of someone processing through their headware was near-instant.

"There's no mention of the samarium in here," EB noted, coming back to reality. The contract covered the digicash and the lanthanum on pickup and delivery of cargo, but no mention of the additional quarter-kilo of even rarer metal.

"Because the samarium is never going to officially exist," the spy told him—and slid a black velvet bag across the table. "There you go. Sign the contract, take the ingot, get out of my office.

"Cargo will be at *Evasion* by oh eight hundred tomorrow. Any problems?"

EB paused long enough to open the bag and drop the ingot into his hand. Like most rare metals, the samarium bar was fixed with a stabilizer. Where a bar of gold would be ninety-nine percent pure, the bar of samarium was only roughly seventy-five percent pure—which meant that the "two-hundred-and-fifty-gram" ingot actually weighed three hundred and forty grams, according to the stamp.

"None." The ingot went back into its bag and the bag slid into his pocket. "Send me any intel you have on the blockade. I have some work to do before we get there."

3

"DID YOU TAKE THE JOB?"

Trace didn't even need Ginny to ask the question. She could see EB's pleased grin as he rejoined them in the mall.

"Of course Dad-E did," she told the engineer, watching her adoptive father wince at her nickname for him. *Dad-E* was EB. *Dad-V* was Vexer. Even Trace would freely admit that Vexer had got the better end of that deal.

"I did. We talked about this before we came aboard." EB shook his head at Trace, his glance taking in the several large bags she was carrying.

"We'll talk more details back on the ship. What *did* you buy, Trace?"

"A surprise," she said with her own pleased grin. She trusted Ginny to keep her secrets—at least the important ones, like that she'd bought her dads presents.

EB looked like he wanted to challenge that but finally just sighed and shook his head.

"Do you two need anything else? I'd like to get back to the ship and call a family meeting."

"We got the stupid." Trace hadn't been a big fan of any of the options, but she'd settled on a program that used a soft-spoken male engineer as the teaching hologram. And if the artificial stupid resembled EB, well, no one was going to be overly surprised at what she found reassuring these days.

"And a few other things, I see."

"You gave her an allowance; I just answered questions," Ginny said brightly.

"Why does that not make me feel better?" EB asked. "I trust that nothing is going to explode on me?"

"Nothing is going to explode, stab, poison or otherwise injure anyone."

Trace's father shook his head again, but the grin hadn't faded in the slightest.

"I'll have to take that on faith. Let's get going."

TRACE GAVE Vexer a big hug after they boarded *Evasion*, then theatrically averted her gaze as her two fathers kissed fiercely. She found their relationship adorable, but she was also thirteen and parental affection was always embarrassing.

Or so she'd pretend, anyway. It was what everyone expected, and her overly melodramatic gestures in that direction amused everyone around her.

Vexer had been standing watch just inside the hatch, overkeeping an eye on the main access to the ship from the Nigahog battle station. Dark-skinned, dark-haired, and dressed in a dark gray shipsuit, someone who wasn't paying attention might have missed him—and he was carrying both a blaster and a stunner.

Evasion's crew had picked up some paranoid habits along with Trace, she knew. She didn't *want* to claim she was responsible...but the Siya U Hestî Cartel had been hunting her as much as EB.

EB had just insulted their leader by refusing to work for her. *Trace* had ended up with an entire database of Cartel passcodes, digital drop boxes, safe houses and similar secrets locked in her head. She'd been supposed to act as a concealed courier to a high-level Siya U Hestî boss, with all of the information encrypted under a key that only the intended recipient would have.

Instead, she'd escaped—and EB and Lan, the ship's doctor, had given her direct access to the database in her head. After she'd stowed away on *Evasion* and brought all hell with her, sadly.

"Seal the door and call everyone to the mess, Vexer," EB instructed when the pair had separated. "All-hands meeting time; need the navigator more than we need watch on the door."

"Everyone's aboard now that you three are back." Vexer stepped back from his lover and tapped a command panel. "Passing the word on the meet now. We took the job?"

"We took the job. I was going to unless it was way off from what I expected, and, well, it's the exact same job as the last one he tried to offer us."

Even *Trace* had heard EB's explanation of what mission Naumov had tried to offer last time—before assassins coming for EB had nearly killed the Nigahog spy.

It didn't sound easy to her, but she had faith in her new family. Plus, a "family meeting" would put both her dads in a room for long enough for her to give them her presents.

BY THE TIME they'd reached the mess, the ship's environment tech, Yijun "Joy" Parisi, had already taken over the food-prep area and was laying out an array of coffees and sandwiches.

"I'm guessing the captain didn't eat while he was on the station?" Joy asked.

"Not that I saw," Trace said cheerfully. "I'm guessing the client gave him coffee but not food."

"That's about right," EB sighed. "I see everyone is conspiring against me as usual."

Excluding Trace, half of *Evasion*'s crew rated as officers and half as techs: EB, Vexer, Ginny and the doctor, Lan Kozel, were officers. Then there were the weapons tech, Reginald "Reggie" Kalb, Joy handling environment, Aurora Narang handling the engines, and Tatiana "Tate" MacNeal handling administration and cargo.

And then Trace, who qualified her own job title as "underfoot" most of the time.

"Trace, pass your dad a sandwich, please," Joy instructed sweetly.

Trace obeyed and EB took it with a grateful nod.

"Folks will drift in over the next few," Vexer announced. "Reggie was asleep, asked for long enough to rinse the gunk out of his eyes."

"We have until oh eight hundred to worry about much of anything," EB said. "We can spare a few."

"And that lets me show you my surprise!"

Trace lifted the two bags she'd been carrying up onto the central table while everyone stared at her.

"Sorry, guys, but I only got surprises for Dad-E and Dad-V," she told the rest of the crew. "Spotted them in the mall and they were *perfect*."

One of the very few things of value she'd acquired from her benignly neglectful foster parents back home had been a strong sense of fashion, instilled by a mix of a nanny with an *astonishing* sense of esthetics and a foster mother who was at the highest levels of both politics and the fashion necessary to *play* politics.

Trace slid a bag to each of her new fathers.

"Go on, open the bags," she told them. "I promised Dad-E nothing would explode."

"Why am I regretting my first initial these last few days?"

EB pulled the bag open as he complained and slid the jacket out. Vexer did the same with his bag, pulling out a perfectly matching jacket.

Both were hip-length synthetic leather in a dark iridescent blue. Unless the measurements in *Evasion*'s fabricator systems, as provided by Ginny, were wrong, they would fit *perfectly*.

The color rode *just* the right line to look good against both EB's olive Hellenic complexion and Vexer's darker Arabic coloring. It also complemented the neutral gray-blue of the shipsuits both men wore.

EB was silent for several seconds, holding the jacket up against his arm to check that exact color match.

"Matching jackets?" Vexer asked with a chuckle. "I like it."

"They're also from the market on the *battle station*, I'd like to point out." Ginny ran her hand down Vexer's jacket. "Inner layer of dispersal webs and expendable heat sinks. I wouldn't trust it to stop a solid blaster hit, but it'll save you from a glancing strike."

"You did not buy this with the allowance I gave you," EB said. "And you're *supposed* to be hanging on to your money for important things."

He wasn't really scolding her, Trace knew. His tone was too gentle for that.

"You and Dad-V *are* important. Plus, well…"

Ginny pulled the third, notably smaller, matching jacket from the bag and tossed it to Trace.

"Now we're *obviously* a family," she said with satisfaction, putting it on. Her dads gave her A Look—but both of them put the jackets on.

"You do all match," Lan told them, the doctor apparently having entered the room without anyone noticing. Trace…wasn't entirely sure what the doctor's deal was, but they were definitely soft-footed.

They'd also saved her headware and probably her brain itself from the consequences of both the Siya U Hestî database *and* her foster father's secret experiments with pediatric neural software.

Trace couldn't say she'd loved either of her foster parents, but she'd certainly liked her foster father better. Discovering that a good chunk of the time he'd spent with her had been playing games with her brain had *hurt*.

But she had new dads. Better dads. And with the three of them all clad in iridescent navy-blue leather, they were a matching family set.

"I feel like I missed a memo."

Reggie was *much* less quiet about entering the mess lounge than Lan had been, the big weapons tech heading straight to the counter where Joy had put together sandwiches.

"Learn from my mistakes, Trace," he told her with a chuckle. "And keep your quotient of rum to a sensible level when the boss is going to talk to the client."

It took Trace at least five seconds to realize that the tech was *hungover*, and she shook her head at him repressively.

"Need a painkiller?" Joy offered.

"Already found some." A plate of sandwiches traveled with Reggie to the table, and he turned to look at EB and Vexer. "Gorgeous jacket, boss. Did we get the job?"

"We already knew we were going to be *offered* the job. But I needed more information before I was willing to take the job."

"And?"

"We took the job," EB confirmed. "Take a look, everyone."

Trace joined the rest of the crew in watching as the captain laid down a holoprojector puck and pulled up a visual of the Estutmost System's habitable planet.

"The destination is Estutmost, but we knew that. Main concern is Dachaigh, the continent of Home."

The globe spun around to highlight the larger landmass. Estutmost had three continents, but it looked like people were almost entirely limited to Dachaigh.

"Dachaigh is divided into Dachaigh a Tuath and Dachaigh a Deas by the latitudinal mountain range of the Snowdens. While the Snowdens are breached by a number of passes across their width, the rebels have apparently triggered a series of avalanches blocking many of them, leaving the main passageway *here* at the west end of the mountains."

An icon flashed on the globe.

"The entire Estutmost System is governed by the Staid Chorporra na h-Estutmost," EB noted. "While the system has broken down into three factions, the Board of Directors of the Staid Chorporra *are* the technical legal and legitimate government of the star system."

Trace blinked as her translation software worked through the name. If EB had been speaking entirely in Gaelic, her headware would have been translating live. Since only the name of the Estutmost government was in Gaelic, she had to specifically ask for the translation.

"The Corporate State of Estutmost?" she asked.

"Originally incorporated out of the Fringe Corporatocracy of Blue Fountain," her dad confirmed. "Standard corporate government structure. All residents of Estutmost are entitled to one voting share of the Staid Chorporra at birth. Additional voting shares are traded on an open market, and the Staid occasionally issues new subscriptions to fund specific projects.

"This structure inevitably concentrates voting power in the hands of those with the funds to acquire additional shares," he continued. "The degree to which even larger agricultural businesses seem to have failed to acquire those shares speaks to some games being played, but the truth is that the details don't matter much to us."

Those details probably mattered a *lot* to the people who'd started a war over them, Trace suspected, but that was...not really their problem.

"We are delivering ninety TMUs to the port city of Llandudno, *here*." An icon flashed, southwest of the pass where the fighting was taking place. "That was requested by the Cinnead rebels. I imagine they're hoping to get the gear we're delivering to the front line ASAP."

"Doesn't that increase our danger level?" Vexer asked.

"Less than you'd think," EB replied. "The Board's troops possess relatively limited anti-space capability. They *do* have high-altitude combat interceptors that could theoretically threaten *Evasion*, but unless we are quite unlucky, they shouldn't be in position to launch on us as we land."

"Because of those," Vexer said grimly, gesturing toward the icons around the globe. "How decent is the intel on the blockade?"

"Better than I expected." A time stamp appeared next to the icons of the orbiting spaceships. "Eleven days old. Estutmost is a full six novas from here with the usual trade routes, though *we* can make it in five with Trace's maps."

Trace sat up a bit straighter and poked gently at the database in her head. Among the many pieces of information the Siya U Hestî database had included was a map of "dark stops"—fully mapped sections of space with enough information to safely nova to that were *only* known to the crime cartel—and Trace Bardacki.

Without updates to those maps, the dark points would slowly degrade into uselessness. Trace wasn't sure how long that would take —but she *was* sure that her dads did know.

"They're running ships through Estutmost more regularly than I would think," Reggie said slowly. "At least every ten days or so with the system blockaded?"

"Could be just one ship cycling through at that rate," EB pointed out. "But yes. Nigahog's Guilds are keeping an eye on affairs, and I suspect the Spacers know damn well who sent in the last ship."

That got *everyone's* attention and the captain smiled mirthlessly.

"Yeah, when we vanished on him, Naumov hired another ship. They couldn't carry as much cargo but they made the run. And when the Spacers successfully intercepted them, they shot down a pair of Spacer sub-fighters."

"And the Spacers blew them to hell," Reggie finished for the captain. "That's not going to help us."

"It could be worse. Knowing where the last ship came in lets us adjust our course," EB continued. "We have options."

The icons above the planet flickered as they highlighted.

"Six nova gunships, only one of which is local, and twenty-two monitors of assorted sizes that *used* to belong to the Estutmost government," he listed. "No number on the sub-fighters, but like the atmospheric fighters, they're not overly relevant. The last blockade runner didn't do their groundwork well."

"You have a plan."

Ginny wasn't asking a question.

"I've done the other side of this," EB pointed out. "So, yes. We've got a plan."

4

"YOU KNOW that if this goes wrong, we can be in real trouble, right?"

EB grunted his acknowledgement of Vexer's comment as he pressed his left palm against a concealed scanner in the wall of his quarters. He wasn't sure at what point his navigator had moved into the captain's suite—mostly because it hadn't been a hard delineation. Vexer still had his own room.

If nothing else, the captain's quarters didn't really have enough space for both of their stuff. The navigator had access to EB's rooms normally, primarily because of the concealed vault that EB was opening.

In the Rim or closer to Sol, secure vaults were part of the cargo space. They were for specialty cargo and similar things. Starships in "civilized" regions had access to credit chits and digital cash drawn on banks that were accepted across dozens of star systems.

Evasion had four such vaults, each the size of a ten-meter unit. And then, because trade out in the Beyond was done in stamped elementals and rare earths, there was a smaller, even more secure vault concealed in the captain's quarters.

The small space contained several neat rows of unmarked, sealed bins. As an authorized user, EB could see the virtual labels hovering above the bins, marking which elementals they contained and in what quantity.

Just maintaining the ship wasn't cheap. Fuel, provisions and parts would absorb a significant portion of the digital cash that Naumov was paying him. *Evasion* had been in and out of Nigahog enough—and Nigahog was a big-enough deal locally—that EB would hang on to some of the cash, too.

But he'd spend at least some of the next day trying to convert about half of those three million marks into stamped elementals of some kind. They wouldn't be able to refuel or restock in Estutmost, which meant that their stop *after* that would require restocking at any price.

Fortunately, as the inventory around him told him, they could *afford* to restock at just about any price. *Evasion* was a far more capable ship than most out in the Beyond, and EB had little difficulty finding work for her.

Even with roughly half of every payment going to supplies and crew shares, he'd built up quite a reserve in the ship's accounts. Technically, some of that money was even *his* versus the ship's, but EB had never needed enough money to have to worry about that.

"Do we even have a bin for samarium?"

"No," EB admitted. "Lanthanum is the highest-value stamped elemental we've been paid in before."

He shook his head and laid his hand on an empty bin, coding it with the new element. New icons appeared above the bin and the lid slid open, allowing him to lay the ingot from Naumov in the bin.

"Cargo arrives in the morning," he told his lover. "I've sent Tate all of the details I have. After that, it's down to you and me to get us into Estutmost without getting shot down."

"And what happens if it goes wrong?"

"Then *unlike* the last idiot Naumov hired, we surrender. Naumov isn't paying for death or glory, and he knows it." EB sealed the bin and glanced around the vault. It *looked* like a lot of money, but he was all too aware of how quickly his resources would run dry if *Evasion* stopped working.

"Fair. The plan makes sense to me. But...I worry about the kid."

"I worry about everybody on this ship," EB observed. "But, yes, especially Trace. We didn't adopt her just to get her killed."

"Being a dad is new on us both, but I think we're doing okay." Vexer squeezed EB's shoulder. "The matching jackets suggest *she* thinks so to, I guess."

"Gods, those are *adorable*." EB was still wearing his and grinned as he looked down at it. "I didn't think there even *was* a color that would work with the skin color for all three of us."

Vexer might be darker-hued than EB, but EB was far from pale himself—and Trace was as pale and þlonde as a human could physically *get* in his experience. The iridescent blue-black somehow worked for all of them.

"Kid has a sense for color that a grumpy ex-fighter pilot and a runaway tech-serf don't even begin to grasp, I think," Vexer told him. "Feeling out of your depth yet?"

"I've been feeling out of my depth with Trace since I found her in our hydroponics bay," EB admitted, turning to embrace his boyfriend. "But we said we'd take care of her, so we deal."

"That we do," his lover confirmed. "That we do."

INSOMNIA WAS an uncommon but familiar friend of EB's. When he finally recognized that he wasn't getting to sleep, he carefully extracted himself from Vexer and walked over to the tiny not-quite-kitchenette in his quarters.

It was quiet enough that he could convince the machine to produce a mug of hot chocolate without waking his lover, and he took a careful sip of the warm beverage. They'd had to pick up new stock of hot chocolate mix on Nigahog, and he wasn't *quite* used to how the planet's biosphere affected chocolate yet.

Even Terran-standard crops produced things that tasted ever so slightly differently from planet to planet. Nigahog's chocolate had an odd umami aftertaste that no amount of sugar or other sweetener could overcome. It took some getting used to.

The warm chocolate soothed whatever anxious twitch was keeping him awake, and he looked back across the room at the bed. Vexer was *starting* to be more relaxed in EB's bed, but even the man's sleeping body language told fascinating stories about his life.

Even when sharing a bed, Vexer slept in a practiced, almost perfectly straight position. The result, EB presumed, of years of sleeping in a cot on a spaceship before he'd jumped ship to navigate *Evasion*.

Even Vexer, a trained interstellar navigator, had been chattel to one of Estuval's Dukes. Owned by and beholden in a way that EB didn't fully understand but which had been very real and very powerful in Estuval's culture. One of the most technically skilled men EB had ever met had been *property*, kept in arguably abysmal conditions to scrape a tiny bit more storage out of the tiny ships that the Beyond world had traded with.

It didn't seem to have hurt the other man's independence, given the way the bisexual navigator had played emotional hot-and-cold with EB before settling. EB was certain that Vexer had been testing him, trying to see who he was *under* the mask he presented the galaxy, before deciding if EB was worth having as his lover as well as his captain.

And since EB *was* Vexer's captain, EB could never be the one to push things to the next level. Even on *Evasion*, which had limited hierarchy at best, the captain held too much power over the rest of the crew for EB to initiate a relationship.

Which was the flaw, he knew, with Ginny's suggestion. He could see the value—at least for Trace—of the pair of them marrying. They were her dads, they were going to take care of her, but a legal and cultural bond between the two men could make that more secure.

Even *EB* wasn't…entirely sure how secure his relationship with Vexer was. That was the downside of leaving the other man in control. He trusted that Vexer was going to be Trace's dad no matter what happened between them, and he *thought* that Vexer was planning on sticking around with EB, but he didn't know.

That was the thought that was triggering his insomnia he realized as he drained his mug of chocolate and slid it into the autowasher.

At fifty-five, a veteran of a bloody war and captain of his own star-ship, Evridiki Bardacki was losing sleep over whether his boyfriend liked him enough to stick around for the long term.

The ridiculousness of it made him chuckle...but it wasn't going to help him get to sleep tonight.

5

THE ADVANTAGE, EB supposed, to being docked at a military space station was that they knew how to handle military hardware and cargo containers. The loading started an hour late—roughly what he expected from military logistics teams—but progressed in half the time he was expecting.

He spent most of the loading time in the cargo office above their pressurized cargo hold, watching each of the ten-meter-long cargo containers go into place on the displays and studying the manifests.

Tate knew her job, and his supervision had nothing to do with a lack of faith in her—and she knew it. She spent the same time switching between six different communications channels and coordinating with the Nigahog logistics personnel to confirm that the TMUs went into the right places to balance their mass.

EB had almost told Tate to double-check that each cargo pod contained a decent distribution of the types of cargo to make sure the Estutmost rebels got a balanced force no matter what—except that he realized she was looking at the same manifests he was and was already coordinating that.

Fifty of the TMUs held pairs of Nigahog's Galahad-2 heavy tanks. EB's manifests probably shouldn't have included full specifications on the combat vehicles, but since they *also* included full training documentation for the locals, it was hard to avoid.

The Galahad-2 was…acceptable to his eyes. He hadn't been a peltast, one of Apollo's naval soldiers, but he'd worked with them enough to get a feel for how Apollo ran their own ground forces.

Nigahog's heavy tank was a hundred-and-forty-ton monster with corner-mounted assault cannon and a main turret with plasma cannon that shared a lineage with a nova fighter's main guns.

The assault cannon—rapid-firing high-aperture blaster weapons—would keep infantry and lighter vehicles away from the vehicle while her main gun could take out just about anything that could be mobile on a planetary surface. Her armor was rated to safely disperse twenty-five percent of thermal energy that hit it…which fell in the range that EB classified as *Why bother?*

Of course, *Apollo* put fifty percent rated dispersal webs on their tanks and had got their nova warships up to sixty before he'd deserted in the face of assassins.

The Galahad-2's last line of defense, in the unfortunate case of facing space fighters, orbital weaponry or over-the-horizon bombardment, was a pod of three Lancelot multi-function high-velocity-terminal missile.

MFHVTMs were conventional antigrav-assisted chemical rockets for the majority of their flight path, that transitioned to a high-velocity mode for their terminal approach. That mode, provided by a sacrificial reactionless Harrington Coil, accelerated the missile to four percent of lightspeed in a fraction of a second—and then vaporized itself and everything attached to it.

On its own, a high-velocity missile suffered from the same problem as everything *else* the Galahad-2 carried: it was a direct-fire weapon that couldn't launch at targets it couldn't see. Mounted to an antigrav-assisted rocket, the HVM became the terminal mode of an effective weapon system.

Effective enough that the MFHVTMs were the core system of the Rakshasa-3 mobile artillery pieces that filled the other twenty TMUs rigged for mobile armor. Each of the Rakshasas was a mobile hundred-ton missile platform with high-power sensor drones, attack drones and vertical launch cells for sixty Lancelots.

It wasn't what Apollo would have built—to his knowledge, Apollo *didn't* build artillery or heavy tanks beyond small prototype squadrons for experimentation—but they seemed practical enough.

Except, of course, for the fact that any kind of interstellar invasion was basically impossible. Under normal circumstances, there was no way that Nigahog could penetrate even the relatively light defenses available to Beyond worlds to land troops on a hostile world.

The twenty-kilocubic fast packet that the blockaders had shot down was about as large as warships and transports built in this region of the Beyond got. Against the fleet of million-cubic-meter monitors that the Spacers had stolen to blockade the system, Nigahog's handful of corvettes and gunships could never have cleared a path for a major landing.

And Estutmost was behind even most Beyond worlds in that they only had monitors. Nigahog had a pair of asteroid battle fortresses that would stand off a good-sized task force from the Apollo Self Defense Force EB had served in.

Space troops, like Apollo's peltasts, made sense to EB. Even aircraft that could do double duty as emergency search-and-rescue or similar civil roles. But actual antigrav hover tanks and mobile artillery?

The only time they'd ever see use was in exactly the situation EB was carrying Nigahog's weapons into: a civil war on a planet. He could get a fast ship past the blockade, at least—but only one ship and likely only once.

EB knew he could do the mission he'd taken on and deliver his cargo to the planet. But while a hundred tanks and forty mobile artillery units might tip the balance of a civil war that had already ground to a stalemate, it would never be enough to *conquer* a planet.

"We're opening the pressurized bay now for uncontainerized cargo, boss," Tate told him.

"What's the manifest for that lot?" he asked.

"Machine tools, more hand weapons, all-weather uniforms… couple of monstrous excavators that wouldn't *fit* in a TMU. Most of the other stuff *could* have been containerized, but I think they're just emptying the station's storage reserves."

EB snorted.

"Makes sense. I think most of their containerized supplies like that went down with the first ship."

"And hopefully, this lot won't go down with us."

He clapped Tate on the shoulder and grinned.

"It won't happen," he promised.

"How can you be sure? I've never seen a blockade like this in my career."

Like most of EB's new crew, he'd recruited Tate *in* the Beyond. She'd been working logistics for the main orbital in her home system when her boss had presented her the choice of sleeping with them or never being promoted again.

Instead, she'd hit up the job boards as EB had been looking for a cargo handler. The rest was history.

"I can be sure because I've seen more blockades than I can count. I've never *run* one, I'll admit that, but I've served in them and I've helped *break* them. I know the moves they need to make better than they do.

"No impromptu force of militia and Beyond mercenaries is going to stop *me* getting a cargo to the surface."

6

TRACE'S PRIMARY "JOB" on the ship was *Hold things and watch people work.*

Her understanding was that was basically how apprenticeships had worked for most of history, and that she was providing at least *some* value while she was learning. She was still catching up on her formal education—she'd been delinquent on that *before* she'd fallen deeply enough into a human trafficker's claws to follow the woman off-world.

Now, well, Vexer and EB wanted her to get a proper education. The holographic teacher they'd acquired on the station was still calibrating to her, but she'd been working through the coursework available on Nigahog's system network.

Fortunately, her foster parents had been obsessed with appearances. That was why they'd taken in a foster, after all—her planet had been swept by a plague shortly after her birth, leaving the area she'd grown up in with a large number of orphans around her age.

To succeed in politics, they'd had to take in a foster and be seen to do right by her. Trace hadn't *enjoyed* living with them, but at this point, she could admit that they'd provided for her every material need.

Her fall into juvenile delinquency and trafficking victimhood had been due to other shortcomings. Still, the education they'd provided her had been top-notch, and she was discovering that she wasn't as far behind where she should be as she'd been afraid of.

Nigahog's educational system said she should have been about a year ahead of where she *was* in differential equations and calculus and suchlike, but she'd thought she'd lost something closer to three years of schooling, all told.

And, more importantly in her mind, she'd picked up quite an education in how a starship operated and ran. Some of it was more hands-on than other parts, but most of it was like what she was doing as they made their run out of the Nigahog System: sitting quietly in the observer seat on *Evasion*'s bridge and mirroring Vexer's screen.

She was even mirroring part of the neural feed going to her navigator dad's headware, though that was less complete. Even what she was receiving of the feed, she wasn't sure she followed—it was a lot of that math that she hadn't caught up on yet.

Maps of their destination were running across both the screen and the feed that Trace was watching. They included everything from what few physical objects were there—basically nothing at a trade route stop —to detailed maps of the gravitational and radiation impacts of the surrounding stars.

Trace didn't follow all of the math, but she was watching over Vexer's mental shoulder as he went through the process of plotting their first nova jump and their overall course.

This nova stop was from the regular maps provided by the Nigahog government, as opposed to any of the dark stops from the Siya U Hestî database. Following her dad's plotted course, though, she noted that the last of the four intervening points was one of the dark stops.

"Hey, Dad-V," she asked quietly. "Why are we using just one of the dark stops?"

Vexer chuckled.

"Give me a moment?" he replied.

She waited quietly as he completed a section of math she could barely *identify,* let alone do. There was a lot of computer assistance in play to let Vexer finish it in the time he did, but it was clear that trying to make the calculation without knowing what the computer was doing would be difficult.

"There." He turned in his chair to look back at her.

Evasion's bridge wasn't large. A two-level room, roughly five meters by four; the back half was lifted above the forward half by one of the fuel tanks. There were two seats on each level, and Trace had never seen the back pair used by anyone except her.

"Course is mostly plotted," he told her. "There are a few tweaks I'll make for our actual entry point when we're ready to make the nova, but those have to wait anyway.

"Now, you were asking why we're using official trade route stops most of the way, right?" He gestured, bringing up a shared image in their headwares of the two star systems and the nova stops around them.

"Couple of reasons. Biggest one is that we can nova up to six light-years, but the trade routes aren't always neatly aligned to star systems. Estutmost is twenty-six light-years from here, so we should be able to make the run in five novas.

"Except that if you follow the official trade route"—the icons flashed on the map—"you see that you have to make five jumps to get within six light-years of Estutmost. The trade route stops are set up to create the maximum amount of overlap for the routes between the half-dozen systems around them.

"More overlap means more ships go through them means more accurate maps and safer novas."

"But the dark point routes are faster?" Trace asked.

"Exactly. That's part of why Siya U Hestî has them. The other part of why they have them, though, brings me to why I'm using regular trade route stops for most of the trip:

"There isn't *much* out here in terms of law enforcement and security outside star systems. Mostly mercenaries, like the Trackers' Guild."

Trace grimaced at the name. While they'd hired mercenaries from the Trackers' Guild to go after Lady Breanna in the end, those same mercenaries had tried to capture her to return her to the traffickers.

Her opinion of the mercenaries wasn't high.

"But the mercenaries and the handful of ships people like the

Nigahog Extraterritorial Enforcement Agency do send out operate along mapped trade routes. Where else would they be, after all?"

"So, the Cartel has the dark stops to avoid bounty hunters and cops," Trace concluded. "But since *we* want to have law enforcement around, we want to use the mapped routes where we can."

"Exactly. But taking that one last stop here"—Vexer tapped the icon in the shared map—"lets us cut a full jump and twenty-hour cooldown out of the trip. *And* it lets us avoid any out-system component of the Spacers' blockade.

"Because of the way the shared maps around here are set up, there's only two nova points that are going to see traffic into Estutmost. If I was blockading the planet and had *any* nova-capable ships, at least half of them would be at this nova point."

"So, we go into the dark to avoid the blockade."

"And then when we nova into Estutmost, we come in from an angle they're not expecting and not watching," Vexer added. "*I* didn't think of that part. That was EB."

"He's…done this before, right?" Trace asked.

"Running blockades? No."

"But…" Trace was confused. EB had seemed *very* certain he had everything in hand.

"He was a fighter pilot, Trace," Vexer reminded her. "He's been *part* of blockades before. He knows how to run them because it used to be his job to *enforce* them."

7

EB HAD a solid-enough understanding of how interstellar bounty hunting in general—and the Nigahog Trackers' Guild in specific—worked to not truly *blame* the mercenaries for coming after him and Trace.

They'd had every reason to trust their central administration offices to be properly verifying the sources of contracts to make sure that they weren't being handed illegal bounties. That was what the admin offices were *for*, after all.

But because the Trackers had trusted their office-side staff, the Siya U Hestî had likely been inserting their bounties into the system for *years*. EB had just been the first with the skills and firepower to stop them in their tracks—and sufficient awareness and desperation to go *back* to the Guild.

Because of him, the Trackers' Guild now knew they'd been used and were cleaning house. He trusted the handful of senior Trackers he'd met to finish that job—and they'd clearly put the word out to the rest of the Guild about what had happened and that the Guild owed *Evasion*.

"You know, I *understand* what they're doing," Reggie observed, "but I really wish they'd do it from farther away."

EB was in full agreement with his weapons tech. A pair of Guild gunships had seen *Evasion* arrive at their second nova point and trotted over to assume a protective escort position near the freighter.

"They're lucky we *do* realize they think they're being helpful," EB said. "When they first started heading our way, I was about to order you to charge the guns."

"Yeah, well, I *did* charge the guns," Reggie said drily. "Self-checks are green on all four cannon. I'm not going to shoot them so long as they don't do anything stupid, but they're making me *twitchy*."

The two gunships were close enough to potentially disable *Evasion* before Reggie could shoot back, and they hadn't so much as said hello.

Given that *Evasion* had two dual-plasma-cannon turrets and each of her four guns were easily twice as powerful as anything the gunships carried, it wasn't a clever means of being friendly.

"It's dumb," he agreed. "But it's dumb in…a big friendly puppy way, not an angry guard dog way?"

Reggie chuckled derisively.

"When it comes to bounty hunters, they're *always* the latter."

"Despite the last few months, I'm not generally used to being on the wrong side of law enforcement, even private interstellar law enforcement like the Trackers' Guild," EB pointed out. "I'll give them a bit of credit. Especially when they're clearly *trying*."

He sighed.

"They're just stupid."

"I'll point out, boss, that *they're trying* has some alternative meanings that also fit the situation," his gunner told him. "Like *they're trying my patience*. I'm *pretty* sure I can't vaporize a ten-kilocubic gunship with one salvo from the guns, and I'm *pretty* sure it would be a bad idea.

"But I'm *twitchy*."

"Stim however you need to, Guns, but keep the twitching away from the triggers," EB warned. "The last thing we need is to create more trouble than this job is already going to give us."

There was a long pause and EB watched the targeting indicators *ever so slowly* drift in the direction of the mercenary gunships. Reggie wasn't aiming the turrets at their would-be escorts.

He was just aiming *near* them.

———

DESPITE THE WEAPONS tech's itchy trigger finger, *Evasion* made it to her third nova point without issue. From there, if they were following the usual course, they'd hit two more mapped points before novaing to Estutmost.

Thanks to the *assholes* who'd decided to use a victimized thirteen-year-old girl as a data courier, he had another option and he was going to use it.

Part of him, though, was hoping that the Siya U Hestî were still using their dark point network and he would happen upon one of their ships. He was never going to object to having a chance to take potshots at the bastards who'd hurt Trace.

Most likely, though, the dark point network was abandoned now. He knew how quickly the usefulness of the data decayed. Trace's database had included the most recent update when she'd escaped the Cartel, but that update would only be useful for another three or four months.

Anyone running off an older update would already be reaching the end of their maps' usefulness unless they were remapping themselves. With the center point of their communication network now in the hands of Nigahog's limited nova military, he *hoped* they'd decapitated the Siya U Hestî effectively.

"EB, take a look at sixty-five by eighty-three," Vexer told him.

The two of them were alone on the bridge together—and if they were less worried, the nova jump might have been made holding hands or something similarly sappy, EB knew. But since the galaxy was seeming a dark and dangerous place of late, EB was simply enjoying his lover's company while they both did their jobs.

And right now, EB's job was to take a look along the vector at sixty-five degrees to the right and eighty-three degrees up of *Evasion*'s nose. In a busier area of space, Vexer might even have given him a distance along the vector, but there it was obvious which ship the navigator meant.

"The corvette?" EB asked anyway.

"Yep. She's running a Staid Chorporra na h-Estutmost beacon."

"Huh."

EB saw that now. He hadn't expected to see any nova warships in the service of Estutmost's corporate state. Naumov had given him the impression that Estutmost either didn't *have* nova warships or that the Spacers had them all.

But the fifteen-kilocubic corvette was definitely transmitting a Staid Chorporra beacon.

"There was no mention of a nova corvette in the data Nigahog gave us," EB finally said. "They flagged half a dozen gunships, but only one of those was local."

"The client, of course, can always be relied upon to give us full and complete information, no matter what. Right?"

"Not really." EB checked the corvette's course. "On the other hand, they *do* generally want us to make our deliveries. And our friend over there isn't heading home. Looks like she's headed to either Blowry or Nigahog herself."

"Surprises when we're tangled up in somebody else's civil war are never good, EB."

"Don't worry, hon," EB said. "We'll watch her and we'll be ready if she decides to cause trouble. But she's far enough away that we're going to have plenty of warning to pop jammers and get the hell out of her way if she decides we're a problem."

Multiphasic jammers completely blocked every known sensor in a region a light-second in diameter. The corvette would need to be a lot closer than she was to put accurate fire on target through a jamming field.

"I know, love, I know," Vexer admitted, reaching across the chairs to squeeze EB's wrist. "But a corvette in Tuathan service seems like something Naumov should have mentioned."

"I guess he only told us what had mutinied to join the Spacer block-ade. Not what the Cinnead or the Staid had under their respective flags. That's a hair I'd rather he hadn't split."

He covered Vexer's hand with his own as he watched the corvette.

Lear Naumov had seemed to be straightforward enough, at least with regards to this mission. He wanted his division's worth of tanks and artillery in the hands of the Cinnead.

Now, though, EB had to worry. He was realizing that he'd taken a job from a spy…and trusted that the spy had told him everything.

He should have known better.

8

EB WASN'T the only one aboard *Evasion* who'd been hoping they'd find a Cartel ship using the dark point when they arrived. His entire crew had quietly turned up to their duty stations as the armed freighter prepared to make the nova.

Reggie had even made sure the main guns were charged and online.

"Nada," Vexer announced about twenty seconds after they arrived. "Everyone can go back to bed."

EB chuckled.

"You heard the man, folks," he told his crew. "While we were somewhere between worried and *hoping* we were going to find some of the bastards here, it looks like we're alone today.

"Go get some rest. In twenty hours, we jump into Estutmost, and we will need to be on the absolute top of our game for that drill."

He waited thirty seconds or so to make sure everyone was settling back down, then logged out of the internal coms net and leveled a beady gaze on his daughter.

"That goes for you too, Trace."

"I'm not on sleep cycle right now," she pointed out.

"No, you're supposed to be closeted with a hologram, learning about the history of ancient Tau Ceti, I believe."

She rolled her eyes.

"If that was the class I was on when I decided to stop doing history lessons, I have more sympathy for past me than I usually do. No drama, no excitement, nothing. Just…"

"Just a complete history of the first world of the extrasolar diaspora, where I suspect everyone involved was *ecstatic* to have a lack of drama or excitement," EB said drily. "You've already seen enough *excitement* to know what adventure is."

"Someone else in deep trouble?"

"That's not how it's usually phrased," Vexer noted. "I've usually heard *someone else in deep shit far, far away.*"

"Huh." Trace shrugged. "I hadn't seen that description."

"So, go back to studying the early diaspora, hon," EB instructed. "And then get some rest yourself. You may not have an explicit duty station, but you know just about enough of *everyone*'s roles to be useful somewhere."

That was a lower bar than EB was implying it was—if nothing else, it was a bar that every member of the crew cleared for each other's tasks—but it was true that Trace had enough training to be useful.

Not least because she was sufficiently *untrained* to know she didn't know what she was doing, which avoided a whole list of potential problems!

EB AND VEXER rotated the bridge watches between them during the twenty hours the nova drive needed to cool down. Trading short watches back and forth meant that they were both rested and ready when the sensors in engineering showed clear.

"Are we good, Ginny?" EB asked.

"For two more novas," she confirmed. "Then we need to discharge buildup. There's no getting out of Estutmost once we're in, boss."

"I know how physics works, Ginny," he said drily. It was still fair for her to point out that limitation. If anyone had built a ship that could handle more than six full-length novas before the tachyon and electrostatic buildup was too severe for the nova drive to work, EB didn't know about it.

Even taking the dark point, they were using up five of those six to get to Estutmost. They could, technically, *leave* the star system. But without a planet to discharge static and tachyons into, they'd be stranded in deep space for twenty *days* instead of the usual twenty hours.

"We can still nova around in the system just fine," Vexer pointed out. "There are a few places to hide and discharge in any system."

"It's only forty light-minutes from Estutmost Six to Estutmost Two right now," EB noted. "We need twenty hours just be able to make the insertion nova from our hiding spot. We can hide and cool down in the asteroid belt at fifty-five light-minutes and go unnoticed, but we'd need to hit Six to discharge.

"And unless the Spacers are more incompetent at maintaining their blockade than I expect, they have at least a satellite watching Six. Our intel says they've got six nova gunships, so they can easily check out what's going on if someone shows up to discharge."

He shook his head.

"We hide in the belt and accept that we can't discharge until we're on the ground on Estutmost itself," he told his navigator and engineer. "It sucks, it traps us in the system for an extra day at least—but it's not like we can offload on the ground in a matter of hours, anyway."

"Tate is still twitchy about offloading on the ground at *all*," Ginny muttered.

"And I'm right there with her," EB conceded. "I've never even landed *Evasion* before. Landing and offloading ninety TMUs' worth of crap on the surface? It's in the design specs, but I've never done it."

Evasion looked like nothing so much as a loaf of bread in a horseshoe. Her four unpressurized cargo bays were stacked two-by-two in a fifty-meter-long box twenty meters across. Above and below the ship were the engineering hulls containing the reactors and engines, with the ops hull and the pressurized cargo hold on the front of the ship.

Thanks to antigrav coils, the forty-thousand-cubic-meter starship *could* land and take off. The TMUs had built-in antigravity systems as well, so they *should* be easily handled and moved in and out of the ship once she was on the ground.

He'd just never done it.

"Aurora and I have gone over every single component of the anti-grav systems with a microscope," Ginny pointed out. "I was ready to replace more hardware in one week than I did most years, but they were honestly in decent shape.

"Whoever built this ship did well by you."

"I had a friend serving as a merc for the local monarch," EB said. "I guess they figured they should be careful with ships they sold to their mercenaries' friends."

Not that he'd exchanged a word with Commander Demirci since leaving that Rim system. She'd decided to go the mercenary route and go back to war, one way or another. EB…had done everything in his power to *avoid* war.

He hadn't been as successful as he would like, though his little campaign against the Siya U Hestî didn't really count as a war. Citizen law enforcement, maybe.

"Main point is that our ship can definitely land and take off again. Cargo offloading…that depends more on whether Nigahog gave us the right kind of cargo containers."

"They put up a billion marks or so of military hardware and are paying us around fifty mill to make the delivery," EB pointed out. The *fifty million* number—a rough translation of the stamped elementals to Nigahog marks—was far more impressive before one realized that every single set of six novas cost *Evasion*'s crew about a million in puri-fied hydrogen fuel alone.

Add in salaries, crew shares, maintenance costs, et cetera…it cost roughly two million marks in whatever the local currency was to make a single trip between star systems in *Evasion*.

Part of that was that many of the things EB needed to run his ship were more expensive out there than in the Rim. But he could run down a lot of money *real* fast if he wasn't carrying cargo.

They were almost certainly going to be running empty leaving Estutmost, too, and he hadn't quite decided where they were going yet —other than *not Icem*.

Trace's Nigahog adoption papers were theoretically ironclad, but he figured wandering through the system her foster parents lived in was something to avoid if possible. If nothing else, given what Lan had discovered in Trace's headware, it would take a great deal of effort not to punch her former foster father in the face if EB was in the same star system.

Pediatric headware software was kept simple and standard for a reason. Headware software modifications were the kind of thing that required complete and explicit informed consent, of the kind that ten-year-olds couldn't really give.

And Trace's previous "father" hadn't even *asked* for consent. He'd just started recoding parts of her software without telling her.

"We're ready to nova," Vexer said, interrupting EB's descent into unpleasant thoughts. "Course plotted to Estutmost's outer asteroid belt. Barring *really* bad luck, we should neither see anyone nor hit anything."

EB chuckled, focusing on the moment and considering the odds of Vexer's "really bad luck."

"I have an enduring faith in your skill, my love," he told the other man. "Let's go."

Vexer nodded and leaned forward to tap a command on the screen. A moment later, the screens around them rippled as reality *shifted*.

The empty space of the dark nova point was replaced with the less-empty space of an outer-system asteroid belt. They were still far enough away from the belt's charted asteroids that nothing was visible to the naked eye, but the screens rapidly updated, zooming in on the nearest chunks of rock and ice.

"Welcome to Estutmost," Vexer murmured.

"Better late than never. Got a hiding spot in mind?"

"Scanning for a nice solid chunk," EB's lover told him. "We're on the outer edge of the belt, so no one *should* pick us out when our light reaches Estutmost itself."

It would take fifty-six minutes for their light to reach the inhabited planet and the orbital blockade. By then, *Evasion* would have vanished into the asteroid belt, hopefully to never be found.

They had a decent chance of not being picked up at all, but hiding in the belt would cover their trail for a day or so. Long enough to cool the drive and make the jump to Estutmost to deliver their cargo.

"That one will do," Vexer murmured. Icons on EB's displays lit up as the freighter's engines flared to life, pushing them toward the four-kilometer-long chunk of ice the navigator had picked.

"I'm dropping a sensor drone here," EB said aloud. "Sending it toward the planet will get us a better vision of what we're looking at."

"We might not be able to pick it up after," Vexer warned.

"I know. That's part of why Naumov paid through the nose for this gig."

EB didn't have many sensor drones, and replacing them was hard. The drones weren't particularly fancy or complicated—the ones *Evasion* carried were SCD tech—but they were sufficiently military that people didn't like to sell them to strangers.

And it had been a long time since EB wasn't a stranger wherever he was.

9

IT WAS A LARGER problem to dispose of heat in space than to create it. *Evasion*, like most spaceships and space stations, was kept at "comfortably warm" through most of her spaces—edging toward *un*comfortably warm in the engineering areas at times.

The main advantage of that in Trace's mind was that if she couldn't sleep, there was absolutely no reason for her not to wander around the ship in her rabbit-patterned pajamas. She did her best to stay out of everyone's way as she peeked through doors at duty stations, but most of the work consoles were empty.

They were about three-quarters of the way through their cooldown, and everyone else appeared to be sleeping. In five hours, they would run the blockade—and Trace wasn't sure what use she was going to be in that particular task.

Finally drifting into the turret-control center down the hall from her room, she spent several seconds making sure the weapon controls were completely locked out before sprawling in the seat and bringing up the sensor displays.

Evasion was tucked in behind a chunk of ice easily fifty times her length and a few hundred times her mass and volume. With the ice asteroid between them and the inner system, all Trace could see directly from the freighter's own sensors was…more ice asteroids. Some rocks. A bunch of empty space.

It all felt very lonely, and a chill ran through her that even the ship's warmth couldn't quite offset.

Trace didn't feel *alone* very often anymore. Her dads and the rest of *Evasion*'s crew had made very clear that she was family now. Empty void still chilled her, though. She hadn't been able to see sensor footage when she'd been trafficked between star systems, but she'd been enough of a "good" victim to have privileges on Lady Breanna's training station.

That had left the void as a bad memory—though she also now had memories of that station in more positive hands.

But that thought brought her into the spiral of the battle for the station, the combat as they'd stormed it…and the room where Breanna had sent her chip-controlled servants, trafficking victims with no control over their own actions, to their deaths to slow the attackers down.

Pushing away those memories, Trace poked at the sensor display and found the extra feed—the sensor data coming in from the remote-controlled drone drifting half a light-second away. That was feeding into a tactical display, and as she watched, a series of datacodes attached themselves to an icon.

"I'm on the bridge," Vexer's voice said in her head. "Going through the sensor data and marking out our next steps."

"I was trying not to bother anyone," Trace replied.

"I'm sufficiently paranoid, much as I trust everyone aboard, to have the system tag anyone who's looking at the tactical display. You doing okay?"

"Can't sleep."

"Want to come up to the bridge and go through the sensor feed with me?"

"Sure." Trace shivered again, pushing away the memories of innocent dead faces. "Could use the distraction."

ON THE BRIDGE, the tactical display was taking up just about every bit of spare volume that Vexer could cram it into. Half a hologram and a quarter on the flat displays, with the rest feeding through headware optics, the three-dimensional model showed the planet and its orbital space in more detail than Trace was used to.

Vexer was standing in the middle of the hologram, *on* the main pilot's seat, studying an expanded version of one of the icons.

"Hey Trace, grab a seat and get comfortable."

"What are we doing?" she asked.

"I'm taking a long look at each of the monitors." He turned, still balanced on the seat, and brought the image of the ship with him.

"Each of them's unique; it's that kind of system," he continued. "Standard spun-up asteroid, though. Take a look yourself."

Trace did. The ship was half a kilometer long and a fifth of that across, a rough ovoid whose origins were still visible in her uneven lines.

"Bigger than a nova ship," she said.

"Much. Monitors are on the same principle as orbital forts. They don't need to nova, so they're not limited by nova-drive volumes, and once you take that out of the equation, well, size doesn't matter so much until you're *much* bigger.

"They take an asteroid of roughly the right size and fire a bloody massive laser into it. Burn a hole roughly three-quarters of the way through and half-melt the entire mass—then start it spinning.

"Takes a few months and the laser isn't cheap to build or run, but when you're done, you have a massive hull to stuff full of tech and mount guns on. This is pretty typical of the type—looks like twenty-two turrets. Might be a few more or less; we're looking at them from a long way away."

"Can they catch us?" Trace asked.

"They can't nova, so no," Vexer told her. "And we're faster than them on Harringtons, too. But...they have the high ground, so to speak. Anyone who is trying to get to Estutmost *has* to go through them."

"And I'm guessing all of that rock isn't great for us doing anything to them?"

"I can't be sure—never can be without examining them at close range—but I'd guess most of their monitors have between ten and twenty meters of asteroid iron for armor.

"The composites, alloys and dispersal networks used for proper nova warships are far more efficient, but there's a lot to be said for being able to have twenty *meters* of armor instead of twenty *centimeters*."

"But we're not going to fight them, are we?"

Vexer chuckled, added two more icons to the monitor's hologram and flipped it back into the overall display.

"If they lock us in, we surrender immediately. We'll probably end up interned for a few weeks until we can negotiate and buy our freedom—and the *cargo* won't get through—but nobody gets hurt on either side.

"EB figures if we play nice once they've got us locked, we can talk our way out."

Trace studied the scattered formation of warships above their destination.

"Is he right?" she murmured.

"I don't know," Vexer admitted. "He knows this better than any of the rest of us. But…"

"But even he hasn't done this before."

"No."

The bridge was silent for a few minutes while Vexer worked, and Trace looked away from the tactical display to a headware feed showing the space around them.

"Is it weird that it feels lonelier out here than it did in deep space?" she asked after a few moments.

"Not really. Intellectually, we know that a star system is a literally incomprehensible size. But that's the problem with *incomprehensible*."

She felt Dad-V's presence join her in the feed.

"We don't—we *can't*—comprehend how big a star system is. And we bounce from system to system like the inhabited planets are the only thing there. If there isn't something in a region for us to visit, we don't go there.

"So, in our heads, star systems have other people in them. And then you end up here…"

Vexer waved a hand.

"There are seven hundred thousand people living and working in this asteroid belt, according to the Nigahog maps," he told her. "They're…*here, here* and *here*."

Three icons flickered on the display. All were in the asteroid belt… and the blockaded planet was closer than any of them.

"I didn't pick this spot at random, Trace," he noted. "We are as far away from the three main hubs of Spacer activity in Estutmost's belt as we could get. The belt is ten light-minutes deep and almost sixty light-minutes from the star. There is a *lot* of mass out there…but even more empty space.

"In some ways, we are more alone here than we would be at a normal trade route stop."

He shrugged.

"So, yeah, feeling alone and lost out here? That makes sense to me. But…"

"That's why we're here?"

"Exactly. The data I'm getting on the blockade is an hour old—but the data we had from Nigahog was over two weeks old."

"War's still ongoing, though," she said quietly. "Guess the people we're here to help wish we'd arrived sooner."

"We had other priorities." Vexer stepped down from his seat and wrapped her in a firm hug. "And we can't blame ourselves for having those priorities, either. I'm not convinced Nigahog's intervention here is going to cause *less* death and trauma when everything is said and done."

Trace shivered and nodded. Part of her had been thinking that their cargo was going to *save* lives and that the delay—the delay *she* had caused—had cost lives.

But Vexer had a point. Almost no intervention in a war was going to make it less violent.

Especially not providing one side with more weapons!

10

EB was linked into the ship's internal network, with every officer and tech online and listening in. He didn't even necessarily need to speak aloud, but habit held true no matter what.

"Engines are ready," Ginny reported, her voice echoing in his head. "Antigrav systems are green. Atmospheric casing checked out as well."

"Guns are ready, though I've been strictly ordered not to use them," Reggie said, melodramatically pouty.

"There is no one we can shoot at today that isn't going to cause us far more trouble than plasma bolts can fix," EB replied.

"Navigation is ready," Vexer said drily, winking at EB across the room. "Course is plotted."

"Medical is ready, though if you manage to create work for me today, I will be very unimpressed," Lan concluded, their voice bored.

"There's going to be enough bumps and starts even if this goes entirely according to plan," EB pointed out. "Be ready with the splints, the bone-knits and the painkillers, doc."

"Oh, believe me, I am," the doctor said. "What happens if you get the nova wrong, Captain?"

"I have faith in Vexer."

"Someone has to," Vexer muttered in response, but he was still smiling at EB. "But to answer Lan's question: there's two ways this can go wrong.

"The first, I cut the jump too short and we emerge either outside the blockade or in the middle of the blockading fleet, in which case I believe our daring and courageous captain is planning on surrendering."

"*Daring and courageous* doesn't give me a reason to get people killed for no reason. Especially not when most of these people will be *us*."

"As I said." The navigator's grin was infectious.

"Given the error radii, though," Vexer continued, "the most likely scenario is that I *overshoot*. In that case, no one will ever know we were here, and the only long-term result will be some very confused seismologists trying to work out why they had a pressure spike."

Even EB had to cringe at that mental image.

"But if that happens, we'll never know. So, don't worry, people. We'll be fine, we'll be prisoners or we'll never know we were dead.

"Everybody ready to nova?"

"Less so than I was a minute ago," EB said drily. "Please curb your enthusiasm for novaing us *into* the planet, if you will, hon?"

"*Boooring,*" Vexer replied. "Trust me."

"I do," EB told him. "And everyone else is ready. You have the big red button, Vexer. Make it happen."

"Nice to be appreciated. Everybody hold on. I'm *not* going to muck this up, but it's still going to be rough as all hell."

EB was already strapped in. So far as he knew, he was the only member of his crew to have ever novaed this close to a planet before. Given that he very specifically did *not* ask about his people's pasts, he might be wrong there—but he, at least, knew what he was getting in for.

"Last chances to find your straps, close your drinks and wish you'd made a better choice of merchant ship, folks. Novaing in five. Four. Three. Two. One.

"Nova."

THE WORST NOVA EB had ever endured in his life had been a Hail Mary ploy during the war between Apollo and Brisingr that had seen a strike group of nova fighters and nova bombers make a full six-light-year jump, in nova fighters, into the upper reaches of a gas giant.

A nova fighter sacrificed a lot of things to cram faster-than-light capability and a useful armament into a hull that was usually three hundred cubic meters or less. One of the things they sacrificed was the shielding that made novas unnoticeable to the passengers on regular ships.

The class two nova drive a fighter used was also far more efficient at short novas. A full-length nova was a strain on the drive, and it let the pilot *know* that.

And to top off the trifecta of insanity of that particular stunt, novaing into an *atmosphere,* however thin at the point of entry, generally fell into the category of *a really bad idea.* They'd pulled off the mission—but six of fifty nova craft hadn't survived the *jump,* let alone the battle that followed.

After that, there would never be any question in EB's mind of what the *worst* nova he'd ever endured had been. But the nova to Estutmost handily managed to jump straight to second place, past every other nova he'd made in an unshielded fighter.

Every muscle in his body tried to cramp at once, and a wave of nausea and dizziness ran through him—not helped by at least nine different alarms going on.

"Vexer!" he snapped, blinking to clear spots from his vision as he tried to work out what was going on.

"Overshot by a thousand klicks. *We're in the fucking atmo.*"

And that explained why this was almost as bad as the gas-giant stunt.

The spots cleared from EB's vision in time for him to grab control of the ship and stabilize them before they hit the planet. Their nova had been plotted to bring them in about eleven hundred kilometers above Estutmost, close enough to allow them to dive to the surface in under a minute.

Instead, they'd emerged inside the Kármán line, crashing an eighty-meter-wide starship into the planet's atmosphere like a breaching whale. A dive that should have been perfectly safe was now massively dangerous, and EB activated every antigrav coil the transport had, hammering them to a painful halt sixteen kilometers above the ground.

They were testing the limits of his ship to protect them from the laws of physics—Harrington coils were reactionless and mostly inertialess, but antigravity coils were most definitely *not*. He ignored where the straps had cut into his skin as he tried to process the scan information coming in around him.

"Closest monitor is at thirty thousand klicks; she has to see us," Vexer warned.

"See us is fine, so long as she doesn't have an angle to *shoot* us. I need to know where we *are*."

There was ground beneath EB, and he took that as a sign to take the ship down—at a more sedate pace than the original near-crash.

"We're above Dachaigh a Deas," Vexer reeled off as he mapped them in. "Should see the Snowdens to the north. Ocean is to the west."

"Got it."

EB locked them in against the map of the continent and found his destination.

Despite everything, they'd got it right. Llandudno was only thirty kilometers away, an infinitesimally short trip for a starship. Of course, whether he could make that trip without being shot down was an entirely different question.

"Sub-fighters in play from the monitor," Vexer warned. "I've got four birds dropping from orbit and coming in fast."

"I'm taking us lower and heading for Llandudno," EB replied. "Get the locals on the horn and tell them I need air cover.

"Reggie, fire a warning shot. Let's make sure they know we're armed. *Don't* hit them; we don't need to make this personal!"

The weapons tech didn't reply verbally, but EB could see the dorsal turret rotating on his displays and grinned as the ship trembled under his hands.

He'd given up being a nova fighter pilot for a thousand reasons, mostly a desire to never be dragged into anybody else's war and a real hope to make it through the rest of his life without killing again.

But *this* was flying like he'd rarely done in a transport, and he'd forgot how much he loved the exhilaration.

"Ginny, how are our systems?" he asked.

His main focus was on the altimeter. They were down to three thousand meters, regular aircraft heights. *Evasion* was probably even less aerodynamic than a brick, and even this speed was bringing heat warnings up on his screens.

"Antigravs are solid as a rock," his engineer told him—in the same moment the dorsal turret fired a single warning shot. "Forward heat shielding is complaining, but everything seems intact. I'll want to go over the tiling whe—"

"SAMs incoming from the pass!"

EB got the alert from *Evasion*'s systems while Vexer was speaking, and swallowed a curse. A dozen surface-to-air missiles were rising from the main pass through the Snowdens. He'd known Llandudno was close to the dueling lines of the main stalemate, but he hadn't thought through how that exposed *Evasion* to the Tuathans' weapons.

And unless he missed his guess, the missiles were the same kind of high-velocity-terminal weapons that *Evasion* was carrying in her own holds. If they got close enough to convert over to their Harrington-coil attack mode…

"Dropping lower," he said grimly, taking the ship even closer to the surface. The altimeter was now reading fifteen hundred meters. He was *way* too deep into the atmosphere to need to worry about the sub-fighters now. They were creatures of space, not air-breathers.

"Sub-fighters breaking off," Vexer said aloud, confirming EB's thought. "Local air patrol is inbound to cover us."

"I'm glad they're in the air, but I don't suppose they have a solution for—"

"Transport *Evasion*, this is Morrigan-Actual," a lilting female voice said in his headware. "Adjust your course thirteen degrees south and add whatever speed you can, please."

There was no *time* for EB to ask what the local pilot wanted. He was less than a minute out from his landing approach—but those missiles were only about *twenty seconds* from converting into crowbars traveling at measurable percentages of lightspeed.

He twisted *Evasion*'s course thirteen degrees to the south and fed more power to the engines. Friction was the main concern there, not engine power.

Their sonic boom probably broke windows as they flashed over Llandudno's southernmost suburb, but the detour bought them about two seconds before the missiles reached conversion range—two seconds in which they were outside the mountain range and in clear line of sight for Morrigan-Actual and the other four stealth fighters EB's sensors hadn't seen.

Lasers ripple-fired through the air as Llandudno's air-defense squadron abandoned their invisibility cloaks and unleashed their antimissile weaponry. The fast-moving aircraft weren't optimized to protect something *else* from surface-to-air missiles, but the course change they'd asked for left the missiles distinctly vulnerable to the jets.

"I see they do have a solution for the missiles," EB said drily.

"Transport *Evasion*, this is Morrigan-Actual," the fighter pilot greeted them again. "Y'all owe us some beers. You're welcome."

"I'll be delighted to buy you all dinner, Morrigan-Actual," EB replied. He looked over at Vexer, who gave him a thumbs-up and cross-loaded landing instructions onto his screen.

"We have final landing instructions from Llandudno Control," he continued. "Are you going to stick around and keep an eye on us for a bit longer?"

"Oh, we'll be here. You just won't see us."

There was a momentary spike of jamming on EB's sensors—and then the combat aircraft were just *gone*. The planes might be backward and out of date by any objective standard, but they were still perfectly able to hide from Rim civilian scanners.

Mostly.

"I've got them," Vexer said after a moment. "Not sure I could have if I hadn't known where they vanished, though. That's an impressive stealth suite for out here."

"And explains part of why this is still a stalemate when only one side can replace tanks and planes," EB murmured. "The Cinnead found themselves some neat toys before the war started."

That raised some *fascinating* questions in his mind about how long the rebels had been expecting this conflict. The implication he'd had from Naumov was that the Cinnead had kicked it off in response to provocations from the Staid Chorporra na h-Estutmost...but somehow the rebels having *stealth jet fighters* made EB wonder about the balance of responsibility there.

It wasn't his problem, though.

"They're directing us to a cargo airport," Vexer warned. "It's designed for shuttles and atmospheric movers. Can we even *fit*?"

EB had slowed *Evasion* down to about sixty kilometers an hour, a snail's pace that was straining his antigrav coils more than his heat tiling, and was eyeing their destination as well.

"My dear Vexer," he told his boyfriend. "We can fit. They're just not going to have any runway left around'us."

He judged the numbers on his screen.

"Or transit ways. Or parking lot. Or... Well, they've cleared it, anyway."

The speed indicator dropped down even lower as he brought the starship in. Finally, they came to a stop with the nose of the freighter about five meters from the main transshipment terminal...and her stern only about eight from the farthest hangar.

"Tate, you're up," he told his cargo handler. "Let's get these people their guns."

11

BY THE TIME EB left *Evasion* through an extended ramp he hadn't even known the freighter *had*, the locals were in motion. A pair of large self-propelled cranes were being carefully aligned with his starboard cargo bays, and a hover-flat sized to carry a single TMU was coming up behind the cranes.

The Cinnead was moving with the alacrity he was expecting…but not the numbers. It would take two cranes to move a single TMU out of the cargo hold, even with antigrav coils reducing the effective weight to nothing.

He would have expected at least four cranes, two for each side of his ship, plus an entire array of transports waiting for the TMUs. But all he saw was three vehicles. Less than a dozen workers all told, in fact.

A chill ran down his spine as he spotted an official-looking black groundcar pulling up. The fact that the woman in a dark olive uniform who exited the driver's seat was the *only* person to leave the vehicle fit the pattern.

So did the military-grade filtration mask she wore over the lower half of her face. There was something going on here, and EB did *not* like it.

The tall officer stopped a precise three meters away from EB and saluted crisply.

"Commissar Enid Owens," she introduced herself. She had the same lilting accent as the pilot who'd shot the missiles off his back, but she was also speaking slowly and clearly to overcome both distance and mask. "I'm damn glad to see you, Captain. After the last transport was shot down, my superiors weren't sure if we were going to *get* the shipment."

"I can't imagine the, ah, *supplier* is known for reliability around here."

Owens chuckled and shook her head.

"Not really," she admitted. "The Cinnead Militia has had decent luck with most folks around here, but one always gets uncomfortable when it's no longer *our* agents cutting the deals."

"Speaking of deals. I was expecting payment on delivery," he told her. "Two and a half kilos of stamped lanthanum. Final tranche of payment for the cargo for the supplier, as I understand."

"We'll want to inspect everything and make sure we've received what we're supposed to." She turned to survey the cranes and single hover-flat with an unenthused expression. "We have a few more bits of equipment coming up, but…that's still going to take longer than either of us would like.

"The Cinnead will make good on your time, Captain, but our resources are currently…constrained."

"What's going on, Commissar?"

EB was following her look and then sweeping the rest of the cargo airport. The place wasn't designed for spaceships—not big ones, anyway—but it should still have been much busier than he was seeing.

Plus, he figured that an armored division's worth of tanks and artillery should be the priority for a rebel militia.

"Mother Nature, on any world, has a funny sense of humor," Owens said grimly. "In the middle of a stalemate, just as it seemed like we might get the upper hand in the mountains, Llandudno got hit with a nasty respiratory virus outbreak.

"Mutation of a known local viral vector, it happens, but the timing sucks. It's…mild enough in some ways, no one has *died* that I know of, but we've had to change up the logistics pipeline to go around Llan-dudno, and I'm short of bodies for work on the ground here. Ones that are conscious and walking, anyway."

"I'd offer to relocate to offload elsewhere, but I doubt I can manage that without getting pinned down by the blockade. My understanding was that delivery to Llandudno was requested."

Owens sighed and nodded.

"Llandudno's a resort and port town, normally. Grain from the entire Dachaigh a Deas transships through here and there's an entire midway strip of casinos and such. There are only two places in Dachaigh a Deas that can handle cargo transfer from a landed starship, Captain, and Llandudno's right next to the pass where the heaviest fighting is taking place."

"It will take the time it takes, I suppose. I'll want to keep my people on board as much as possible to avoid the virus, though," EB warned. That seemed like a reasonable minimum. Without more information, he couldn't properly protect his people.

Short of full bodysuits, he supposed, which they at least *had*.

"That seems entirely reasonable, Captain, though…"

"Commissar?"

Owens sighed and squared her shoulders.

"Our doctors got hit hard before we realized how infectious this latest mutation was," she admitted. "I hate to ask it and it seems silly, but do you have any medical personnel on board?"

A city of a hundred thousand people, plus whatever additional personnel the Militia had brought it, was short enough on doctors to be asking for help from his ship.

That reinvigorated the chill in EB's spine.

"I'll talk to my ship's doctor. We have gloves and suchlike to augment our shipsuits into biohazard gear, so they should be safe to come in. I'm…"

"Not happy to send your people into a city ravaged by an epidemic, I understand. But…if you can help, we'd appreciate it. So long as Llandudno is shut down like this, the entire fate of our rebellion is in danger."

"I'll talk to Lan," EB repeated. "I won't order them to help, but... they're a doctor. They'll probably help."

"Thank you."

———

"LLANDUDNO HAS a population of one hundred and sixteen thousand, with three major hospitals," Lan said in a careful tone. "I can't say for sure how many doctors that translates to, but likely somewhere in the three-to-four-hundred range."

"And they're desperate enough to ask for your help," EB told them. "Up to you."

"Oh, I'm going, I'm going," Lan replied. "I swore an oath, a long time ago. I studied epidemiology, at one point. I might even be able to help them synthesize a vaccine or even a counterviral.

"I'll have to run their files, but I could almost certainly use extra hands," they warned. "Vexer is the best-trained medic on the ship after me."

"He is?" EB asked. That wasn't something he'd realized.

"He's no doctor, but I've given him some refreshers on his first aid and emergency medic training from Estuval. He may be rusty, but we'll mostly just need people to swap out IV bags."

Lan chuckled.

"Heck, I could probably use just about anyone from the crew. A lot of what's needed to handle a respiratory infection wave like this is gopher work. Any pair of hands could help."

EB sighed.

"You can ask for volunteers," he told the doctor. "We're not going anywhere until our cargo is offloaded, and it's going to take them three days at this rate.

"We may as well do some extra good while we're here."

Even if he had a damn good idea *who* was going to volunteer when asked to help people!

12

THE MESS HALL aboard *Evasion* was grimly quiet after EB and Lan laid out the situation.

"These poor people," Ginny said first.

Trace could only nod. Plague and viruses figured heavily in her own world's history—she didn't even *remember* her biological parents, carried off by a local mutated viral before she was even toddling.

"My phrasing was slightly more professional, but yes," Lan confirmed. They were pacing back and forth by the entrance to the mess, their hands shoved in their pockets. "I've already requested a vehicle to pick me up.

"I will be taking half of our stock of general antiviral medication—EB already gave permission—as well as half of our personal protective equipment. Anyone who comes with me will be in full-body prophylactic equipment until we have returned to the ship and sanitized."

Lan shook their head grimly.

"The locals are assuming that, like most respiratory viruses, this is entirely based on an inhalation vector. I refuse to assume that until I've had a chance to examine the bug myself, so we will be excessively careful."

"We novaed this ship *into* atmosphere and flew her at full speed at low altitude," Aurora nearly whispered. The engine tech was almost always soft-spoken, her black hair plastered against sallow skin in a way Trace was pretty sure was unhealthy.

But then, the teenager had hoped to connect with the second-youngest member of the crew and been coldly, if politely, shut out. She recognized her biases.

"Aurora is right," Ginny conceded. "She and I need to go over nine-tenths of this ship with that microscope again. Engines, heat tiling, environment... I need to stay. So does Aurora. So does Joy."

Joy looked like she was about to object, but then sighed and nodded.

"Especially if we have a local viral vector," she conceded. "I need to go over our external scrubbers *yesterday* if that's the case."

"We had no warning. No one could have *given* us warning—or we'd have landed somewhere else," EB said. "But I agree. The three of you need to focus on the ship. Tate and I have to support the cargo offload."

He turned to Reggie and Vexer.

"That leaves you two gentlemen."

Trace looked at them herself and swallowed a surprised sound. Vexer was nodding in response to EB's comment, clearly planning to volunteer to her eyes. *Reggie,* on the other hand, looked as close to *terrified* as she'd ever seen the weapons tech.

She'd seen the big blond weapons tech from the Rim strap on armor and wade in against a dozen Cartel assassins without so much as a pause.

"I...I can't do viral, boss," Reggie finally whispered. "Just...just can't."

"That's fair; it's not everyone's favorite enemy," Lan said instantly. "Most folks prefer a threat they can see."

"I like ones I can shoot," Reggie agreed. "Sorry, doc."

"I'm in," Vexer said. "Just the two of us then, Lan?"

"And me," Trace said, before she could think too hard about it. She wasn't going to let one of her dads charge off into craziness with just Lan for support!

Lan was looking at her, and there was something in their eyes that made her shiver.

"You already have more medical trauma than any doctor wants to see a patient have, Trace," they said gently. "Are you sure?"

"None of the shit that was done to me was done in a *hospital*," Trace snapped. Both her foster father and the Siya U Hestî Cartel had fucked with her headware. The Siya U Hestî had even installed *extra* silicon into her brain without asking—always a nerve-wracking thought.

But none of that had been done in a hospital. And none of it had involved sick people.

"I want to help," she assured the doctor, though her gaze was focused on her dads. "I'm not doing anyone any good sitting here aboard *Evasion*, twiddling my thumbs!"

THE "FULL-BODY PROPHYLACTIC EQUIPMENT" was both more and less intimidating than Trace had feared. The standard day-to-day ship-suit of life aboard a starship was only a set of plumbing connections and a helmet away from being a spacesuit, after all.

That meant it was capable of sealing to the skin and preventing air flow in or out when instructed. For this purpose, Lan helped Trace put on a pair of flexible plastic gloves and link them into the suit—the emergency gloves the suit concealed were obstacles to any kind of working dexterity.

Then she put on thin plastic boots over the shipsuit feet and double-sealed them. Once all of that was in place, she had to recalibrate the shipsuit settings from her headware.

Her skin wasn't a great fan of being completely cut off from external air, so she needed the suit to provide airflow over it. Like everything else, though, the shipsuit was designed to do just that.

"Here," Lan told her, handing her what looked like a thick white plastic torc. "Emergency oxygen supply and purification system. Purifier uses ultraviolet and a contained heat cell to kill anything alive in the air."

They snorted.

"What's left isn't necessarily pleasant to breathe," he admitted, "but it is definitely *safe*. Which is important."

Trace put the torc on, linking it to her shipsuit both physically and digitally, then took the hooded mask Vexer passed and did the same. She felt like a monster from some horror film, but at least the hood and mask were transparent.

"I'll be running a scanner as we go," Lan told the other two, tapping a long black device attached to his left sleeve. "If I tell you to switch to canned air, do it immediately. No questions asked until after, okay?"

"Okay," Trace confirmed.

"Canned air is what, four hours?" Vexer asked.

"Yep. Plenty of time for us to get back to the ship, no matter what goes wrong. I don't see any reason we'll need to do that, but we want to be ready for it regardless."

"What if the hood gets damaged?"

Having gone through the whole system, that was the only piece Trace could see getting damaged at all—but it also felt surprisingly frail.

"It should autoseal in ten seconds or less. If it doesn't, here." Lan passed her a package the size of two decks of cards. "Emergency patches.

"Of course, once your air is contaminated, we'll need to quarantine you on return to the ship and pump you full of countervirals *anyway*," they admitted. "So, don't tear the mask."

"Reassuring, thanks." Vexer clapped Trace on her shoulder. "You don't need to come with us, Trace," he continued. "I don't get the impression that this is going to be a place for a kid."

"Am I going to help or hinder if I come?" she asked bluntly.

"Help," Lan conceded with a glance at her dad. "Even if all you do is run to supply closets for me so I don't have to, you'll help. If the situation is as bad as the Commissar was implying to EB, every set of hands might make a difference."

"Then I'm coming. Not really in question, is it?"

"Was she this much trouble *before* we adopted her?" Vexer asked wryly.

Trace glared at him.

"I think I might have been *more* trouble before that, Dad-V," she told him sweetly.

13

EB WATCHED the gray utility vehicle roll away across the airport tarmac with a feeling of trepidation. He couldn't put his finger on the exact cause, but seeing his lover and his daughter drive into a city ravaged by epidemic and within spitting distance of a major front line left him plenty of possible sources!

On the other hand, he also had plenty of things to do, and he turned his attention back to the masked woman with him.

He wore the same full body coverage gear that Lan had insisted their companions wear, and Commissar Owens didn't seem bothered. Just exhausted.

"Have you made contact with your superiors with regard to the cargo and my payment?" he asked her.

The locals had offloaded exactly one container so far. It hadn't even been moved out of the airport yet. The hoverflat had delivered it into the hangar, and a trio of olive-uniformed officers had vanished into it twenty minutes earlier.

"I have." Owens' gaze was following his own. "We linked our major cities with fiberoptic cable before the war. My communications are quite reliable, Captain."

"You were very prepared for this," EB observed. "When do I get paid?"

"I'm authorized to release the first kilogram once we've confirmed the contents of three containers and offloaded ten," she told him. "At that point, they'll dispatch the rest from Dinas Fferm by armored courier."

EB grimaced. Dinas Fferm was the Cinnead's capital, a space and naval port on the very southern tip of the continent.

"You don't have it all here?"

"We weren't sure that the request to deliver to Llandudno had made it through. And, well…Dinas Fferm is the easier place for a starship to land. If someone tried to run the blockade on spec, we'd want the elementals to hand."

She shrugged.

"Plus, that's where our government and treasury are located, and we have more secure facilities there."

"Again, you seem to have been well prepared for this."

"Everyone knew this was coming for a long time, Captain Bardacki," Owens murmured. "Every year that rolled around, the Tuathan corporations increased the costs of the inputs we needed to feed the planet—and the Staid Chorporra increased their quotas and fees.

"Again and again, we saw the results. Cinnead farmers—family businesses and agricultural coops—driven under by the opposing demands of the governments and the suppliers. Then they were bought up by Tuathan agricorps."

"Whose owners sat on the Staid Board; I'm guessing?" EB asked. Conflict of interest and abuse of power were stories as old as time, after all.

"Exactly." She sighed. "So, we began preparing. Importing weapons and aircraft, laying aside elementals where we could. The Cinnead isn't really a nation the way you likely think of us, Captain, but we managed to muster more resources than the Board expected."

"The Cinnead…" EB considered how they'd been described to him. The word meant *Clan*, after all—which went well with Dinas Fferm, which basically meant *Farm City*. "I'm guessing it's a glorified cooperative of agricultural cooperatives with extensive family and blood ties holding it together? Plus a healthy dose of e-democracy and anarcho-communism, I presume."

Owens chuckled.

"You may understand what we are better than I thought," she conceded. "Most people assume we are either a corporate spinoff like the Staid Chorporra or a disorganized revolution. We are neither of those things, and we prepared for this war for some time."

The preparation may well have added a weight of its own toward the conflict, EB suspected, but it wasn't his planet to judge. His own homeworld had its own issues—his government had unofficially authorized their former enemies to assassinate the heroes of the war, after all.

He still wasn't sure what had been going through the Council of Principals' minds when they'd agreed to *that*, but he'd been driven from Apollo by the results.

"I hope it goes the way you want," he murmured. "I've seen very few ground wars in my time. I served in a more-traditional nova conflict, but even that..."

He shook his head.

"War is never a pleasant thing, and it never goes the way anyone expects."

"No. We thought that this kind of stalemate would bring the Board to the negotiating table, but from what people have told me, they're not talking to us."

EB wasn't sure if Commissar Owens was the woman in charge of all Cinnead Militia in Llandudno or not. She wasn't, he assumed, the civilian leader of the city—but either way, she was senior enough that she would know if the negotiations were taking place.

"I'd have expected there to be some talks," he admitted. "From what my contacts on Nigahog said, this war has been stalemated in the Snowdens for over a month now."

"Six weeks. This was the plan. But...we expected the Spacers to support us or at least stay out of things entirely. We knew the mutiny was coming, but... The blockade is only neutral on the surface—the only factories that can produce combat vehicles are in Dachaigh a Tuath."

"You figure the Board is relying on that to win?"

"And your arrival is going to change the entire calculus, Captain. You've done more for us than you'll ever know."

"I'll be gone, hopefully, before you ever deploy any of these systems in your war," EB agreed. "I'll only find out how this ends if the news catches up to me as I travel the galaxy. You have a lovely planet, Commissar Owens, but I have no desire to get caught up in your war."

"The blockade will impede you leaving as much as it did you arriving."

"They didn't stop me getting here, and they won't stop me leaving."

A second container finally slid out of *Evasion,* and he held his breath for a moment as it balanced precariously on the edge of the cargo bay. The crane handlers knew what they were doing, and the second crane was in place to stabilize it.

"True enough, Captain. But know that you have changed the world for us!"

14

LLANDUDNO GENERAL HOSPITAL was the tallest building Trace had seen in the coastal city so far. It towered over the six-story apartment buildings and multiple styles of housing that surrounded it, a step-pyramid-style structure twelve stories tall.

Despite none of them ever having seen the building before, Lan seemed to know exactly where he was going. Trace and Vexer followed in his trail like they were on invisible leashes as he strode into the main reception area, leaving even their Militia-guide looking befuddled.

"Can I help you?" a stressed-looking nurse asked. "You are?"

"I am Dr. Lan Kozel, of the Kolter System," Lan barked crisply, putting their hands on their hips as they surveyed the entry area. "I need to speak with the head of your epidemiology department. We're here to volunteer our services for as long as we can."

"I...I see," the nurse replied, studying Lan's broad form and shaven head. He looked a bit taken aback by Lan's forthrightness.

He also might have just been exhausted, Trace figured. She doubted anyone working in a hospital was getting enough sleep to keep up with their workload, not with an epidemic going on.

"Give me a moment to establish where Dr. Wilson is," the nurse said, his eyes going unfocused as he linked into his headware.

"Of course."

By the time Lan had finished speaking, the nurse's gaze had refocused.

"Dr. Wilson is in the lab on the top floor. He is delighted to hear that we have a doctor volunteer, but he can't be interrupted right now. He suggests that you see Dr. Langdon on the seventh floor."

"That is fine for my companions," Lan said calmly. "But if you have a contagion lab on the premises, that is where *I* need to be. I am trained in epidemiology and contagion management."

They'd said that on the ship too, Trace remembered. Which was weird, because *she* thought their specialty had been headware hardware and software. He'd certainly managed the repairs to her abused silicon neurons with a skill and finesse she hadn't expected.

Trace would freely admit she was only a kid, but she didn't think doctors generally had more than one specialty. There was probably a difference between "trained in" and "specialized in," she supposed.

"Perhaps you should have that discussion with Dr. Langdon?" the nurse suggested. "There's an ambulance about to arrive and I'm going to need to triage the patients."

"Of course," Lan said with a swift bow. "Vexer, Trace, come with me please."

"How do you know where you're going?" Trace asked as the doctor strode firmly away from the reception desk toward what she guessed was the elevators.

"I downloaded a map as soon as we entered range of the hospital's network," they told her. "And I have a great deal of experience with reading hospital maps!"

DR. LANGDON TURNED out to be a redheaded woman even shorter than Trace. Her hair had clearly *been* longer and roughly chopped off to get it out of the way. The unevenly cut ponytail matched the bags under her eyes and the visible pressure line where she'd adjusted her mask.

"Front desk said you were coming," she said abruptly as they approached. "What have you got?"

"I'm a trained epidemiologist and I've worked with contagion quarantine before," Lan said swiftly. "My companion, Vena Dolezal, is a trained emergency medic—and his daughter is a willing set of hands that has no opportunity to be infected."

Langdon snorted.

"Off the starship that just landed? 'Cause those are the only people I'd guess haven't been exposed."

"Exactly."

"And you're willing to help? I didn't expect that." She studied the three of them. "I won't say no to anybody, even a willing set of hands. Dolezal, what was included in your medic training?"

"Shipboard emergency care," Vexer told her. "General first aid, bone-setting, injection administration, IV management, fluids administration, t—"

"I need IV management and fluids admin," Langdon said. "If you can do those, you're a godsend. Nobody is dying of this bug, but it's taking everything we've got to keep it that way. Even the worst cases, it's mostly just that they can't keep water down."

"If we keep them properly hydrated, all signs are that we're not going to lose *anyone*, but we have fifteen *hundred* people on IV in Llandudno General alone."

"Show me where to scrub in," Vexer said. "I'll have Trace gopher for me and the other nurses in the ward?"

"So long as she's scrubbed in, even that'll help." Langdon gave Lan a look. "I need to get back to patients, Dr. Kozel. Wilson is doing a test cycle upstairs in full quarantine. You won't even be able to get in to help for another hour.

"But I can damn well use another doctor down here until then."

"Then give me a patient list, Dr. Langdon. We have work to do."

TRACE LOST track of Lan in the chaos that followed. Vexer helped her link her headware into the ward's support network—and it took her no time at all to find the request queue.

There were four doctors and twenty-two nurses and paramedics trying to keep on top of three hundred patients in a ward designed to hold…less. People were making runs to storerooms and such for supplies as they could, but the queue for requests was growing faster than anyone had time to fulfill them.

She threw herself into the task. The network could tell her which storeroom had which medication or supplies, but the records didn't narrow it down much further than that.

After the first hour, she'd learned where to find the key supplies, at least. The main thing she was running around was saline bags—and she could tell that there was going to be a problem with the supply of those far too quickly.

Still, the only thing she was qualified to do was run supplies around. Except that with the shortage of trained hands, even that was worth it. She managed to keep in touch with Vexer throughout, but she did the best she could: start at the top of the request queue and work her way down.

Five hours in, one of the older nurses looked at her as she was delivering the request pack of compress bandages and swore.

"Kid, have you eaten?" she demanded. "Drank? *Sat down?*"

"Has anybody on this floor?" Trace asked.

"Yeah, but we're not, what, thirteen?" the woman replied. "Answer the question."

"Can't. Exposure risk," Trace said.

"At least go sit down. Ten minutes," the nurse ordered. "The request queue is a third of the length it was this morning—and I've seen you running around all day. Go. Sit. Down."

Trace nodded and obeyed. She found a seating area near the elevators, scrubbed down again and was about to take a seat when she got a ping from Lan.

Trace, where are you?

At the elevators, she told them. *Nurse told me to sit down.*

She was considering her shipsuit and the hooded mask. There had to be something in the hospital that was sterile enough to drink if the mask had a way for her to get it through. A straw or some such.

Wait there. I need…a second brain. One without biases.

Trace had no idea what the hell Lan meant by that, but the doctor arrived less than a minute later. As if they'd been listening to her thoughts, they were holding a foil drink packet and passed it to her.

She looked at it in frustration for a moment before Lan touched the side of her face and pulled a drinking straw out of the mask. It rotated in the mask, presenting the straw to her dry lips.

"Didn't know that was there," she admitted.

"I should have said; sorry. Drink package is steam-sterilized inside and out. It's a meal-replacement smoothie; should get your brain back running."

Balancing the multiple points of contact designed to minimize exposure while drinking took all of her focus for a few seconds before Trace managed to swallow back a mouthful of strawberry-flavored drink.

"What do you need me for?" she asked.

"I need to go over what I've found with someone who isn't local and who doesn't have my blinkers and predispositions," they told her.

"I don't know if I'll understand," Trace admitted. She was nervous to be alone with doctors, too. She trusted Lan, but the hospital bothered her less than the doctors did.

"That's part of the point," they admitted. "Because if you see what I saw, then we definitely have a problem."

15

LAN TOOK Trace up to the top floor, still drinking her liquid lunch, and guided her into a side conference room.

"I stole all of Dr. Wilson's data," they said bluntly as they gestured her to a seat. "Not that he was being unreasonably secretive or anything; they are at war and I am a stranger. But I saw some oddities and I wanted to validate them."

"Okay," Trace said slowly, still not entirely sure what purpose she was going to serve that couldn't have been served by one of Lan's stuffed toys.

She supposed none of those had come with the doctor, though they filled every available space in the medbay on *Evasion*. Based on the one they'd given her—a stuffed cat named Mistopheles that was as close to a nonhuman emotional support as Trace had—Lan's stuffed animals were all of a grade to go through an autoclave for easy sterilizing.

But they weren't of a size that made them easy to drag around a foreign city.

"So." Lan gestured a holoprojector awake. "Let's start with easy. *This* is the most recent mapping and visualization of the virus."

A misshapen blob appeared in the air, with a slew of icons, letters and numbers that Trace didn't even begin to understand hanging next to it.

"And *this* is the original mapping and visualization they did when they first hit a hundred hospitalizations for the same symptoms," they continued.

A second misshapen blob and legend appeared in the holograms. Trace glanced from one to the other, then back to Lan.

"What am I looking for? I can't even read the codes."

"Don't need to, not really. Do you see the differences? *Changes* in those codes, shifts in shape, those kinds of things."

Trace studied the images in the air for a moment, then ran a comparison program in her headware to confirm her initial impression.

"There aren't any," she said.

"Fuck."

"Lan?"

"That's what I saw too, and I was hoping I was wrong," they told her. "Viruses mutate, Trace. It's what they *do*. They're always different. *Always*."

"And this one isn't?"

"Exactly. It's possible that there's a labeling error or something in the data files, but…"

Lan spread their hands.

"Started poking at other things after that," they noted. "Not many diseases are this…balanced. Low lethality—not zero, despite what they told us. Three people *have* died—but extremely low. Hyper-contagious. They defaulted to labeling it as a respiratory virus and managing it, because we have population protocols for that, but…"

"Hence full-body PPE," Trace said.

"Exactly. I don't think you can get much more contagious than this little *fucker*." Lan waved a hand, dismissing the duplicate image and expanding the newer one. "Aerosol-to-skin transmission. I cough, it hangs in the room for five to ten minutes, and if one of those droplets *touches your skin*, you are at risk of infection."

"That sounds…bad."

"As bad as it can get. Rarely occurs in nature. Worse, most combinations of this level of lethality and infectiousness are…well, *benign* is the wrong word, but mostly harmless? Ninety-nine percent of the evolutions of the common cold, for example, just make the patient feel like crap but leave them functioning.

"This one…"

"There's a thousand people in this building alone who are feeling worse than that," Trace said.

"Yeah." Lan was glaring at the image of the virus in a manner that made Trace worried.

"What is it, Lan?" she asked.

"It's a biostabilized virus with minimal detectable mutation. It has a ten-day incubation period, which the patient is infectious for at least five days of. Once it hits, the patient is bed-ridden with vomiting and nausea—completely out of commission.

"On the other hand, treatment is easy. Consumes readily available resources, mostly just requires living or robotic hands to do the work. At the same time as the infected are being floored and new infected are coming in—because your patients were infectious for a week before they ever made it to the hospital.

"Maybe half of your patients can self-manage, but they're still out of commission. Deaths are rare but inevitable when the virus gets into the vulnerable populations, because its *target* is the healthiest."

They trailed off, continuing to glare at the virus's shape in the air. In the silence, Trace followed Lan's spoken thoughts through to the only possible conclusion.

"It's artificial, isn't it? A weapon."

Lan exhaled a long sigh.

"I was really hoping that the kid who didn't know what a bioweapon looked like would draw a different conclusion," they told her. "But that's my assessment. It's a tactical bioweapon, designed to disable a defensive position for a period of a few days."

"But this isn't the defensive position," Trace said, then paused. "Llandudno is the supply line for the front, isn't it?"

"Yup."

"You said everyone was infectious for a week before they knew. So, half the city was probably contagious before anyone actually was falling sick?"

"Yup."

"Did the data you stole include medical reports from the militia?" Trace asked in a very small voice, considering everything they'd just gone through.

"No. But I did the math. First hospitalized cases here were nine days ago. If it was deployed in Landudno to spread to the Snowden lines, they started seeing hospitalizations four to five days ago.

"By now, at least half the soldiers at the front line are puking their guts out—and half of what's left is keeping the first half hydrated. And you can play all the games in the galaxy to disguise your weakness, but if your enemy knows what's coming..."

"We have to tell the locals," Trace said. "They need to know this was an attack."

"We do," Lan admitted, but shook their head. "I'm just...not sure it's going to make any difference."

"Why not?"

"Any soldiers they send into those fortifications will get infected. If they had enough troops to cycle through the way they're going to need to, they'd have already won the war."

***

"DR. KOZEL. DID YOU LEARN ANYTHING?"

Sam Wilson eyed Trace curiously, but their main attention was on Lan. Like *Evasion*'s doctor, Wilson had shaved their head. They wore subtle makeup to blur the lines of their cheekbones as well, though the makeup was badly smudged.

"I did and I don't like it," Lan said bluntly. "I lied when I said I was an epidemiologist specialist, Dr. Wilson."

"What?" they snapped, some of the fatigue clearing from their face as they surged to their feet. "Why would you—"

"Because I worked in *bioweapons*, Doctor! I've done a lot of things over the years, and I try to forget that *particular* stint, but I remembered the protocols, the analytics, and the contagion protocols.

"You have a biostabilized targeted tactical bioweapon in your city, Dr. Wilson," Lan concluded. "Designed to disable the population of fighting age to clear the path for an enemy assault to punch through your fortifications in the Snowden mountains and storm this city."

"A…a *bioweapon?*"

"And it has been a spectacular success. Give me three days and everything you have on this floor, and I'm pretty sure that we can synthesize a target counterviral that will get people back on their feet, but you're not going to have three days.

"Unless the Tuathans are far more incompetent at using their bioweapons than they are at designing them, they did the same math I did and recognized that the fortifications are probably at their most vulnerable *today.*"

Wilson collapsed back into their chair like their strings were cut.

"We'd hoped we'd kept it away from the front," they whispered. "But…I'm not Cinnead, they only trust me so far, and I don't get medical reports on the Militia. They wouldn't *tell* me if it had reached the lines."

"Which should have been an answer in and of itself, shouldn't it?" Lan asked. "I didn't expect to see this sophisticated an artificial organism out here, I'll admit. It took me longer to realize what I was looking at than it should have."

"The colony's founding members included a biotech company that was testing terraforming bacteria," Wilson told them. "The Board has always made sure to keep their grip on the bioengineers tight—hell, as it was explained to me, if we don't win this war in the next twelve months, the damn soil will start *un*-terraforming under our farms."

Trace swallowed a curse that wasn't appropriate around adults, especially in this situation.

"No wonder they launched a war," she said instead.

"We need to get out of here, Doctor," Lan told the local. "The medic I brought, Dolezal, I need to find him."

"Still in the floor-seven ward. I can page him…I can… I can't… I can…"

"You need to activate whatever contingency plans you have, Doctor. If I were you, I'd be hoping that the Board is planning on leaving the hospitals alone. It's a reasonable hope…but you may need to prepare for the alternative."

"*How?* We don't have enough hands and doctors to—"

An explosion tore through the air, dragging all of their eyes to the window. Outside, a fireball falling from the sky helped locate where a squadron of jet fighters was now swarming toward Llandudno.

"It's too late," Lan whispered. "It's begun."

16

THE SOUND of the tank engines coming alive was far less impressive than EB figured Owens was expecting. Antigravity coils were entirely silent, after all. The turbines that drove the combat vehicle were well contained and shielded as well, leaving only a vibrating hum to emerge from the Galahad-2 as it lifted off the ground.

The assault cannon on the corners began to rotate a moment later, the commander inside the tank testing the secondary weapons first.

"I suppose even being quieter than I expected doesn't make it actually *stealthy*," Commissar Owens finally said as the missile pod and main turret went through similar test rotations.

"Not in the slightest," EB agreed. "The *Spacers* probably know you just powered up a main battle tank. She's got a few stealth features, according to the manual, enough to make her hard to hit at range or from orbit, but…that's a fifty-megawatt fusion power core, Commissar. You aren't hiding her from any serious scanners."

"I imagine the Board's Gallowglass tanks aren't much harder to pick out." She reached out a hand to touch the tank. "Sadly, until we break open a few more of those storage containers, we don't have the kind of aerial drone surveillance necessary to *find* them. We can stop them getting their drones in too close, but they have the tech advantage here."

The tank shifted and Owens stepped back, allowing the vehicle to smoothly slide forward through the hangar.

"Or they did, anyway."

"Three containers," EB reminded her, gesturing at the three TMUs sitting in the hangar. "And you've confirmed that at least one of the tanks works."

"Six tanks and a light battalion of infantry won't turn the tide here, Captain." But she chuckled and sighed. "But that's the metric for your first payment.

"Walk with me."

He fell in behind the olive-uniformed local. Militia or no, the Cinnead troops were professional and well trained—the Galahad couldn't be fought with just one tech inside, but the officer who was testing the tank out definitely knew their work.

Stepping out into the daylight, Owens turned away from EB to grimly study the mountains to the north.

"I don't suppose you'd be open to some mercenary work on the side while you're here?" she asked.

"*Evasion*'s no warship, and I don't think my three suits of powered armor are going to make a huge difference in your war."

"I suspect *Evasion*'s guns would make an ugly dent in the Tuathan fortifications in the pass," Owens said. "But that's fair. All of *our* power armor is up there."

"Along with your antitank weapons, tanks and artillery, I'm guessing?"

"Not the tanks. We weren't planning on launching an offensive without the weapons you delivered, Captain, so we held the tanks back. Just in case."

He nodded, following her gaze.

"I'm honestly surprised they're not negotiating," he murmured. "You do control the food, after all."

She laughed bitterly.

"I see some of Estutmost's secrets remain our secrets."

"Oh?" EB wasn't sure what she meant. "I know your supplier is *very* interested in your terraforming tech. Said it was unlike anything they had. And Estutmost's soil is hostile to human-compatible crops by default."

"The Dagda Combined Fertility System would probably be useless to Nigahog," Owens told him. "I'm farm-born and -bred, Captain. Dagda is why my family could make a living. It's how the Cinnead can exist. It's how *Estutmost* can exist.

"But Dagda is not a true terraforming system. It's a temporary solution via a suite of artificial organisms that are intentionally rendered sterile before deployment. And it's controlled by the Staid Chorporra."

"So, if the war continues…"

"We made sure to have stocks of Dagda on hand, but they didn't *want* us building reserves," Owens concluded. "We've used them up for the current round of crops, and the soil *should* be good for one more without additional applications.

"But after that, we're fucked. And *they're* fucked, because the crops are just as bioengineered as the soil, and the *Cinnead* control those."

She sighed.

"But Estutmost has always had amazing biotech, and there are enough crops and scientists north of the Snowdens that the Staid's Board thinks they can keep the population fed until *we* starve."

That was a cluster far beyond anything EB had expected. It also, thankfully, wasn't his problem.

"Fortunately, my employers didn't expect payment in terraforming tech," he said drily.

"Stamped elementals, I know. They're in the car."

She turned away from the mountains and headed toward the gray sedan she'd arrived in. EB followed, glad to finally get at least some of the payment Naumov had said was waiting for him.

The last thing he expected was for the sky to explode above them.

―――――

"WHAT THE *HELL*?"

"Owens, get *down*," EB snapped, grabbing the Cinnead officer and pulling her behind the car. A second aircraft detonated in the air, and he could see missile traces when he looked up.

The whole sky was breached by a bolt of thunder as *someone*—Llandudno's air defense squadron, he *thought*—fired an HVM.

"Sandoval, report," Owens barked. She wasn't talking to EB, but she clearly was giving in to the unconscious urge to speak aloud.

"Fuck."

"Owens?" he asked.

"The cable from the Snowden Line has been cut," she told him. "We've lost contact with the fortifications—but the Tuathans wouldn't send aircraft over the mountain without a purpose."

Pillars of light and fire marked the antiaircraft laser turrets positioned to the north of the city firing—but the fire only lasted moments before it was cut off, with aircraft still dueling in the sky above Llandudno.

"Why did the turrets stop?" she whispered to herself.

"Because they're gone," EB said grimly, looking to the north and spotting pillars of blacker smoke. And as if in answer to an unspoken question, he heard a distinct whistling sound. He'd never heard that *exact* tone before, but he could guess what was coming.

"What the—"

EB was running, dragging Owens behind him as the shells dropped out of the sky. Purely ballistic projectiles, they detonated two hundred meters up and scattered seeking bomblets across the airport.

Owens' car was close enough to the targeting criteria that at least three weapons hit it, obliterating the vehicle. The cranes working to offload *Evasion* were also hit, explosions toppling the massive machines to the ground in pieces.

Dozens of bomblets smashed into the roof of the hangar storing the cargo containers they'd already offloaded. Designed for peacetime cargo handling, it lacked the armor or structural support to withstand artillery bombardment.

Evasion, on the other hand, was a spaceship armored against high-velocity micrometeorite impacts. She was no warship, able to stand off plasma strikes, but the bomblets of an area-strike artillery shell were no threat to her.

Not in the first few hits, anyway.

"They shouldn't have…"

"They're getting targeting data from the aircraft," EB told her. "But if they're shelling Llandudno, they're moving on the city. They've cut the coms to the fortifications and they're shelling here—your Snowden Line is *gone*."

"Right."

Owens gently removed herself from his grip and surveyed the devastated cargo port. The unloading equipment needed to empty *Evasion* was wreckage—and the crew working them was dead.

"You need to get to Dinas Fferm," she told EB. "We can't offload *Evasion* here and we need those weapons more than ever!"

Thunder split the sky again as more HVM strikes smashed through the aerial battle. This time, EB was looking up and he saw the angles.

"Those aren't fighter-launched," he said softly. "Those are…those are the same damn missiles I'm delivering to *you*."

Owens nodded, her eyes stony.

"They must have retrieved them from the first ship," she guessed. "Which means that the Snowden Line is being overrun by Nigahog heavy tanks as we speak—and they'd already been weakened by the same virus that hit Llandudno."

"You didn't mention that part."

"We weren't exactly going to advertise our weaknesses." Owens was glaring at the debris of the warehouse. "Chauncy, report."

She apparently *got* an answer as she nodded a moment. "If the engines are what they *should* be…push right out."

A few seconds later, the debris shifted and the sound of turbines whining was suddenly audible across the cargo port. Lifting from the chaos like a phoenix from the ashes, the Galahad-2 heavy tank rose out of the debris, wobbling as the pilot mis-balanced the jets for a moment, and then headed toward them.

"You need to go," Owens told him. "I'm going to get in that tank and take command of the defense, as best as we can, but you need to get your ship and the weapons aboard her to Cinnead Command in Dinas Fferm."

"I'm here to make a cargo delivery, not turn the tide of your war,"

EB said. "And my kid and boyfriend are out there—not to mention my ship's damn *doctor*."

"I'll get the word to the troops around the hospital," Owens promised. "We'll protect your family and crew, Captain, but you need to leave *now*. Before they get enough of those HVM platforms out of the pass to seriously threaten your ship."

"I'm not—"

"Captain, *please*," she said. "There's a trio of atmospheric fast movers set aside for evacuating wounded. We'd be overwhelmed trying to evacuate all of the sick from the hospitals, but I'll have them load your family aboard and send the plane to Dinas Fferm.

"But you have to go now or my people are doomed. We need those tanks more than ever."

EB could see more artillery shells hammering down to the west of the city—most likely on top of either a fortified position or a mobile force of the Cinnead Militia.

The rebels' main defensive line was lost. The city he was standing in was lost—he was surprised Owens wasn't trying to beg a ride aboard *Evasion*. Without the tanks and artillery still aboard *Evasion*, the Cinnead's cause was lost.

And if the Cinnead's cause was lost, he was never going to get paid.

"You'll get them out?" he demanded.

More olive-uniformed troops were filtering in to the wrecked airport now, noncoms clearly directing them toward the debris. EB wasn't sure they'd manage to dig out the tanks in time, but there were five more of them in the shattered hangar.

They wouldn't make a *difference*—but six heavy tanks the Tuathans hadn't anticipated might well make a *point*.

"I will do everything within my power," Owens promised. "But I need you to get that cargo to my people."

"And you?" EB asked. He would think worse of her if she wanted aboard *Evasion*, but he'd take her anyway.

"That tank has better communications systems than my command center," she told him, then grimaced. "Plus, my command center is being shelled about three times a minute. No one is getting in or out today."

EB hated himself for it, but there wasn't anything he could do in Llandudno. Even if he tried to use *Evasion* for ground-fire support, he couldn't do enough to get his family out.

"All right, Commissar. I'll go."

17

"GINNY, get the antigrav system and the Harringtons online. I need them by the time I make it to the bridge!"

EB could close the ramp himself, thankfully. A mental command from his headware started the process as he continued deeper into the ship. A second command summoned a status report into a corner of his vision.

There were a bunch of orange warning lights across the top of the ship where the cluster munitions had struck, but his real concern was the exterior hatches highlighted in blue—including one of the cargo bays.

"Tate, I need you to get all of the exterior hatches closed," he ordered. "We're going to be in motion ASAP, and we can't risk friction or air-pressure losses."

"What the hell is going on, EB?" Ginny demanded. "Coils are already spinning up; they'll be live in sixty seconds."

It would be a toss-up whether he managed to make it through the ship by then. *Evasion*'s operations hull wasn't that big, but the ground-access ramp was positioned to be conveniently stored, not to provide easy access to the bridge.

Landing the ship hadn't been high on the list of design criteria, after all.

"The Tuathan forces are shelling the city, which means the fortification line has been breached. They want us to relocate the cargo to Dinas Fferm—and *I* want to move before they dial us in accurately enough to start dropping HVMs on us!"

In the Staid Chorporra's place, he'd use the *threat* of HVMs to keep *Evasion* grounded until he could seize the ship and her cargo. The tanks and artillery still in his bays might well be the Cinnead's last chance not to lose the war.

"Closing the bay doors," Tate reported. "What about Lan, boss? Vexer? *Trace?*"

EB grimaced. His family were at the top of his own thoughts, but what could he do? *Evasion* couldn't even withstand serious shellfire. Cluster munitions were one thing, but if the artillery starting dropping hundred-millimeter-plus shells on his ship, she would be crippled or destroyed in short order.

"The Cinnead are going to evacuate them," he told his crew. "I don't like it, but we can't do anything for them ourselves—and we're not getting paid unless we get this cargo to Dinas Fferm.

"They've promised they'll do everything they can, and we have to trust them."

"I don't like it," Reggie interjected. "There has to be *something* we can do."

"Spin up the guns and take shots of opportunity as we fly," EB told his gunner. "It looks like the Tuathans got the cargo from the first ship, which means they have Galahads and Rakshasas. Put a plasma bolt into a couple of those—or their homebuilt artillery—and we'll help *everybody*.

"Including our family."

He was at the bridge at last, the doors sliding open in response to his silent command as he half-ran into the room. He didn't have as much practice at dropping into *Evasion*'s bridge seats at a run as he'd once had for Apollo's Hoplite interceptor, which meant he spent precious seconds getting into the chair and taking full control of his starship.

By then, all of his systems were online, and the last exterior hatches were closing. His sensors showed that the Cinnead were being surprisingly effective at getting the Galahad-2s moving from the debris field that had been their hangar—the cargo containers had kept the tanks clear of debris, but getting them out was *still* impressive, and two more of the antigrav vehicles were now on the tarmac.

Commissar Owens' people might not know how to use the heavy tanks to full effect, but *some* functions were basically automatic when turned on. As EB watched, two of the tank's secondary guns opened fire into the air at something he couldn't see on his own scanners.

Shells struck by blaster fire exploded in the air, reduced to hopefully harmless debris by the tanks' defenses.

"And that's our bloody cue, boss," Reggie said in his headware. "I *can't* shoot down incoming shells or missiles. So, as they start dialing us in…"

"We get vulnerable. We're coming back for our people, I promise."

EB's words were directed as much to himself as his crew. It was his daughter and his boyfriend they were leaving behind, after all. Lan was a good friend too, even if Trace and Vexer were definitely the priority in EB's mind.

Evasion didn't like being this close to a planet's gravity well, but she answered to his commands readily enough. Antigrav reduced her weight, if not her mass, to something that made her lack of aerodynamic qualities irrelevant.

She wobbled in the air as she rose, but EB directed her away from where the Cinnead tanks were still shooting down incoming projectiles. Another tank had joined the impromptu armored company taking shape in the cargo port, but it seemed pretty clear that the Tuathans knew what was going on.

"They're using the planes for targeting, but the local air cover is *gone*," Reggie warned in his ear. "I can't get a solid lock on the fast movers, so I *really* hope they used up any HVMs they had in the dogfight!"

"Me too."

Heat signatures spiked on several displays as the ship rose above the city. EB stabilized *Evasion* in the air, and then ran power to the

Harrington coils. He couldn't go to full power—in atmosphere, *Evasion*'s full thrust would result in something more comparable to a giant HVM than actual *travel*—but he could take her to levels that were generally considered unsafe.

Safety was relative, however, and a risk of coil burnout was a very different thing from a risk of being hit with hyper-velocity missiles.

"Magnetic-tube artillery, hundred-twenty-millimeter," Reggie suddenly reeled off. "*I see you, you bitches.*"

Two of *Evasion*'s turrets opened fire, cycling as fast as Reggie could feed them plasma. Bolts of energy designed to cross fifty thousand kilometers of pure vacuum flashed across thirty kilometers of air, a series of fireballs highlighting the pass through the mountain.

For his own part, EB focused on flying the ship. He almost certainly shattered windows in Llandudno as he pressed *Evasion* to Mach one. Mach two. Mach three. Heat warnings flashed on his screen, warning him that the forward heat tiling was in a danger zone.

It didn't matter. He had seven hundred and twenty-three kilometers to go to reach Dinas Fferm—and every minute he was in the air was a minute for the Spacers to send a nova gunship and a sub-fighter squadron to force him to surrender!

"Well, *now* I can see the fighters," he muttered to himself. Four of the Tuathan fast movers were trying to come after him. Without the sheer power of *Evasion*'s Harringtons, the combat aircraft were going higher, heading into the range of "suborbital flight"—not a bad plan from their perspective, since they pretty much *had* to know where he was going.

Of course, there was also a distinct downside to going that fast and that high when chasing prey with guns designed to engage at deep-space ranges. Atmosphere badly degraded a plasma cannon's range and power—but not *that* badly.

Three of the planes vanished under Reggie's fire, and the fourth broke off and away at a speed and angle that suggested either great skill or absolute terror.

"We're clear."

"Eyes up," EB ordered. "I make it six minutes to the air-defense perimeter around Dinas Fferm, and until we're under cover of their missiles and lasers, the Spacers can pin us down."

The only thing making this stunt even *possible* was that there were batteries of surface-to-orbit missiles positioned around the Cinnead capital. Within two hundred kilometers of the city, the Spacers weren't going to come after him.

"I've got a monitor moving into position above us, but I think they're trying to stop us making a break for it," Reggie told him. "They may not be sure what we're doing yet."

"And if I had any other way to keep them guessing, I would."

Evasion was never meant to fly this low to the ground. EB was running her at less than half a kilometer of altitude, low enough that the Spacers couldn't risk orbital fire on her. They *had* to come down to catch her, and if they hesitated *enough*, he'd be clear.

"Gunship swinging around."

"She won't risk a nova," EB told Reggie. "Too-short range. Our risk point is gunships farther out, and I don't see any."

There were two timers running in his head. The first was the obvious one: the four minutes left until they hit Dinas Fferm's air-defense perimeter. The *second* was fuzzier: the timeline until a sub-fighter deployed from any of the monitors EB could see couldn't drop low enough to force *Evasion* off course.

"Monitor is dropping fighters!"

EB nodded silently. Big as the asteroid-built monitors were, their volume was inefficiently used due to their construction method. None of the Spacer ships would carry more than a dozen sub-fighters—not least because the only *real* use of sub-fighters, in his educated opinion, was as a defensive measure against *nova* fighters.

And no one in the Beyond had any real numbers of nova fighters.

Four sub-fighters now plummeted away from their mothership, letting gravity do much of the work of pulling them downward to *Evasion*.

"Three minutes," EB said quietly. The sub-fighters were a real threat. If they got into position to fire without hitting the planet, he'd have to honor that threat and obey their orders.

"I can hit the lead pair from here," Reggie offered.

"The moment we kill a Spacer, this becomes *personal*, Reggie. And when it's *personal*, they'll run the risk ratio of whether there's likely to be someone in those empty fields below us."

So long as it was mission and duty, it wasn't *quite* a game, but even small risks would be avoided. The Spacers didn't want to get their hands dirty. They were going to let the blockade do the bloody work for them.

As soon as their own people died, it became *personal*—and then freighters got shot down from on high. Nothing EB could do could protect *Evasion* for more than a few seconds if the monitors opened fire on her.

"Blockade runner, this is Armstrong-Gamma-Actual. You are under the guns of our monitors. Stand down and head for orbit."

EB ran the angles in his head. The lead sub-fighter was still well above the Kármán line, at least five hundred kilometers in the air. They couldn't shoot at *Evasion* without threatening the farms beneath them…and they were still only using gravity to drop.

"Boss?"

"Do *not* fire," EB ordered. "Ignore them."

"*Ignore them?*" Ginny's voice was incredulous.

"Ignore them," he repeated. "And tell me the moment any of our heat tiles hit red."

"What?!"

She hadn't even finished complaining when EB juiced the Harrington coils again.

This *was* going to cost him thermal-protection tiles. But that was what the protective armor systems was *for*. They could source replacements in Dinas Fferm—or just take the flight up very, very slowly.

Now the sub-fighters brought their own engines online, augmenting gravity as they dropped into deep dives. No starfighter was designed for atmosphere, but they were as capable of flying in it as *Evasion* was. More so, in many ways, because ancient tradition kept both sub- and nova fighters built in similar styles to aerospace fighters.

They cut through the atmosphere like the birds they resembled—but they were too late.

"What are you thinking?" he murmured as the fighters continued to blaze toward him. "You can't get angle to force me up. Are you going to fire or not?"

Seconds were ticking away and seconds were everything. The fighters would have to pull out before they entered the air-defense perimeter of Dinas Fferm—they'd have to bring a lot more than four sub-fighters to challenge those batteries—but they could fire *into* that perimeter.

They could no longer force *Evasion* back to orbit, but they could still shoot her down. The Spacers couldn't force EB to surrender, but they could still enforce the actual blockade.

If they were willing to kill all of his crew and destroy whatever *Evasion* landed on—plus the inevitable damage from misses.

He could *see* the moment the sub-fighters got the order. One second, they were descending from the skies like bats out of hell, their prows and guns pointing toward his ship as he barreled for Dinas Fferm.

The next, they almost stopped dead in the air, reorienting to bolt back to orbit before the Cinnead missile batteries could target them.

"I'd feel bad for ignoring them," EB said with a rush of relief, "except that they don't even have the courtesy to tell me they're letting me go!"

18

TRACE FOLLOWED Lan through the chaos of the hospital corridors in a near-daze. She'd known they were landing in a war zone, but all of the adults around her had seemed to think that they were going to be perfectly fine—and while her opinion of *most* adults was scatological, she'd learned to trust the judgment of her new family.

For a second, she lost sight of the doctor. Inhaling sharply, she pressed herself against a wall as a trio of soldiers—out of uniform and identifiable only by their helmets and guns—rushed past with a stretcher.

"Trace!" Vexer was suddenly there, grabbing her hand as she tried not to hyperventilate. "Come on. We need to get back to the ship."

Lan found them at the elevator, the doctor moving through the chaos like it was a calm day. Even through the shipsuit and full body PPE, they seemed to radiate authority and certainty that led to people giving way to them.

"There you are. Can't take the elevator. Follow me."

Trace glanced helplessly at Vexer, but her dad just nodded grimly and went where Lan indicated. Vexer seemed almost as lost and over-whelmed by the situation as she felt. The doctor's certainty was enough to get her following them—hopefully, they knew what they were doing!

Lan led them into a stairwell around the corner from the elevators. A uniformed soldier with no visible weaponry was standing inside, directing traffic toward the ground floor. She held up a hand, pausing the flow of people long enough to get the trio of *Evasion* crew into the queue.

And not one moment longer, Trace realized. Still holding Vexer's hand, she had a stranger breathing on the top of her head, and Lan was almost walking *on* the person in front of them.

The soldiers managing the evacuation were doing everything they could to keep people moving. There was no way Trace and her adults could break from the line they'd been inserted in, forcing them to move with the rest of the crowd until they were finally outside of the step pyramid of the hospital.

Then Lan grabbed Trace's free hand and pulled her and her father to the side of the parking lot.

"We have to get back to the ship," Vexer said grimly.

"We can't," Lan replied. "Listen."

Trace listened. There was a whistling sound she didn't recognize… followed by the sound of explosions, which she very definitely *did* recognize now.

"They're shelling the city," the doctor told them. "EB has to get the ship out now or he never will. He'll hate every second of it, but he'll leave us behind. We need to see to our own safety."

Trace swallowed and held tightly to the two adults' hands.

"How?" Vexer demanded. "I'm a freighter navigator, Lan. Trace is *thirteen*. I can't… I don't…"

"I can. And I *will*," Lan snapped. "But you need to listen to me. We can't get back to the ship, and we almost certainly can't get out of the city before the government forces get here. We need to go low and go dark, and we need to do it *now*.

"Follow my lead, do what I tell you and we'll still be here when the captain comes back for us. Can you do that? Both of you?"

Trace looked up at Lan in a new light, wondering just who the *hell* was working as a doctor on her dads' ship.

"Yeah, I can do that," she promised.

IF TRACE HADN'T ALREADY SUSPECTED that Lan was the best companion she and Vexer could have for this situation from *Evasion*'s crew, she realized it two minutes later when the doctor finished hotwiring an aircar.

"Get in," they instructed.

"Do you know where we're going?" Vexer asked.

"I have a plan, yes," Lan confirmed. "But it won't do you much good if we get separated or killed, so there's no point in me sharing the first draft while I'm percolating."

"Coordinates are in your headware. Fly low, fly safe, keep us out of sight."

Trace was already in the back seat before Lan shuffled over to let Vexer take the controls. Her dad looked askance at the loose wires yanked out of the control panel—one of which had been plugged into Lan's neck a moment earlier—but he seemed to know what do with the controls.

The light air vehicle took off smoothly, and Vexer flew them away from the hospital. Pillars of smoke rose throughout the city, easily visible even staying within a few meters of the ground.

"They're not randomly shelling," Lan said as Trace stared at the smoke. "They're hitting power grids, known military bases, key infrastructure. They know *exactly* what they're shooting at—the planes are providing sighting."

"How do you even know this?" she demanded. "You're a *doctor*."

"The question I prefer not to answer, young Miss Trace, is *who* I was a doctor for." They shook their head. "My guess is thirty minutes until the lead elements of the government forces hit the city perimeter."

"I thought they were held up in the mountains," Vexer argued.

"Half or more of the Cinnead troops in the mountains were down with that damn virus. Speaking of..." Lan tore their hooded mask off. "Locals are using face masks, not full PPE. We can't draw attention. Here."

They handed Trace and Vexer standard personal nano-respirator masks, presumably *borrowed* from the hospital.

Grimacing, Trace took off her own hood and followed suit with the mask.

"Doesn't this make us vulnerable?" she asked. "You said it was skin-contact contagious."

"I'd rather rig an IV in a safehouse to keep us all hydrated than see us identified and detained by the Staid Chorporra na h-Estutmost," Lan said bluntly. "Catching the virus is now a far lower risk factor than being identified as strangers."

"We're at the coordinates you gave," Vexer noted. "There's nothing here."

"Of course not; it's a parking lot," the doctor confirmed. "We ditch the car and the PPE here. If we could ditch the shipsuits, I'd say do that, but I don't think any of us have enough other clothes on us to make that work."

"There's a couple of bags in the storage back here," Trace told them as the aircar settled down. "Maybe we should check if there's anything that fits? Can't hurt."

"Can't hurt at all. Next step is a hotel, about two minutes' walk from here."

"How are you this calm...this *prepared*?" Vexer asked.

"I learned a long time ago to have a plan to escape any room I ever entered," Lan replied. "Come on; I'm going to rig the car to self-ignite once we're on our way, so let's check those bags!"

WHOEVER THE OWNER of the car had been, they'd had much the same tall and slim build as Vexer. The conservative dark blue suit they stole fit Vexer perfectly, though the clothing didn't do much good for Lan or Trace.

One of them was no longer obviously starship crew, which Trace hoped would help. She understood the threat environment, at least, but she wasn't sure what she could or couldn't do to help them disappear.

The general panic in the town didn't help her mood—nor did the smell of burning plastic and electronics the wind wafted past them from the parking lot they'd left behind.

It had never even *occurred* to her that an aircar's high-density batteries could be turned into bombs. She'd grown up in an era where even the vehicles in the Beyond were so overdesigned for safety that even human-caused accidents were rare and more embarrassing than fatal.

Except it had taken Lan under a minute to rig the aircar to light itself on fire. Their PPE, the original owner's clothes, Vexer's clothes… all of it was a smoldering wreck behind them now.

And Trace Bardacki was never going to look at any vehicle the same away again.

"In here," Lan finally said, turning under the sign of the third hotel they'd passed on a street of several.

"Why this one?" Vexer asked.

"You'll see."

The doctor strode through the lobby with the same certainty and confidence that had carried them through the hospital earlier. The hotel looked cheap to Trace's eyes, though she knew that she hadn't been exposed to ordinary hotels when traveling with her political parents on Icem.

The walls were painted an uninteresting gray. A few pieces of art that she was relatively sure had been public-domain before the diaspora from Earth hung on the walls. There were a handful of fabric couches, clearly designed as much for ease of cleaning as anything.

Most importantly, though, was that there wasn't a single living human being visible in the entire space. An artificial stupid hologram of a gorgeous Black woman stood behind the counter, waiting with the kind of unquestioned patience only an AS could manage.

"Welcome to the Black Lotus Hotel. How can I assist you?"

"I need the Shíguāng Dàoliú Special," Lan told the stupid. "Starting five days ago, book for three weeks."

"Rú nǐ suǒ yuan," the stupid said instantly, then returned to English. "And how will ser be paying for their stay with the Black Lotus?"

"Verified silver ingot."

There was presumably some silent addition to the conversation after that, because Lan paused for a few seconds, then reached inside a pocket of their shipsuit and selected an ingot. They slid it into a receptacle that opened on the counter, which promptly chimed happily.

"You are in the sixth day of your stay with the Black Lotus," the stupid said cheerfully. "I am sorry that you lost your room cards, ser. Please see the receptacle on your left for replacements."

Lan nodded to the hologram. An opening had appeared on the counter, and they grabbed three black cards out of it.

"Come on," they said. "Let's get sorted before curfews start locking in."

THEIR ROOM WAS a two-bedroom suite with a fold-out couch that Lan immediately claimed for themselves.

"You two can fight over the rooms," they instructed.

"Don't care," Vexer admitted. "Left?"

"Sure." Trace dropped down next to the doctor. "What now, Lan?"

"I've got a grocery order coming to the room in about thirty minutes," Lan replied. "I'll investigate the kitchenette before it gets here; hopefully, I did it a disservice in my planning.

"After that, we don't open that door for at least twenty-four hours. We hunker down, we keep an ear and an eye on the news feeds, and we stay safe."

They shook their head.

"So far, the news media isn't sure what's going on, but they're pretty sure the shelling was reasonably well aimed."

"And has stopped," Vexer said slowly. "Because...damn."

It took Trace a while longer to link into the news feeds and find the updates than either adult, but she saw what Vexer was swearing at before they could explain.

Every feed was showing fire descending from the sky onto the slopes of the Snowden range. Most of them weren't overly clear on *where* the plasma bolts were coming from, but flipping through them,

Trace found one with a decent shot of *Evasion* blazing across the sky toward the south.

"EB got out, good," Lan finally said. "And bought the city a few hours along the way, looks like."

Vexer growled.

"I don't feel overly bad about the people lobbing artillery shells into a civilian city, regardless of how well aimed. And that's *not* considering the void-cursed *tactical bioweapon*."

"That we're going to catch now, aren't we?" Trace realized aloud. That thought made her curl up on the chair she was, tucking her legs into her chest as she shivered.

"That's part of what we're hunkering down against." Lan waved a hand around the room. "The Black Lotus was mentioned on a few discussion boards I checked into, for multiple reasons. They have really good sanitation protocols, so the room should be fine.

"The groceries should *also* be sterile-ish…so unless we caught it in the street, we'll be fine."

"You need to work on your reassurances, doc," Vexer said. "What happens if we did catch it?"

"Trace, there's a small diamond button on the right side of your emergency collar," Lan told her. "Press it, please."

Running her fingers over the oxygen supply and filtration collar they'd given her when she put on the PPE, Trace found the button and hit it. The entire right side of the torc-like collar popped open with a hiss of escaping air.

She reached into the compartment and pulled out a carefully wrapped package of vials.

"Apologies, you had an hour less air than you thought you did," Lan told her. "On the other hand, that's three full courses of countervirals. If we did get exposed, those should keep us upright and functional through the worst of it."

Trace removed the collar with a sigh.

"What about clothes?" she asked. "I'm not the biggest fan of living in the *same* shipsuit for days on end."

"We'll cross that bridge tomorrow or the day after," Lan said. "For now, we stay low. This city is about to be invaded, after all."

"How did you even know that the hotel would let you book into the past?" Vexer asked.

"Discussion boards," Lan replied brightly. "All of Black Lotus's records now say we've been here for five days. That makes us much less suspicious, given that *Evasion* arrived today.

"As Trace has found before, there are always dark web boards that can only be accessed if you know the right key phrases," the doctor continued. "Trace has a stack of them in her database, but there are also some keys that open doors just about everywhere.

"And like I said, I make sure I always have an escape plan. Old habits die hard."

There was a long silence, then Trace coughed.

"So, do the people you used to make bioweapons for *know* you fled to the Beyond?" she asked innocently.

Lan sighed.

"I never made bioweapons for anyone, except in the most theoretical of senses," they explained. "I was..." They were silent for a second, then sat up on the folding couch and studied her for several long seconds.

"I was covert ops," they admitted. "Twelve years in Kolter Planetary Security Counter-Intelligence, six years in KPS Extraterritorial Services. Most of my time in Counter-Intelligence was working in bioweapon prevention.

"I did do a stint designing theoretical bioweapons for training exercises, but most of my time was making sure that we had measures to make sure nobody loosed a bioweapon in Kolter."

They shook their head.

"My first four years in ES was as support staff, actually being a doctor. The last two years... Well. There's a reason I'm on *Evasion*, and I've already said more about my past than I want to.

"I just need you to trust that I *can* get us through this."

19

DINAS FFERM HAD AN ACTUAL SPACEPORT, unlike Llandudno, which made putting *Evasion* down easier. The city was both larger and more vertical than Llandudno, but the spaceport was on the southern edge, next to the harbor.

Like Llandudno, Dinas Fferm was a transshipment point. Rails and roads from across the Dachaigh a Deas converged on the two cities, one at the northwest end and one at the southeast, carrying the fruits of Estutmost's terraformed soil.

In Llandudno, the cargo was loaded onto *water*-borne ships and orbital movers and mostly sent north to the Dachaigh a Tuath. Much of the food that arrived in Dinas Fferm went the same way, but the ships and spaceships that came through the larger city also carried supplies to the Spacer settlements throughout the system and the smaller settlements away from Estutmost's main continent.

While the downtown was filled with the office towers that held the administration for twelve million people and the agriculture and logistics that fed the system's forty-five million souls, the region around the harbor and spaceport was more industrial. The vertical structures around *Evasion* were the oldest type of their kind: grain silos.

"Reggie, keep the dorsal turret powered up," EB instructed as he set the ship's maneuvering systems into shutdown. "Swap off with whoever you can get to volunteer—I want human eyes and hands on our upper gun twenty-four-seven so long as we're here."

"How long are we expecting to *be* here, boss?" Reggie asked. "It doesn't feel right to leave our own behind."

EB couldn't argue with that. He wasn't entirely sure just *what* Reggie had done before being recruited. He knew the weapons tech came from Redward, the star system where *Evasion* had been built, but he'd *hired* Reggie in a star system almost eighty light-years away from Redward!

He had reason to believe that Reggie's previous profession had been less than legal, but the deal he'd offered everyone who signed on to his ship was simple: no questions were asked about pasts. He didn't want to explain that his own home government had sacrificed their fighter aces to enemy assassins as the price of peace, after all.

But whatever Reggie's life had been—mercenary or pirate or cartel enforcer or proper soldier—he'd been of the breed that didn't leave their fellow soldiers behind.

It had been part of the dogma of EB's own Apollo Self-Defense Force, too.

Plus...

"They're my *family*, Reggie," EB said quietly. "My daughter. My lover. Not just my XO, my doctor and my stowaway.

"The Cinnead promised they'd be extracted, and we couldn't stay. So, we check in with the locals, see what the timeline looks like for that extraction, and we deliver our cargo."

"And then?"

"Then we shall see, won't we?"

WITH A PROPER SPACEPORT came proper cargo-handling tools, designed to handle and work with TMUs in multiples. Instead of paired cranes and regular float trucks, EB exited his ship to see specialty cargo lifters rolling up to the back of his ship.

Multiple platoons of olive-uniformed soldiers were spreading out to secure the area surrounding *Evasion*. There were even troopers in powered combat armor, even if the ratio was far lower than any Rim military would tolerate.

A closed-top infantry fighting vehicle was approaching across the nanocrete, a remote-controlled turret slowly rotating to watch potential threat vectors. The six-wheeled vehicle came to a halt ten meters back from *Evasion*'s ramp and disgorged a pair of olive-uniformed soldiers who spread out in clear bodyguard fashion.

They weren't given enough time to *actually* secure the area before the passenger unfolded himself from the back seat. A tall man with tanned skin, pure white hair and a gold star on his shoulder, EB recognized the family resemblance before the local reached him.

"General Owens, I presume?" he greeted the Cinnead officer.

"Thomas Owens, yes," the General confirmed, offering his hand. "Evridiki Bardacki?"

"With the cargo and waiting for payment," EB said drily.

Owens nodded sharply and one of the soldiers returned to the IFV.

"Half of your promised payment on delivery immediately, including the amount you were supposed to receive in Llandudno," the general said crisply. "The rest when we complete unloading."

"I was also promised extraction of my crew—my *family*—from Llandudno."

"We've lost contact with Commissar Owens," the elder Owens told EB as the soldier returned with a metal case. The trooper passed the case to EB, but his focus was still on the General. "Either she or the Tuathans triggered a short-range multiphasic jammer shortly after you left the city. Any non-wired communication is completely hashed, and their fighters hit the cable link."

EB swallowed. That took both extremely precise piloting and perfect intelligence.

"Commissar Owens is…"

"My daughter."

"She was alive and locking herself in a Galahad-Deuce when I left," EB offered.

"That was the last report I had as well," General Owens told him.

"Unlike your family, Captain, I know my daughter is not being evacuated. Llandudno…"

He sighed heavily.

"Llandudno cannot hold, but it is Enid's task to try. We owe it to the people of the town."

"So, what now?" EB asked.

"The Tuathans have the edge in combat vehicles, but we know this continent and they do not," the Cinnead General said grimly. "The Galahads and Katyushas you have delivered will tip the balance back in our favor, we hope, but we need time to learn to use them."

He shook his head.

"Twenty hours' drive for the Tuathans' tanks to get here," he observed. "It'll take them a hell of a lot longer than that."

"Once the cargo's offloaded and you've got my people back to me, it'll be time for us to go," EB said. "I wish you and yours luck, but this isn't my war."

"No, it's not," Owens agreed. "But you've helped win it anyway. We won't see the evacuation aircraft from the hospitals for a few hours yet, but your family was supposed to be escorted to Llandudno General's fast movers by our troops.

"They'll be here, Captain. My daughter swore it would be done—which means it *will* have been done."

EB HAUNTED the bridge for the following hours. He'd barely managed to make himself count and store the five quarter-kilogram stamped ingots of stabilized lanthanum they'd been paid.

With the exception of that nearly momentary break, he spent his time on *Evasion*'s bridge, watching the sensors like a hawk. He watched the Cinnead defensive air squadrons sortie. He watched mechanized companies that had been quartered near the harbor roll out, as the Cinnead Militia prepared to contest the open plains between Llandudno and Dinas Fferm.

There was no sign of incoming air traffic from Llandudno. Standard colonial database aerial fast movers were jet-propelled aircraft with antigrav systems. Runways weren't truly necessary for most of them, but the complete lack of traffic suggested that the Staid Chorporra troops had shelled the civilian airport along with the cargo airport.

Or that the government aircraft were shooting down any aircraft that tried to evacuate from Llandudno. That would be a war crime, and so far at least, everything EB had seen suggested that the locals were trying to abide by generally accepted rules of conflict. *Mostly.*

Not least because the Spacers were staying neutral. If the people who'd taken control of the orbitals and blockaded the planet decided to pick a side, well, the war wasn't going to last much longer.

Atrocities were a losing game in that scenario.

And yet no one was arriving at Dinas Fferm's airports. The jammers were keeping news from leaving the city and all EB could do was wait.

Wait and curse himself. He'd allowed himself to believe that the locals could get his family to safety. Now Vexer and Trace were in a city that was under siege at best, occupied at worst.

"Boss, you need to rest."

He looked up in surprise. He hadn't heard Ginny enter the bridge, and she was now standing right behind him.

"I'm watching for the evacuation planes," he told her.

"I know what you're doing," his engineer replied, taking a seat in the empty forward chair. "And it's not going to change anything. You staring at a sensor screen isn't going to magically lift the jamming or find Vexer or keep Trace safe."

"But it means I won't miss them arriving."

"I'll wake you up when they arrive," she promised. "But you need to do anything *other* than sit here and beat yourself up for your choices."

"My *family* is out there, Ginny," EB whispered. "Vex… Trace… What have I *done*?"

"The only rational thing to do. Doesn't make it any less fucking awful, but it was the only thing you could do. Daughter, boyfriend, doctor…they'll either be fine or they won't."

EB flinched at that dichotomy.

"I wish I'd sent Reggie with them. I wish I'd *gone* with them. I…"

"If wishes were fishes, this ship would stink of seawater."

He snorted, a weak attempt at finding humor in the situation as he looked back at the sensor screen.

"It's a three-hour flight at most. It's been six."

"I know." She rested her hand on his shoulder and squeezed. "There's nobody on this ship who isn't worried about them, EB. I know Trace and Vexer are special to you, but we're all family here. You know that."

"Me and Vexer as dads to everyone, you as mom whether you like it or not?" EB asked. "Void curse it. I…"

"I told you that you should marry the ass," Ginny noted. "Wouldn't have changed this, but at least he'd know how much you care. There's *I love you* and there's *I love you enough to spend my life with you.*

"Pretty sure you two have made it to the latter, but *someone* is a stubborn prick who thought it wasn't worth acknowledging."

"Don't know if now's the time for that, Ginny."

"The bad times aren't the time for anything." She fell silent, her hand still on his shoulder as she stared up at the displays.

"What do we do if they don't get out?"

EB barely realized the whispered words were his.

"How's that even a question, boss?" she asked. "We go after them. Ship, armor, guns…whatever it takes. We end this fucking war for the locals, if that's what we gotta do.

"Blood of the covenant is thicker than the water of the womb. We made a *promise* to that kid. I'm not her mother, not the way you and Vexer are her dads, but she's *the* kid to all of us. This ship—this crew?

"We walked into hell to save you and Trace once. We'll go right back in for her and Vexer and Lan. The Staid Chorporra doesn't have a big-enough army to stop us getting our family out!"

20

Vexer's instruction was sharp enough to be clear over the sound of Lan in the kitchen. The doctor was sorting through the grocery delivery they'd arranged, organizing into self-prep, easy-prep and actual-cooking categories.

Or at least, that was Trace's interpretation of the organization. She hadn't asked what they were doing. She'd repositioned the big stuffed chair she'd claimed to cover the door and claimed the one stunner Lan had sneaked onto the planet in their own oxygen collar.

"Which one?" she asked Vexer.

His answer was a silent link, which she accepted and then grimaced at as an olive-skinned man with flaming red hair appeared in front of her.

A background filtered in as she activated a virtual screen, showing that the stranger was standing on the steps of what looked like some kind of government building—and a subtitle promptly confirmed that it was the Llandudno City Government House.

The stranger wore camouflage fatigues, the digital cloth frozen in gray-and-black urban instead of actively shifting, with a black shoulder lapel on each shoulder displaying three thick gold stripes and a small gold star.

"Citizen-shareholders of Llandudno. I am General Valentine Griffith, commanding officer of the Second Division of the Staid Chorporra na h-Estutmost Security Forces. I have been appointed the military governor of Llandudno by your Board of Directors."

Behind him, several people in business suits were being led away in handcuffs by camouflaged soldiers. Trace guessed that those were either the elected city council or "just" local bureaucrats.

"By the authority of the Board, the civil government of Llandudno has been temporarily dissolved. Soldiers of the Second Division are assuming law enforcement and security roles throughout the city, replacing the Llandudno police force."

Trace might have been behind in her education, but she was pretty sure that the historical track record of using soldiers as police replacements was unpleasant. However General Griffith was presenting his role, he was the commander of an occupation garrison.

"For the moment, Llandudno Harbor has been declared a security reservation," he continued. "For your own safety, please remain outside the designated security blockades. As the Cinnead rebels continue their terrorist campaign against the elected directors and government of our star system, we must secure areas of Llandudno against potential infiltrators and saboteurs.

"To maintain the security of the city and its citizen-shareholders, an eight PM curfew is now effective in all districts. We recommend strongly against unnecessary travel outside your home, to protect yourself against the epidemic ravaging the city and potential rebel action or unhandled munitions from the conflict in the city.

"Any interference with security operations will not be tolerated. Obey orders given by soldiers of the Second Division and remain home where possible.

"I assure you all that the military government and these restrictions will be a short-term measure. Once the so-called Cinnead Militia has been properly contained and managed, we will be able to hold proper elections for the formation of a new civil government under the Board's supervision.

"Thank you."

The image dissolved into a more standard datafeed of local news with *Do you want to know more?* buttons, and Trace waved it away, checking the door before she glanced over at the adults in the room.

"So, the Cinnead lost."

"No surprise there," Lan said grimly. They were leaning on the kitchen counter now, watching the other two. "The locals had relatively few forces in the city itself. Once the Snowden line fell, they couldn't hold Llandudno."

"So, what now?" Trace asked.

"I was assuming the city would fall," they admitted. "So, we follow the plan. Stay low here for a few days, then relocate somewhere else. Obfuscate the trail as best as we can. The Board's troops will be looking for anyone from *Evasion*—if they can hold a lever on EB, they will."

"He'll have the cargo offloaded in a day or two at most," Vexer said. "After that, is EB really of value to them?"

"He ran the blockade once," Trace noted. "They might want him to do it for them. Spacers aren't letting *anyone* through, after all."

The hotel suite was silent and Lan sighed.

"There are too many advantages to them being able to lean on EB for them to let us go," they told their companions. "So, we need to stay low and quiet, out of everyone's sight and everyone's notice."

"What about local resistance? Do we make contact?" Vexer asked.

"Eventually," Lan agreed. "We want to get out of the city and down to Dinas Fferm, but I doubt there's many folk crossing the plains right now. The news is pretty censored already, but the Staid Chorporra's security divisions bypassed the city once it fell. Discussion boards show tanks and other combat vehicles heading south.

"This war just got a lot more mobile—but while the Tuathans have the vehicles, the Cinnead know the territory. I know how my old military colleagues would have planned out this fight. I imagine the Cinnead's leaders know the game too."

Trace didn't know the game, but she believed Lan when they said the locals did.

"So, we just…sit here and wait to be found?" she asked.

"We sit here and hope we *aren't* found. And then we move to a new safe house."

Lan shook their head.

"I'm still watching those dark web discussion boards," they reminded them. "Hopefully, someone will flag on there if Black Lotus starts looking compromised."

"And otherwise, we sit." Trace sighed and glanced back at the door. She clenched her hands around the stunner and silently nodded to herself.

She'd waited through worse. She'd survived being trafficked as a potential sex slave by cooperating until she saw a chance to run.

That had found her EB and *Evasion*. It had worked out for the best, but the journey there had been a nightmare. One she'd survived by endurance and patience.

She could wait.

21

THE SECOND TIME EB saw General Thomas Owens, the starship captain went to the militia commander instead of the other way around. A civilian groundcar carried EB through the city to an ordinary looking office building.

The General's "office" was on the fifteenth floor of a sixty-story office tower. It had been an open-plan workspace at some point, with a slightly sunken space to allow for shared planning or some such.

All of the original furniture had clearly been replaced. Heavy armor paneling had been set up around the edge of the room, blocking out any view from the outside. More armor paneling blocked one of the two exits from the elevator column at the center of the building, though the security at the entrance into the space was minimal at best.

The room was filled with computer equipment, displays and holograms. EB's headware told him there were hundreds of secured datafeeds or more whizzing around him, headware connections he couldn't access.

Olive-uniformed soldiers were everywhere he could see. Many were seated, lost in virtual worlds as they worked away on stations that were half in their heads. Others were carrying messages, drinks, papers, hardware—and even now, new equipment was being set up wherever they found space.

His guide took him through the buzzing hive of chaos to a central holographic display that looked like it had begun life as some corporate executive's latest efficiency toy. It was too decorative to have been built to be military, in EB's mind.

The display tank was currently muted, focused down on a single image: that of a tanned man with flaming red hair in a gray uniform.

"The Board of Directors of the Staid Chorporra na h-Estutmost has authorized me to release a list of rebel prisoners taken in Llandudno to the so-called Commission of the Cinnead," the stranger was saying as EB reached the central section of the command center.

"While there continues to be debate in the Board over how to treat the members of your rebellion, the position that this is a military conflict bound by the Geneva and later Conventions maintains sufficient support for the security forces to proceed on that basis.

"It is, of course, in the best interests of all involved if the Commission were to lay down their arms rather than continuing this pointless loss of life."

There was movement, and EB watched a squat blonde woman step away from the others gathered in front of the holographic display. A small lighting setup illuminated her as holographic pickups activated —a clever setup, he realized, as it made it very clear what was being picked up versus not.

"General Griffith, while your gesture may well represent the minimum level of necessary courtesies, it is appreciated nonetheless," she told the holographic figure.

She spoke with the same lilting accent as the rest of the Cinnead EB had heard, but there was a sharper burr to her tone that he hadn't heard before. It was closest, in fact, to the accent of the man who'd been speaking on the hologram.

"You can inform the Board of Directors that we are well aware of the laws of war. Their violations are being recorded, and there will be consequences for them when this is over.

"The Commission will not lay down arms in the face of your bluster, General. Justice will still be served."

"As a soldier, Em Innes, I always find it fascinating the degree to which all sides always claim to be fighting for justice," the Tuathan general said calmly. His hologram bowed. "I suppose we shall see who is right in the end."

The hologram vanished, and the broad blonde woman glared at the holodisplay as the lighting shifted. She turned and saw EB standing at the edge of the small cleared area and peremptorily gestured him over.

She seemed to know who *he* was, even if he had no idea who she was. He obeyed, concealing a sigh of relief when he saw General Owens in the small cluster of people around the woman.

"Captain Bardacki, please meet Commissioner Siwan Innes," Owens said, the Militia General stepping up to stand by Innes. "She is the Chairwoman of the Commission of the Cinnead."

"Prior to all of this, Captain, my theoretical job was running a supply purchasing cooperative," Innes noted. She was examining EB with a sharp look that he found uncomfortable. "Now I have apparently become the involuntary head of state for twelve million people."

Somehow, EB had to take *involuntary* with a grain of salt there. The Cinnead had been far too well prepared for this war for it to have been as much of a surprise imposed on them as they pretended.

"I was asked here to speak to General Owens, Em Commissioner."

"You were asked here to speak with the Commission, Captain," Innes told him bluntly, gesturing at the scattering of people behind her. "Join us."

He wasn't in a position to argue. He followed her into the middle of the cleared area around the holodisplay. A faint buzzing in his ears and a warning from his headware told him that a security barrier had been lowered around them.

Unsurprisingly, the entire conversation with General Griffith had been held as publicly as they could—and the story of the Commission's defiance was probably already winging its way through the Cinnead's military and civil ranks.

Now, though, the seven people who ran the Cinnead were sealed behind a curtain of white noise. Unless someone had a listening device in this tiny open space, they would never be able to know what was discussed.

"Cargo offloading was completed two hours ago," EB told them. "You have received your vehicles and guns. I have not yet been paid. Nor has my family been evacuated from Llandudno."

"Yours or anyone else's," Innes snapped. "The evacuation aircraft from Llandudno General Hospital was shot down by Tuathan forces who failed to check identity beacons and confirm she was a medical transport.

"Forty-seven wounded soldiers were on board. All were killed. Your people, however, were *not* on board, as our soldiers were unable to *find* them, Captain."

That shouldn't have been good news, and there was a reason the woman had phrased it in that order. She'd *wanted* him angry.

She'd succeeded, but EB suspected it wasn't directed the way she'd want.

"Our last confirmed location of your crew was in the quarantine lab in Llandudno General with Dr. Sam Wilson. Your Dr. Kozel confirmed what the Commission had *thought* was a…garbage conspiracy theory was true after all."

"I don't understand," EB admitted.

"According to your Dr. Kozel, the epidemic that swept Llandudno and undercut our defenses in Snowden was no accident," Owens told him. "He judged it to be a 'biostabilized targeted tactical bioweapon.' And given that it was responsible for allowing the Tuathan security forces to sweep through the Snowden Line with ease, it adds up."

"And is a war crime," Innes growled. "Not that anyone who matters seems to believe us or *care*. If they're willing to deploy the same biotechnology that this whole war is about as *weapons*, I don't know if we can win."

From the shuffling feet around her, that wasn't an opinion the rest of the Commission necessarily disagreed with—but it also wasn't one they wanted her to say *aloud*.

Innes made a chopping gesture, and the holodisplay lit up with a map of the Dachaigh a Deas. EB carefully controlled his surprise as the map filled with icons in various colors. This was the full strategic map available to the Commission of the Cinnead, and he could probably have sold his headware recordings to their enemies for a significant sum.

It was a sign of either trust or desperation…and EB didn't think he'd done anything to deserve that level of trust.

"The situation is deteriorating, Captain," General Owens told him, stepping up to stand beside Innes and gesturing toward the map. "The Tuathans know where Dinas Fferm is and recognize that this city contains the majority of what industry we have.

"Their security forces have concentrated the majority of their available strength into a single armored column, anchored on the Galahads they retrieved from the previous blockade runner, and are pushing directly here."

EB had already read that off the map. Five mechanized divisions, led by about two hundred tanks—mostly homebuilt—were following a straight path directly across the Dachaigh plains.

Six brigade-level formations—another two divisions' worth, if he was reading the icons on the main formation right—were deployed around the main column, protecting logistics and sweeping up smaller points of resistance.

An eighth division marker was in Llandudno, bringing the total Tuathan forces south of the Snowdens to eight divisions and about a hundred and forty thousand soldiers.

The Cinnead forces only had brigade markers on the map. Six brigades were dug in around Dinas Fferm to protect the capital. Ten, marked as *high-mobility brigades*, were playing cat and mouse with the escorting brigades around the main government column.

Assuming the organization structures were comparable, the rebels had sixteen brigades to the government's twenty-four. The high-mobility brigades appeared to have ten tanks each, all homebuilt. EB guessed that the Cinnead tanks weren't up to the same level as the Tuathan gear—but both sides clearly felt that the Nigahog Galahad-2s were better vehicles than anything Estutmost had buit.

There were twenty-five of those leading the main column. He'd just delivered over ninety—enough to even the armor numbers between the two forces and hand the rebels the qualitative advantage.

If the rebellion survived long enough to use them.

"We're having some success degrading their logistics, but the Staid Chorporra security forces know what they're doing," Owens admitted, gesturing at the raider brigades EB had identified on his own. "They have a fifty percent edge on us in numbers of infantry and light combat vehicles—and almost double our number of tanks.

"Thanks to you, we've evened that up, but we need to buy time to get them deployed."

"Tell him what we want, Owens," Innes snapped.

The General sighed and nodded.

"You still owe me over a kilogram of stamped lanthanum," EB said mildly. "I have no real side in your war, General, Commissioners. I've made my delivery. I want to collect my payment, collect my people and get out of here.

"Nothing else."

"You'll get your money, Captain." Innes glared at him. "And we want to *hire* you again."

"I'm listening. But I'd listen harder if my family wasn't behind enemy lines and I'd been paid."

The Cinnead's leader did *not* like that. She looked like she was about to tear his head off but then simply shook her head and gestured to Owens.

"You'll be paid," the General repeated. "The money is on its way here as we speak. But we *do* want to hire you and your ship again."

He waved a hand at the map, and two pictographic charts appeared above it. Both showed multiple types of aerospace fighters and fast movers, but one set was highlighted in red and one in green.

"We started this war with fifty-two aerospace fighters acquired from the Icem System," Owens told EB. "Our intelligence at the told us that the Staid Chorporra security forces possessed eighty-six armed fast movers, all built in the Dachaigh a Tuath, and that the production line had been shut down and repurposed two years ago.

"As of an hour ago, between our pilots and antiaircraft systems, we have confirmed kills on ninety-four Staid aerospace fighters and probable kills on another twenty," the General said drily.

"Pilots exaggerate." EB had been one after all. "But they don't generally exaggerate that much."

"No," Owens agreed. "We badly misestimated the strength of our enemy's air forces."

"But we have forced them to a draw in the air," Innes interrupted with fierce satisfaction.

"If by *draw* you mean *mutual massacre*," the General murmured. "We have six aerospace fighters left to provide air security for Dinas Fferm. We believe that the government has a similar number, despite their losses to date.

"Neither of us possess sufficient aircraft to attempt aerial operations outside the protection of our antiair defenses. Their assault column has the HVM pods of the Galahads and AA laser systems on some of the other vehicles, but they have no air cover at this point.

"They are utterly vulnerable to air attack...and our air strength is completely exhausted."

"And you have a starship," Innes told EB. "You shattered their first assault wave at Llandudno and took out most of their artillery. A single pass by your ship's guns would break up their column and delay them at the very least!"

"I understand that *Evasion* is no warship," Owens continued. "But her turrets are a devastating weapon applied in a planetary context. You could single-handedly turn the tide of this war."

EB swallowed his initial sharp retort. He had, after all, not yet been paid for the delivery.

"The range and power of a plasma cannon designed for space is heavily reduced in atmosphere," he noted first. There was, though, a reason ground wars weren't normally fought. Only the fact that the Staid's orbital guard had mutinied and joined Spacers—and decided to be neutral—was allowing this war to be fought at all.

"Not by enough to prevent you from devastating their column," Owens said. "They have no defenses that can stand off your ship. *Evasion* could end this war in ten minutes—which would make it far easier to retrieve your crew from Llandudno."

"The problem, General Owens, is that everything you've suggested about *Evasion* is true of every ship available to the Spacers," EB reminded the locals quietly. "So far, they have chosen to attempt to intercept *Evasion* instead of shoot us down, because everything we've done has been either direct self-defense or simple cargo delivery.

"But if we become directly involved in this war, we become an unquestionably military target and a threat. Unless they are secretly on your side—which I've seen no evidence of!—they will shoot *Evasion* down."

He shook his head.

"My freedom to maneuver is entirely contingent on the Spacers' unwillingness to risk hitting the surface and inflicting catastrophic damage. It's not a question of money or desire, General, Commissioners.

"I literally *cannot* use *Evasion* as a fire-support vessel. She's not designed for it, she's not truly equipped for it—and so long as the orbitals are hostile, it would be suicide."

Innes growled at him.

"Not much use, are you?"

"You have over twenty thousand cubic meters of military hardware that you didn't have a week ago, thanks to me," EB replied. "A cargo for which I have only been partially paid—and a cargo I brought to Dinas Fferm on the assurance that my family would be safe.

"I have some sympathy for the situation that led the Cinnead to war. But this is not my world and it is not my war. To function in this region, I must act with *discretion*. Turning my freighter into a fire-support ship is neither discreet, wise nor *effective*.

"I'll take my money for the delivery, if you please, but after that, I do believe our business together is concluded."

The Commissioner hadn't really stopped glaring at him at any point. Now she stalked over, invading his personal space and glowering at him in a way that fully negated his ten-centimeter height advantage.

"Most people, Captain, know better than to be demanding when in the hands of their employers," she hissed.

"Most rebel governments know better than to threaten the only people who've successfully run the blockade keeping them from getting weapons." She was an intimidating woman and he suspected she was used to that clearing her way.

He sincerely doubted she was *actually* going to have him jailed. He was a bit concerned that she'd refuse to pay him, but he would not be intimidated.

And truthfully, even if they didn't pay the last one-and-a-quarter kilograms of lanthanum, he'd done decently out of the deal. He'd just lost his boyfriend and daughter along the way, and he needed to find them.

EB and Innes glared at each other for at least ten seconds before Owens cleared his throat.

"Your payment is waiting for you with an armed escort in the lobby, Captain," the General declared. "We keep our word and our contracts, Captain Bardacki. If it had been within our power to deliver your crew to safety, we would have.

"We lost them ourselves. We lost…so many, ourselves."

Owens' voice broke as he spoke, and much of the tension drained from the room like a lanced boil.

"She's not on the list, is she?"

For the first time since EB had met her, Commissioner Siwan Innes moderated her tone as she looked at her officer. Her voice was soft, her words gentle.

"I didn't…expect her to be," Owens admitted. "She took those tanks right into the teeth of the assault force to cover the harbor evacuation. All of them were destroyed."

There was no response EB could make to that. He wanted to get his family out of Llandudno…but the woman who'd promised to do so had *died* trying to get *everyone* out.

He couldn't say the Cinnead hadn't done what they could.

22

WITH THE ARTIFICIAL stupid left behind on *Evasion*, Trace was reduced to once again doing coursework from a planetary datanet. She was picking modules at random and currently studying truly ancient history: the fall of the Roman Republic and the birth of the Roman Empire.

Her current primary conclusion was that Julius Caesar had been an unmitigated *asshole*.

She'd finally left the task of watching the door to Vexer, as Lan had left to do…something. The doctor was being troublingly opaque about what they were doing, just asking for trust.

Given that Trace had once trusted them to open up her brain and poke at the Siya U Hestí's silicon, she figured this should be easier. She was learning she'd figured *wrong*, but she did trust the doctor.

Even if they were a spy.

Her own occasional poking at dark web discussion boards had been much less fruitful than Lan's. She suspected the codes in her database gave her as much access as they had—Lan had access to a copy of the database on *Evasion* and presumably was using the same information she was using—but she had far less of an idea what she was looking for.

Her own experience was such that she could have easily sourced them drugs or a rave, but the "skills" of her descent into juvenile delinquency didn't seem like they were going to help them today.

The boards she'd found had let her get a feel for the state of the occupied city. Unsurprisingly, the news feeds were painting a rosier picture than the reality. The security forces weren't kicking down doors at random, but they were making a *very* thorough sweep of the city for remaining Cinnead troops and operatives.

The consensus of the semi-criminal user base of the boards she was surveying was that the occupiers were really just arresting anyone who'd been an employee or customer of the Cinnead. A good chunk of the city fit into that category, and the populace was getting nervous.

Her boards were *also*, however, figuring that any actual resistance or guerilla force left behind would have had any paperwork tying them to the Cinnead wiped. Working through the payroll and customer lists of an agricultural cooperative that had organized food production for an entire planet wasn't going to shake the covert militia out of the woodwork.

Trace wasn't sure how to find the Cinnead's resistance. She knew it had to exist, and she hoped that finding the resistance would be *helpful* to them—if nothing else, she doubted they were going to be able to get out of the city on their own!—but *finding* them was entirely outside her skillset.

She guessed that most thirteen-year-olds weren't made *quite* so aware of the limits of their skills as she currently was. It sucked.

The sound of a sharp knock on the door interrupted her moping, and she dismissed her unread page on Julius Caesar's modifications to the Roman dictatorship and checked that Vexer had the door covered with their single stunner.

A second and third knock came in the pattern Lan had promised, and she relaxed. Slightly.

She didn't fully exhale until the door opened and the enby doctor propped it open with a foot to allow them to bring a set of bags in.

Lan had changed at some point while they were out and now wore a dark green blazer over a set of slacks with an incorporated frilly skirt.

They dropped the bags on the floor with clear relief and closed the door behind themselves.

"The whole city is on a knife's edge," they observed. "Any trouble?"

"We didn't order room service or cleaning, so no one has even bothered us," Vexer said. "You?"

"Nothing unexpected."

Lan walked a bag over to Trace.

"New clothes," they told her. "So you can get out of the shipsuit."

That was a relief, though looking in the bag brought a new realization that made Trace shiver. Lan had, of course, bought her underwear to go with the new clothes. The *last* time someone had bought Trace underwear, it had been far more in the *sexy lingerie* category than any preteen should have been wearing.

Her comfort level with Lan buying her clothing was skittering on shattered glass as she checked the clothing. The underwear was, thankfully, as far from sexy as imaginable. It looked comfortable and practical, exactly what she needed—though the size was wrong.

The bras were a size bigger than the last ones Trace had bought. Considering the size unwelcomely for a long few moments, she realized that was probably about right.

Puberty *sucked*.

"How did you know my size?" she asked to distract herself, looking up at the doctor as they passed a bag of clothes to Vexer.

"I'm your *doctor*, Trace," Lan pointed out drily. "And it's not like top surgery magically disintegrated my ability to buy bras."

Turning back to the bags, Lan pulled a heavy-looking package wrapped in brown plastic from Vexer's clothes and laid it on the coffee table.

"I also acquired a few *other* things," they noted. "Three proper police stunners and two blasters—sorry, Trace, but I'm *not* giving you a lethal weapon. That's not something you need to live with just yet."

Whoever had wrapped the package had put real effort into disguising its contents. Trace didn't think the weapons were illegal in Llandudno—the stunners definitely weren't, at least—but she did have to wonder where Lan had found an *open* gun shop in a city under military occupation.

Probably much the same way she'd have found party uppers if she'd decided she needed them, she supposed. She knew where to find the contacts; she just didn't know the right questions.

The ex-spy definitely *did*.

"Last bag is food?" Vexer asked, grabbing two of the weapons from the table. "I don't want to draw attention by ordering room service, but we're running low on most things already."

"Yeah. We'll need to move on quicker than I'd like, though, so I didn't pick up too much," Lan warned.

"I thought we'd covered our tracks," Trace asked.

"As best as we can, yes, but the more layers of concealment we can add, the better. I've got a line on an actual safe house, not a hotel room. Black Lotus is a known entity in the underworld. While that provides us some security, it also means that the Staid Chorporra is inevitably going to specifically check it out at some point.

"We need to not be here when they do."

"What about the resistance?" she said.

"It exists," Lan conceded. "At least a few hundred Militia troops are still in town, with gear and hiding spots. But they're keeping their heads down and letting the security troops get comfortable."

"Two days isn't enough time for that," Vexer pointed out. "We're talking weeks."

"So, how this goes will depend entirely on the war," Lan said. "If the war drags on long enough for the resistance to feel they can move, things may get messier in Llandudno. But if the war is over quickly… Well."

"We might almost be better off if the rebels lose, wouldn't we?" Trace whispered.

"Might be easier to rendezvous with EB and get out, yes," Lan agreed. "But while I'm not inclined to pick a side in somebody else's war, I *also* know that the government would very much like to have us in a cell somewhere.

"For leverage on our captain, if nothing else."

23

A TINY HOLOGRAPHIC ship blazed into the sky and vanished in a flash of blue radiation. A dozen metrics flickered around it in EB's head, modeling of the impact of gravity and atmosphere on the nova jump.

It wouldn't be a clean jump, and it definitely wouldn't be a long jump. Jumping from Estutmost's atmosphere, there was no way *Evasion* could make a full six-light-year nova. On the other hand, any *short* jump would leave EB and his crew exposed to pursuit by the blockading gunships.

If he had access to the orbital sensor network, he'd be more comfortable making a jump of a few light-hours. As it was, the simulation called for a fifteen-light-minute jump straight "up" relative to the system's ecliptic plane.

The nova drive would cool down from that jump in about thirteen and a half minutes, allowing him to make the full six-light-year jump to the trade route stop before the light of his nova returned to Estutmost and the blockaders.

It wasn't the most graceful or riskless maneuver, and he'd be novaing far lower in the atmosphere than he liked, but his estimates of the Spacers' response time were clear. If *Evasion* went straight up, she'd get to about three hundred kilometers before she was swarmed.

The simulation was for a nova at one hundred and fifty kilometers' altitude. He didn't even need Ginny to tell him that the ship would require repairs after that, but they'd be things they could handle out of onboard resources.

At least enough to be able to make the journey to Blowry, a star system that EB hoped wasn't involved in any of the wars, crime syndicates and other bullshit this region of the Beyond had dragged him into.

He wasn't in the Beyond because he wanted to draw attention to himself. Like his entire crew, he was running from something. The failures of discretion that had dragged him into a war with the Siya U Hestî still frustrated him.

Not that Lady Breanna had given him much choice in the matter. He'd either needed to become one of her captains, helping her traffic kidnapped and terrified children and young adults to a dozen unpleasant fates, or he'd needed to…well, piss her off, run away from her bounty hunters and eventually turn on her and wreck her secret headquarters.

That hadn't been the choice she'd presented him—but that was how it had worked out.

But EB knew his skills and his limits. He'd made the jump calculations and he'd done them well. *Evasion* would survive the jump—but he suspected that *Vexer* could run calculations that would get them through unscratched.

Even with his numbers, the scenario that had just played out on the bridge's holoprojectors was an abject failure in his mind. They could run. They could flee the star system, abandoning three of his crew. Abandoning his *family*.

Except…

He couldn't run.

He *wouldn't* run.

EB knew his weaknesses and his limits. He wasn't a physical coward—he'd served through an entire war, after all—but he *was* afraid to die—and he never wanted to have to kill anyone ever again.

He'd fled from assassins back home. Fled again from becoming a soldier in the Rim. But when Trace had shown up in his life and needed help…he'd found a place to stand and people to stand for.

He hadn't hired a mercenary fleet and destroyed the Siya U Hestî Cartel to save Trace only to abandon her now.

The problem was the *other* scenario he'd been running. The one where he made a run for Llandudno—and no matter what he did, either Tuathan HVMs or Spacer plasma cannon wrecked *Evasion* before he reached his family.

———

EVASION'S MESS was a solemn and silent place when EB joined his crew there. The only person missing was Reggie, still in the dorsal turret keeping watch on the sky. The fact that the Staid Chorporra no longer had aircraft only partially reduced the need for that.

He looked around at the tired faces. They'd been in Dinas Fferm for three days now. Everyone *should* have rested. Should have found some measure of equilibrium.

It was very clear that his crew had done no better at that than he had.

"So, we got paid," he said quietly. "Two-point-five kilograms of lanthanum, as Nigahog promised. Tate, I'm guessing there is nothing in this city that we could load for export?"

The cargo mistress shook her head.

"The only thing this place exported was food, and they're hanging on to every scrap of that they've got," she said. "We're leaving empty."

"That at least makes her easier to fly, right?" Ginny asked. "A few of the systems are a bit shaky after the run from Llandudno. This ship is not supposed to go that fast in atmosphere."

"I know. What else were we going to do?"

Nobody answered him. The four women were all watching him, like tired and depressed hawks waiting for a mouse to move.

"I've run the numbers," he told them. He wondered if his tone sounded as hollow to them as it did in his own ears. "We can get high enough to make a short nova within the system before the

Spacers are on top of us. Then we can hit the trade route and get out of here."

"We're not doing that, though, are we?" Joy asked. The dark-skinned environmental tech straightened in her seat, not quite glaring at him. "We can't leave our crew behind."

EB looked around again, swallowing hard.

"I…have considered our options," he told them. "I've programmed the course into the computer, and the first jump will be almost automatic. Reggie and Ginny between them know enough to make standard nova jumps along the mapped routes.

"You'd go to Nigahog and check in with Naumov. I can make sure there's enough money in the ship accounts to keep you all paid and able to wait for a few months, until I can catch up."

"'Catch up'?" Ginny echoed. "You want us to leave *you* behind?"

"The easiest, if not fastest, way to get back to my family is by ground vehicle," he explained. "I don't know if I can get Vexer and Trace and Lan *out* of Llandudno, but I *do* know that my place is with them."

"Your place is also on this ship."

The other three women nodded confirmation of Ginny's firm words.

"We're not leaving you behind, Captain," Tate said. "And we're not leaving anybody else behind, either."

"Somehow, I figured that was the conversation going on," Reggie interrupted from the door.

The blond weapon tech stepped over to join the group.

"If you're staying, boss, I'm staying," he told EB. "And while I'm not going to speak for anyone, it doesn't sound like I'm alone in that."

"We're going after Trace and Vexer and Lan, Captain," Ginny said firmly. "We're not leaving your boyfriend, we're not leaving your daughter and we're not leaving the ship's only doctor.

"So, how about you pull up those numbers you were talking about and we look at finding a better plan as a crew?"

24

TWO HOURS OF SUGGESTIONS, simulations, discussion and reassessments later, EB was left with the same conclusion he'd walked into the mess with: the only *sensible* plan was to make a run for it.

But when sensible was unacceptable, sometimes you had to do something stupid.

"It's about speed and stealth," Reggie noted, leaning back with a beer in his hand. "The problem is that, from the perspective of this kind of mission, we don't have *either*."

"*Evasion* can't make the run to Llandudno in less than twelve, maybe even fifteen minutes," Ginny said grimly. "We strained the hull too badly coming the other way. A thousand kilometers in eight minutes…that's a tad over Mach six on average, and the systems say we peaked at Mach eight.

"We can *definitely* make Mach three. Probably Mach four. Anything faster and we're risking hull integrity."

"The Spacers almost intercepted us making the run in eight minutes," EB reminded his people. "Four to seven more? Add in that Llandudno doesn't have an air-defense net that's going to welcome us?"

"Llandudno isn't going to welcome us at all," Joy pointed out. "Even if we get there, how do we find our people?"

"We tell them the truth." EB managed not to clench his fists. "They let us find our family and we leave. They *don't*, and we demonstrate why the Commission wants to hire us as a warship.

"There's no way in the *universe* the Spacers are going to shoot us down from on high while we're above a city. I'm betting we can do a serious number on their occupation garrison hovering over the city—but, truthfully, I'm betting that the government commander would far rather let us land and be gone than fight us."

"But none of that changes the fact that we can't conceal our flight from the Spacers and we can't make the trip fast enough to stop them dropping sub-fighters on us," Reggie said grimly. The weapon tech was looking at the holographic display in the middle of the room and clenching his beer.

"I'm with you all. We're not giving up our people, we're not leaving anyone behind, but I'm not seeing an answer, either."

"The only thing I can see us doing is heading up and novaing out," EB said. "And I'm not leaving Estutmost."

"The planet? Or the *system*?" Ginny asked, staring at the hologram again. "How far was your first nova again?"

"Fifteen light-minutes," EB replied. "We won't have sensor data for anything longer."

"But we calculated our nova *into* Estutmost from almost a light-hour away," Ginny said.

"Vexer did, yep. Wait…"

EB stood up and changed the scale of the map. New data flowed in as he gave it mental commands and a new scenario took form.

"You're thinking we nova out and nova back, aren't you?" he asked his engineer.

"It's going to *suck* for our systems," she admitted. "But once we're on the ground, I can make any repairs we need over a few days. Before we try to make the same stunt to get out."

"And it will suck less than taking a plasma bolt to the manifolds."

EB shook his head at his gunner and ran the numbers again.

"I'm not Vexer," he warned Ginny. "He made the nova into

atmosphere smoothly enough that we didn't take any material damage. I can't do the same. I'm a better *pilot* than he is, but he's a better navigator."

"Put us on the ground in one piece and I can fix anything you do to our baby," Ginny repeated. "I promise you."

From fifteen light-minutes away, he'd be able to get enough data to calculate the jump. Hopefully before the Spacers had enough information to locate where *Evasion* had emerged.

Given that micro-jumps were the bread and butter of the nova fighter pilot he'd been, he'd be certain he could plot the jump if it wasn't for the whole *atmosphere* component.

"We can do it," he murmured. "It's going to be rough and it's going to be risky."

He looked around his crew.

"You don't have to come with," he told them all. "I know some of you are in for the long haul, but for others…there are going to be quiet spots you can settle in here and ride out the war. Spots that will be safer than making a nova jump into atmosphere between two hostile forces."

"I'm in," Reggie said, setting aside his empty beer. "I've done dumber things for worse reasons, and I don't leave people behind."

"There's no way in hell we're abandoning Trace," Ginny added.

"Or Lan," Tate said.

"We're in," Aurora concluded—and Joy just nodded.

"Everybody's in, EB," Ginny told him. "There's no way we're leaving any of our people behind on this planet. We're not going to ask *you* to leave Vexer or Trace behind, even if any of us were willing to consider leaving *Lan* behind."

"Which we're not," EB admitted. "I'm not going to pretend I'm not more motivated by Vexer and Trace, but I wouldn't be leaving our doctor behind, anyway. They're *all* family."

"And family means nobody gets left behind," Reggie finished for him fiercely. "I'll plan in some ground-bombardment patterns. If the Staid Chorporra wants to be a pain, we'll *show* them pain!"

"I really hope not," EB told his gunner. "But we'll make it work. We're getting our people, my friends.

"One way or another."

THE LAST STEP before they left was a walk-around of the exterior of *Evasion*, using a handheld scanner to double-check that Ginny had replaced all of the heat tiles. EB fully trusted that his engineer would have done everything right and even checked herself, but an extra set of eyes never hurt.

The scanner also showed him that she wasn't kidding when she said that they couldn't do the Mach six run again. The replacement tiles were ever so slightly less capable than the ones *Evasion* had been built with.

Some of that was that Dinas Fferm didn't have the best tech available in Estutmost for heat tiles. Some was that Estutmost's tech was behind even that of the Rim. Much of it, though, was just inevitable in replacements. The initial set had been installed with the main hull and as a set. The replacements were individual pieces, shaped to size and placed in gaps.

A perfect match was impossible. The difference was irrelevant for most circumstances—but a Mach six rush in a breathable atmosphere was far from most circumstances.

The sound of a vehicle drawing up behind him warned him he wasn't alone, but he made sure to finish his sweep before turning around.

For his part, General Owens appeared to respect the need for that and was waiting patiently, leaning on the IFV he used as his personal transport, when EB walked over to talk to him.

"You're leaving us."

It wasn't a question.

"You didn't get my family out. So, now I have to."

"That's a brave move, going to Llandudno. Think you can pull it off?"

"Seventy-thirty," EB admitted, glancing at the armored car. He didn't know who was driving the vehicle, though he *presumed* anyone shuttling General Owens around was trustworthy. "Not going to give you the details, no offense."

"None taken. Given that every estimate my people have made is that you will be shot down or captured on the way, I wouldn't *want* you to risk revealing your plan," Owens told him. "My daughter died trying to hold that city, Captain Bardacki. I'd move worlds if I thought I could save her still."

"And my daughter is alive in that city."

"We owe you still, Captain. Is there anything we can do to help?"

"Nothing that comes to mind, General. I appreciate your limitations, but I have to do this because your efforts failed."

Owens winced but nodded. He was silent for a few seconds but held up his hand as EB turned to walk away.

"Seventy-thirty, huh?"

"It's risky, but I think we can do it. I don't think anyone else could."

"Are you willing to take on one more contract, Captain? For going the way you're already planning to go?"

EB considered the General silently for a few moments of his own, then sighed.

"You want me to deliver troops to Llandudno. I don't think I can deliver enough to retake the city, General. Not unless you have something that fits in an unpressurized TMU hold and self-deploys."

That told Owens that they were going into space, he supposed, but that would be obvious about ten seconds after they took off.

"I don't have the brigades to spare even if you could carry them. I was thinking more on the order of a couple of companies of commandos and person-portable crates of weapons for the resistance already taking shape behind enemy lines."

"Entirely organically, of course," EB noted drily. "There were never any preparations for such a contingency."

"Not enough, as it turns out." Owens turned away to look at the city behind him. "Our resistance cadre suffered the same problem as the Snowden Line and the city's intended defenders: that bioweapon left them puking their guts out as Tuathan troops rolled in."

"And the occupying force has the vaccines and countervirals to protect the city from the virus. Of course."

"Of course." EB followed the man's gaze. "Nothing comes for free,

General. I sympathize with your personal situation, but I'm not exactly sold on *any* side of this war. I just want to get my family out."

"I chose my side a long time ago," the Cinnead General said calmly. "But I understand. I'll have to see what resources I can break free, but say…a quarter-kilogram of stamped gold to transport two hundred troopers and a thousand cubic meters of cargo? To move them a thousand kilometers, it seems almost ridiculous."

"They won't be traveling a thousand kilometers, General, because we both know that if they tried to travel that distance on their own, they'd never make it. The open plains are a battlefield right now, aren't they?"

"We are delaying their advance, but we are not winning," Owens conceded. "But every day I get to exercise the two new heavy-strike brigades…give me six months, and I'd back the soldiers who are training with the tanks you brought us against the best the Staid Chorporra can deploy.

"But I have six *days*, Captain. I need every edge I can get, which means I need Llandudno fighting them."

"We're making the trip anyway," EB conceded with a sigh. "We'll take your quarter-kilo of gold, General, and we'll deliver your soldiers and your guns. But I can't promise it'll be clean. I *was* planning on offering to just take my family and go. If I'm delivering your people, they may need to exfiltrate from *Evasion* on their own.

"I'm certainly not fighting the Tuathans for them."

"The Commission would *love* to hire you for that, but I understand why you don't want to get that involved," Owens said. "No, the people I'm thinking of will be perfectly fine if you kick them out the back of the ship halfway to orbit.

"That's what the ORCs trained for."

EB arched an eyebrow.

"Orbital Recon Commandos." Owens smiled thinly. "They *were* an elite section of the Staid Chorporra's security forces, but they defected to us as a unit."

"Like the Staid's orbital forces defected to the Spacers?" EB asked.

"Exactly. That alone, Captain Bardacki, should give you an idea of whose side you should be on in this war. Some of the Staid Chorporra's best looked at a war their government didn't expect to lose…and chose to fight with us."

"Or, in the case of the Spacers, decided that they shared more with the folks living in the orbitals and the asteroids than they did with their bosses groundside," EB murmured. "Which is far from as uncommon a story as those bosses would like. Or ever seem to realize."

"The Spacers, too, have their axes to grind with the Staid Chorporra," Owens told him. "Someday, they'll realize what side they should be on, and this war will get much shorter."

"Maybe someday," EB agreed. "For now, I'll hold twenty-four hours for your money, your troops and your guns.

"That's all. We were almost ready to go, and I'm not willing to wait to rescue my family."

He had to hope that Vexer and Lan were keeping Trace safe. He wasn't sure *any* of the three of them were qualified to survive in an occupied city…but the Cinnead could still make his life *damn* complicated if they wanted.

And, so far, he *liked* most of them that he'd met. He was willing to give them that much rope.

TRACE HAD to read the discussion board post three times to be sure of what she was looking at.

Someone talked. Black Lotus is compromised. Whoever needs to know, get out now.

The problem was that the board she was looking at had been defunct for at least a month and had been a Siya u Hestî digital dead drop, according to her database. She was paranoid enough to think that someone might be trying to game *her*—but the other option was that there were Siya u Hestî people in the hotel.

Or that one of their informants was putting up a red flag in case someone was still watching.

She dismissed the datanet with a wave of her hand and charged out into the main area of the suite.

"We have to go," she told the two adults—to realize that Lan had looked up as she came in and said the exact same thing.

They arched an eyebrow at her.

"I have a source saying the Lotus is compromised," they observed. "But I found a local discussion board where one of the still-employed cops is leaking intelligence like a sieve. You?"

"One of the Siya u Hestî digital dead drops went active with a single message," Trace said. "Lotus is compromised."

"I was about to get you," Lan told her. "Troopers are moving through the streets *now*. Whatever Second Division learned, they decided it was urgent. Grab clothes and guns; we're moving."

"Where to?" Vexer demanded. "You've only left three times. What kind of backup location do we *have*?"

"I need to lean on a contact I was hoping to spend more time solidifying. But if I've guessed *right*, we'll make rendezvous with the Cinnead resistance."

Trace hoped that was a good thing. She didn't want to get caught up in somebody else's war, even if the Staid Chorporra was *really* getting on her nerves right now. She wasn't a fan of being hunted.

"I'll get my stuff," she promised. "How long do we have?"

"Two minutes would be fine; *now* would probably be better," Lan admitted.

***

TRACE HAD BEEN WARNED that their exit, when it came, would be in a rush. She'd packed the clothes Lan had bought for her into a backpack that the doctor had also acquired and had been living out of that as best as she could.

Now the toiletries in the bathroom and the inevitable bits strewn around the one room were swept into the backpack. She tucked the stunner into the small of her back and threw the light jacket Lan had bought over it.

She was wishing she had the jacket she'd bought for herself. The matching set for her and her dads had included light but real armor and dispersal webs. She very much didn't want to get shot by anything, ever, but the armor would have been a reassuring presence today.

Vexer was checking a pair of shoulder holsters against the cut of his stolen blazer when she came back into the main room. The blazer wasn't designed to conceal weapons, but it was also just a bit bigger than Trace's dad. It worked well enough to conceal the blaster and stunner he was carrying as he buttoned it closed and looked up at her.

"You good?" he asked gently.

"*Good* is a stretch, Dad-V," she admitted. "But I've got my stuff."

She was also mentally poking at an application she'd been assembling while she was waiting. Ancient history was boring. Coding and digital security breaching were *fun*.

Finally unleashing the specialized worm she'd been building, she held her breath for a moment as it hit Black Lotus's digital defenses. Trace had copies of a lot of the software Dad-E had brought with him from the Rim, and it should…

She grinned triumphantly as the worm inserted itself into the datafeeds for the surveillance system and started sending her a feed of everything…and then swallowed.

"Dad, Lan, they're here," she snapped. "Armored aircar is touching down out front *right now*."

"What?" Lan asked. "How…"

"I'm in their surveillance feeds." She flicked a link to the ex-spy to let them see what she saw. "Don't know the aircar type, but those are definitely *somebody*'s soldiers."

Trace had enough exposure to recognize clamshell light body armor and blaster rifles. The soldiers' armor and fatigues were set in a fixed gray urban camo pattern rather than the automatically adjusting mode she figured they had to have, but these soldiers were *meant* to be seen.

"Back door it is," Lan declared. "Follow me."

"You have a plan and the schematics, I'm guessing?" Vexer asked as he held the door open.

"Of course."

Trace had her attention split as she followed the two adults. A screen hanging in her vision showed her the approach of the dozen gray-armored soldiers as they spread out, securing the front entrance.

The lack of staff at the Lotus made it an odd procedure to watch. The soldiers had clearly been expecting to be detaining people in the front lobby, and the absence gave them pause.

Trace's feed didn't have audio, but she could see one of the soldiers barking commands at the hologram, which seemed to just stare back in confusion. It likely had been intentionally programmed to be unable to respond to the questions it was getting.

"Groundcars are only a couple minutes out," Lan told their companions as they opened a NO ENTRY door on the second floor. "Aircar team hasn't split up to cover the back exits, so we still have time."

Trace had to pay more attention to her own surroundings as they headed down a surprisingly rickety set of stairs in the staff section of the hotel. The drone lift next to the stairs was *far* better maintained than the path built for humans.

Still, it held up well enough under their feet as they traipsed downward. There were fresh footprints in the dust as well—whatever staff the Black Lotus had clearly didn't use these stairs, relying on the drones instead for cleaning and delivery, but someone else had headed out this way before them.

The bottom of the stairwell had several doors, some of them specifically sized for drones but three sized for humans. Despite an apparent effort to make everything look the same, it was easy to identify the exit.

It was the one where someone had failed to override the lock and had cut it open from the inside. The double-layered security door hung slightly open, latch and lock-bolt both severed by an extremely sharp blade.

"Well, that helps," Lan said as they pushed the door open. "Groundcars are *here*. We need to move."

Turning her focus back to the surveillance feed, Trace grimaced as she saw Lan's point. Two ground vehicles—more trucks than cars, each disgorging another dozen soldiers—had pulled up in front of the hotel.

But she could see more in the distance from the other exterior feeds. They were spreading out to secure the entire hotel block and all of the exits.

"We're out of time," she murmured.

"Not quite. Follow me."

Lan took off down the alleyway and Trace followed. A glance backward confirmed that Vexer was right behind her.

She wasn't sure where the doctor was taking them until they

reached the door on the far side of the alley. As Lan paused, kneeling at the door and prodding the lock with a tool of some kind, she could hear bootsteps as the soldiers started sweeping down the alleyway.

"Clear; in here," Lan ordered as the door swung open.

Trace and Vexer obeyed, the ex-spy following them in and closing the door.

"What is this place?" Trace asked, glancing around what appeared to be a storeroom of some kind.

"I have no fucking idea. It was just the first door I saw. Keep moving west."

Despite everything, Trace had to chuckle at Lan's admission—but she followed the instructions, pushing through the door leading from storage into what appeared to be the bathroom access for a restaurant.

The lack of a cooking smell suggested the place was closed, which was both good and bad. Good because no one was going to be wondering why new people were coming out of the bathroom—and bad because any troopers in the street were going to wonder why people were coming out of the restaurant at all.

Trace was the first out into the actual seating area of a plain-looking Italian restaurant. White plastic tables gleamed, waiting for the checkered tablecloths neatly folded up on a prep counter along one wall.

Fortunately, the windows were tinted, and she hadn't wandered out into plain view of the pair of Second Division troopers standing just outside the restaurant.

"Shhh!" she hissed at the adults as they followed her into the space, then pointed at the two soldiers.

Not watching this space, Lan's voice said silently in her head. *General patrol. If we're lucky, they'll move on.*

They know about the raid one street over, though, Vexer noted. *They have to. Nobody is* that *incompetent.*

Trace didn't have anything to add. She was eyeing the tinted glass at the front of the restaurant, trying to judge how close she could get to the double glass doors without being seen by the troopers.

She figured she was better off waiting. If they moved on…

Heard back from my contact, Lan told them both. *We have a contact point. It's not close, but we can make it on foot.*

Could be a trap.

Lan shrugged back at Trace. They didn't need to say more—paranoia was unavoidable in their current position, but they had to do *something.*

"They're moving," Vexer whispered. "I think they saw something."

The two soldiers certainly seemed to be striding away from the restaurant with distinct purpose, their hands on the slung blaster rifles as one of them shouted words Trace couldn't hear through the glass.

"Come on; let's go."

Lan's strange tool opened the front doors almost instantly once the soldiers were far enough away, then they led the way out onto the street and away.

Now they could hear sirens heading in their direction.

"Soldiers first, then police to lay a bigger cordon," Lan said. "We need to keep moving west, get clear of their perimeter before they establish. Then we can head for the rendezvous."

Vexer suddenly winced at something Trace didn't hear. Lan raised a questioning eyebrow at him, and he grimaced.

"I have hearing augments," the navigator reminded them both. "And I hear blaster fire. Someone didn't get the warning in time—and either they aren't going quietly or the soldiers have orders not to take them alive."

"The farther we get from that mess, the happier we all are going to be," Lan concluded. "Come on. That street over there looks like it heads in the right direction."

There was only one right direction right now, Trace knew, and it was *away.*

26

TRACE WAS BARELY A TEENAGER, with all of the energy of that age, but she'd also spent most of the previous year living on stations and spaceships—and a good chunk of that under extremely constrained conditions as a prisoner.

She didn't have the endurance or the practice at long hikes she'd acquired growing up in a terraformed nature reserve anymore. By the time they reached the park Lan said was their contact point, she was feeling the drain of the hike out of Llandudno's downtown core.

Reaching a park bench, she collapsed into it and took several long deep breaths before looking around. The park was full of Estutmost's native plant life—both as a preserve and to limit the resources applied in terraforming.

The multi-trunked trees with their webs of vine-like leaf-branches looked strange to her eyes, and not just because she'd grown used to spaceships. Denton, the Icem System's inner world and her home planet, had native life that much resembled Terran-standard plants.

Estutmost did not. Even the bushes and ground cover more resembled spiderwebs of tiny vines than leaves or grass. It was strange to her eyes but also surprisingly pretty.

It was also, as she understood it, completely inedible to humans.

Eating Estumost plant life would provide slightly less nourishment than eating plastic.

"Wasn't there supposed to be someone here?" Vexer asked, collapsing onto the bench next to Trace. "There's a few folks around, more than I expected in truth, but…"

"We were supposed to *meet* someone here," Lan corrected. They had a hand on the back of the bench Trace and Vexer were on, leaning on it for their own support. "I wasn't expecting them to be here when we arrived."

"Took us long enough to get here."

Trace managed not to snort at her dad's whiny tone. Vexer, it seemed, hadn't enjoyed the walk any more than she had.

"So, we wait?" she asked.

"We wait," Lan confirmed. "For a bit. Not forever. Still could be a trap, after all."

Trace grimaced and nodded, leaning forward to check that she could still reach the stunner holstered at her back. The two adults had their blasters as well, but she was grimly certain that if they ended up needing *any* of the weapons, they were in real trouble.

Her stomach rumbled as she looked around. Hopefully, they wouldn't have to wait too long—or if they did, that there was at least *one* open vendor in the park!

THIRTY MINUTES LATER, Trace was searching the park's datanet site to see if she could either locate somewhere selling food or identify the small furry animal that was playing peekaboo with her across the pathway.

She was having more luck with the critter. There was an image list of creatures expected to be found in the park, and it was near the bottom as one of the rarer beasts to see during the day. Of course, it was also just called a chipmunk.

Trace had grown up in a biosphere reserve intended to duplicate the ecosphere of the Great Lakes in North America as closely as possible. She knew what a chipmunk was supposed to look like—and while the Estutmost version definitely checked off the *small, striped* and *adorable* boxes, it had four too many limbs and a clearly prehensile tail.

"Normally, there are four food carts cycling through this place," she muttered to Vexer. "All of them are missing today."

"I'm not surprised."

"Look alive," Lan hissed at them both. "And not at the critter, please."

The chipmunk chittered again, hissed at the approaching pedestrian, then vanished back into the bush.

Trace wouldn't have guessed the approaching man as much older than her. He was a shaggy-haired teenager wearing jeans and a T-shirt that had both seen better days—and the shirt was too big for him.

Which helped cover the stunner he had holstered in his mid-back. She might have missed it if it wasn't the same style of holster she was wearing.

Even if she had, though, she figured Lan had spotted the weapon at a distance. They were definitely watching the youth as he seemed to casually wander through the park, getting ever closer to them.

Finally, he stopped in front of them, appearing to look into the bushes on the other side of the trail.

"Dr. Kozel?" he whispered, just loud enough to be heard.

"Last I checked."

"Wait a minute, then follow me north out of the park. Surveillance drones' schedule shifted; this isn't as secure as was planned."

Apparently not finding what he was looking for, the teenager took off again toward the north side of the park.

Lan sighed.

"I suppose my expectations of decent tradecraft were doomed to frustration," he murmured. "But here we are, and we work with what we've got."

"He's just a kid."

"Nineteen, I'd guess," Vexer told Trace. "Six years older than you. Old enough to make his own choices."

"And I'm not?"

"You're a special case," Lan reminded her. "Galaxy didn't give you much choice in growing up. We do everything we can to keep you safe, but we can't change that.

"Come on; minute's up and he can only dawdle so long before it looks suspicious."

Trace levered herself up, tentatively testing her legs to see if they'd recovered from being jelly. She could walk, but she hoped that they wouldn't be going very far!

TO TRACE'S DELIGHT, their guide left the road after less than a full block and entered an ice cream shop. When they joined him, the restaurant was empty other than them, the teenager who'd got them to follow him, and a doughy older woman behind the counter.

A doughy older woman who, unless Trace missed her guess, had her hand on a blaster under the counter.

"Apologies for the extra confusion, Dr. Kozel," their guide told Lan. "You can call me K-Five. This is the titular Shelly of Shelly's Frozen Sweets, and she has *terrible* eyesight."

"Absolutely awful," she agreed cheerfully. "I do see that I have customers. Want some ice cream?"

Trace raised an eyebrow at Lan. She wasn't sure what they had in terms of local money, but the doctor produced several bills from his coat and passed them over.

"Four of your best and most portable."

"Fair 'nough," Shelly told them. "Vanilla-spice waffle cones, coming right up. Watch the door, Kie—"

She cut herself off mid-name and simply nodded as the teen turned to watch the entrance.

Practiced hands flew across the machines and storage containers, setting four cones to bake simultaneously and then preparing the ice cream balls as they cooked.

"You'll go out through the back once you have your ice cream," she continued. "K will stick with you as guide and introduction. There will be a van waiting with a driver: MacEalair Furniture Delivery Service.

"MFDS is a white-glove service, so they have seating you can use.

You won't be able to see out of the van, and you'll want to keep the door closed."

She passed the first ice cream to Trace.

"We know who you are, but you'll forgive us our secrets," she continued as she began to efficiently assemble the second ice cream. "Well." She chuckled. "K knows who you are. *I* have terrible eyesight."

"Absolutely atrocious, I can tell," Lan agreed. "Thank you. The ice cream smells delicious."

"K's is the same as yours, in case you were worrying about drugs or something," Shelly noted. "Good luck to ye."

The teenager scooped up a random ice cream and passed the last to Vexer.

"Come on," he told them sharply. "Ice cream is good, no argument there, but every Tuathan noncom in the city has Dr. Kozel's face in their morning brief. The sooner we have you in the safe house, the safer you are and the happier we are!"

27

THE VAN WAS EXACTLY what they'd been told: a windowless box with uncomfortable seats designed to hold a team delivering specialty items. Without the ability to look out the window, Trace focused on her ice cream in a form of self-defense.

She'd still barely finished it before the van rolled to a gentle stop.

"Come on," K-5 told them. "We're here."

Trace shared a look with Vexer. They hadn't gone very far, though the sealed box of the van meant they had no idea where they were. They were, for the moment at least, at the resistance's mercy.

She left the van last, stepping out into a dark garage of some kind. Their driver had also exited the vehicle and was holding up a lamp set just bright enough to keep them from tripping over things.

"Follow me."

K-5 stepped past the driver, who was clearly angling the light to keep their face shrouded in darkness, and led the way to a door deeper into whatever building they were in.

The corridor outside the garage was at least lit. It was an institutional space, of a type that Trace wasn't entirely familiar with but guessed at some kind of office. The doors she could see had windows that had been covered over with paper to provide some semblance of privacy.

The corridor let out into an open space that Trace figured needed at least ten more levels of decoration or thought to give it *any* personality. She wasn't sure what it had been supposed to be—from the plain carpet and wide-open space, she suspected it was supposed to have portable furniture of some kind dividing it up.

Instead, the windows had been covered with more paper and the room had been set up as a cross between a cafeteria and an armory. Open crates of small arms and body armor were laid out in neat rows on one side of the room, with three neat rows of folding tables holding two dozen seats.

A dozen of the seats were occupied by a mix of men and women whose ages ranged from K-5's *way too damned young* to a white-haired woman who made EB look like a spring chicken—but who clearly knew what she was doing with the dissembled blaster rifle sitting on the table in front of her.

The old woman looked up as K-5 led Trace and her adults into the room and cleared her throat sharply, gathering everyone's eyes to her.

"Clear the room," she ordered softly. "Need to chat with these folks."

The others collected their trays of food and rose from their seats. There was no rush, but clearly no one was going to disobey the older woman, either.

One of the younger boys got distracted by Trace, staring at her for at least ten seconds before K-5 cleared his throat sharply. The stranger flushed and vanished from the room at speed.

Given that the youth still had at least five years on Trace, she found herself shifting behind Vexer slightly, her hand slipping to her stunner.

"Prick," K-5 muttered. "Sorry about that, kid."

The woman in charge gestured for the trio of *Evasion* crew to sit, then leveled a gaze on K-5.

"Less commentary on your fellows, more privacy, please, K," she told him. "You also need to take a walk."

"Wilco," the teenager said cheerfully. "I'll check the door locks."

"You do that."

Trace waited for Lan and Vexer to take seats, then dropped herself between the two adults. Something about this place was making her nervous. It was institutional enough to bring up bad…vibes, more than bad memories.

K-5 did a quick circuit of the room's exits before slipping out the last one himself, leaving the four of them alone.

"Dr. Kozel, Officer Dolezal, Em Bardacki," the resistance officer greeted them one by one. "I am Major Aderyn Vaughn. So far as *you* need to know, I am the senior remaining officer of the Cinnead Militia in Llandudno.

"I am not, unfortunately, in contact with Cinnead Command except in the most roundabout of ways. However, we did receive very specific orders with regards to you three."

Only Vexer taking her hand and gripping it tightly under the table kept Trace from panicking at that. The phrasing was ominous.

"We were supposed to get you out before the city fell," Vaughn continued. "But the people running the evacuation lost track of you before they could get you on a fast mover."

She grimaced.

"Which may have been for the best, since only one of our evac fast movers made it out of the city, and that one was shot down in error by the government forces. If we'd managed to evacuate you as planned, you'd be dead."

"Always wonderful to realize a disaster worked out in my favor," Lan said drily. "Since I don't believe that we can be extracted at the moment…what are your orders?"

"Secure and protect your persons until I can make contact with Command. Then attempt to coordinate a covert evacuation."

She shrugged.

"Commissar Owens promised Captain Bardacki that we'd get you to safety and get you out in exchange for him moving *Evasion* to Dinas Fferm. We failed to get you to Dinas Fferm to meet him.

"But we *are not* going to fail to keep you safe." She waved a hand around her. "This is one of our primary command-and-control centers. *Nothing* comes here or goes from here directly.

"We have a small number of offices that have been converted into apartments, and we'll put you up in one of them until we manage to sort out what we're doing with you."

"What happens if EB comes back for us?" Vexer asked.

"From what I understand of Captain Bardacki's history and achievements, that will be a very bad day for the Staid Chorporra's Second Division," Vaughn replied. "But *I* will do everything in my power to make contact with Captain Bardacki and arrange transport for you to meet him.

"You are not part of my organization, and I have no intention of asking you to get involved in our operations. All I ask, in exchange for our protection and assistance, is that you never tell *anyone* anything you see or hear here. Fair?"

"More than," Lan told her. "I am also willing to place my medical knowledge at your disposal, Major. In fact, if you have any kind of biofabrication equipment, I believe I've gone over the information I have on the Tuathan bioweapon sufficiently to begin fabricating a counterviral."

There was a long pause as Vaugh blinked, clearly processing.

"I don't have a biofabrication unit *here*," she conceded slowly. "But I believe I can source one. We'd been assuming that we'd have to wait for the virus to burn itself out amidst the population before being able to do anything about it, even once we knew it was a weapon.

"It helped confirm *that* when the Tuathans immediately rolled out vaccination clinics within twenty-four hours of taking control."

"Get me a unit and I should be able to rig up both a counterviral and a vaccine," Lan told her. "The first will get your people out of their beds; the second will protect those who haven't *been* infected."

They spread their hands.

"Given that none of the three of us have caught the thing yet, I very much want to get that vaccine underway!"

"I will see what I can do," Vaughn promised. "Regardless, all three of you are safe here. So long as this command center is secure, no harm will come to you."

That was probably a larger condition than the Cinnead officer wanted it to be, but Trace also figured that was as good as they were going to get in a city under occupation.

28

"ARE our new passengers all settled in?"

"Yep. They're even trying to pretend they're comfortable, which makes me suspicious."

EB sighed and tried to wrap his brain around Reggie's worry.

"Because they're not griping?" he finally asked.

"What soldier *doesn't* gripe about whatever is to hand? Let alone bites their tongue when asked to spend the trip in an empty pressurized cargo bay?"

"They'll bitch to each other, not the crew flying them."

"True, true. Feel like maybe we should get them some padding or safety harnesses or something? Coming in the first time was pretty rough."

"We warned them." EB checked his datafeeds. The last of the commandos had joined Reggie in the cargo hold.

In the end, Owens had sent him more commandos and fewer guns than expected. A hundred and twenty commandos could *fit* in a cargo bay designed to hold eight thousand cubic meters of cargo. It wasn't comfortable or spacious for them, but they fit.

They'd also brought sixty crates of what EB assumed were guns, armor and munitions. He'd done enough scans of the gear to confirm they didn't contain anything likely to damage the ship or somehow get him in even *more* trouble, but he hadn't had anyone open the boxes.

While Reggie was correct that they didn't appear to have any extra gear to secure themselves safely, EB also knew how the ORCs were supposed to make their insertion into Llandudno.

"I wouldn't worry too much about them," he told Reggie. "Make sure to point out the anchors on the walls and leave it to them from there. They're supposed to be making a HALO jump out the bay door as we go in, so I'm guessing they have *some* kind of harness."

He watched through the feed as his weapons tech followed his instructions. As expected, the Orbital Recon Commandos were wearing low-profile HALO kits—kits that readily produced snap-release cords they used to tie themselves to the wall.

"Everyone is secured," Reggie reported. "Heading to the dorsal turret control. Need anything else, boss?"

"If I thought anyone on this ship prayed, I'd make a real request for thoughts and prayers. As it is, strap yourself into the turret and stand by. If you have to do anything, it's a bad day for us, but we may need those bombardment patterns."

"I'll be ready."

EB turned his attention to the rest of his checklist. There were a hundred systems he needed to make sure were solid before they attempted this run. No part of the run wasn't risky. No part wasn't audacious as hell.

"All gravity systems are green. Power generation is green. Nova drive is green." Ginny's voice echoed in the back of his head as she worked down her own checklist.

"I confirm the same," he told her. "I'm working through the list. Anything on your end?"

"We're green across the board. I'll take every second you want to wait to check and double-check, but we're into excessive redundancy now. Whenever you're ready, EB."

EB exhaled a long breath and nodded to himself. There were a few more things on his own checklist, but he seemed to be the final holdup.

He interrogated those systems, and *Evasion*'s computers happily confirmed everything for him.

"All right, everybody. Time to roll." His voice echoed through the ship, a warning to everyone, passengers included.

"There is going to be a quiet and easy part of this. It's not this part. I strongly recommend that everybody who doesn't absolutely need to be on their feet strap in."

He checked the vector projections of the orbital monitors on his screen and nodded sharply again.

"I make it an eighty percent chance we're getting out of here without being shot at, but if they decide to start firing, I'm going to be flying without much thought for our poor abused inertial dampers."

One final run through the datafeeds confirmed what he was hoping for: only Ginny and Aurora were outside of proper safety harness, and the engineer and engine tech were as secure as they could get while still being ready to jump into action.

He didn't know how this trip was going to end, but he had a plan and he knew how it was going to start.

With a deep breath, EB brought *Evasion*'s systems online.

***

THE FIRST FEW seconds were slow and careful as EB balanced the antigrav coils and a tiny bit of thrust from the Harringtons. The freighter lifted a few meters into the air as he scanned the surrounding area for potential hazards or any poor bastards who might have been in the effect area.

No one at the spaceport *should* have been in the launch effect area, but it happened. Today, at least, they were clear.

The space above them wasn't so clear. From what he'd seen on his sensors and the information the Cinnead had provided him, the Spacers had parked one of their monitors directly above the city to make his escape harder.

Of course, they *probably* thought they'd made his escape impossible.

Grinning at the thought, EB increased power to the Harringtons. *Evasion* started to rise rapidly, and he began to run the update on the nova calculations on a secondary feed. Everything looked good—but he needed to breach the Kármán line before the atmosphere was thin enough to nova.

And that gave the Spacers over a hundred kilometers to shoot at him in if they chose to. His acceleration was limited in atmosphere as well, but the higher he got, the faster he could go.

Ten kilometers. Twenty.

"Monitor is maneuvering to clear her guns," Reggie reported. "I have sub-fighters on the screens as well. Four bogies incoming and *fast*."

"They learn quick."

These sub-fighters weren't relying on gravity to pull them down. They had their own Harringtons pushing them down into the gravity well, descending even more rapidly than *Evasion* was rising.

Thirty kilometers. Forty.

"Intercept point is one hundred ten kilometers," EB said aloud. "Reggie, hold your fire."

"Your call."

Fifty kilometers. Sixty.

"Blockade runner, this is Aldrin-Alpha-Actual. You are under the guns of our monitors. Stand down and head for orbit at minimum acceleration. Any attempt to divert, any attempt to nova, will be met with lethal force. We're done with games, Captain."

EB grinned. Seventy kilometers.

"You might be done with games, my friend, but I am still playing you," he whispered.

Ninety kilometers.

"Sub-fighters will have clear line of fire before we pass the Kármán line," Reggie warned.

"But will they shoot?"

EB's hands were on the physical controls, his attention buried in the screens and datafeeds as he watched the descending fighters. There'd be no time to evade after they fired. He needed to make the judgment of whether they were going to shoot him *now*.

His grip shifted almost without him planning anything, twisting *Evasion* into a sharp upward spiral as a single plasma bolt from the starfighter flashed across his screens.

A warning shot.

And a hundred kilometers.

"We're clear!"

He triggered the nova drive even as he spoke and the world *rippled* around him. Atmosphere, sub-fighters, monitors, Estutmost…all of it vanished in the blink of an eye and a wave of nausea.

Only empty space remained around *Evasion*. They'd made it.

EB exhaled a sigh of relief and checked the engines.

"Ginny? How we looking?"

"Strained but intact," she told him. "I'd like twenty minutes to go over some of the couplings, but I'm guessing we don't have it?"

"We can nova again in ten minutes. They can see where we went in fifteen, so we nova in ten. Can you check what you need in that?"

"We'll do what we can," Ginny promised. "And it *looks* like every-thing is fine, but…"

"We'd rather be certain. But the options are *good enough* or *people shooting at us*. We're going with *good enough*."

IN EVERY STAR system EB knew of, the majority of the mass was distributed along the ecliptic plane with the planetary bodies. He didn't pretend to understand the math or physics beyond that—his knowledge of astronomy was extremely specialized—but he knew that it meant that a star system had a lot of places to run to, if not neces-sarily hide.

Once the light from his emergence reached Estutmost, they'd know exactly where he was. If he was still there when they inevitably sent a gunship to investigate, he'd have to either fight or run.

The plan was that he'd be back at Estutmost before they ever knew where he'd gone. If they saw where *Evasion* was sitting, the Spacers might well guess what he was up to—and there were a few ways they could make his nova back into Estutmost's atmosphere harder.

Right now, he was collecting every scrap of data *Evasion*'s sensors could detect and feeding it back into his nova calculation. Given that his data was ten minutes out of date, there was always a piece of a nova calculation that was guess work.

It was both an art and a skill, one that the computers couldn't replace. That skill didn't make that much difference in the normal turn of events. A few thousand kilometers either way was irrelevant in deep space. Even formation-keeping was straightforward enough, so long as the ships involved shared calculations.

Jumping into a planetary gravity well, though, was a lot harder. That was where Vexer's skill at nova navigation had served them well —and where EB was missing his lover's talents most.

It wasn't the only reason he was missing Vexer, even if it was most pressing at that moment. He was surprised by just how large a hole he was feeling in his life with Vexer stuck on the planet. *Evasion* felt wrong without his boyfriend or daughter aboard.

He was fixing that. The numbers on his screen were as settled as they were going to be. The drive was cooling down, and they were almost ready.

"Couple of the metrics still look fuzzy, boss," Ginny told him. "I think we're good, but…"

"I know, I know," EB conceded. "I'm getting the updates, feeding it into the calculations."

The navigation software dropped a green sphere onto his hologram of Estutmost. If he'd got everything *right*, they'd appear in that green sphere. It was a target zone roughly two point seven kilometers across —two hundred and seventy *million* kilometers away.

If they dropped into that zone, they'd be inside the Spacers' blockade and heading down toward Llandudno before anyone knew they were there. The sub-fighters were faster than *Evasion*, but not enough faster to get beneath her and stop him getting through.

Vexer would be certain he'd made it work, EB knew. If it had been a short jump through space with a fighter's nova drive, EB would have been perfectly fine.

But this was a fifteen-light-minute jump with a freighter's class one nova drive—and a nova into a planetary gravity well and upper atmosphere. EB *thought* he'd done it right, but he'd never done this before.

"Are the locals ready?" he asked.

"Just checked in on them," Reggie reported. "They're unstrapping and prepping their drops. They seem more comfortable with this than we are."

"Apparently, they drop from orbit all the time," EB said. "Just another day at work. Same for us, right?"

"Right," Ginny said. "Engineering is as good as it's going to get, boss. Cooldown complete. We're ready to nova."

"Understood."

EB stretched his hands out in front of him and pinged the ORCs' commander. There'd be a *very* narrow window for the commandos to make their jump. EB doubted they'd actually make the jump from orbit, but he wasn't supposed to be making allowances for them.

They'd either jump when they thought they had the line, or they'd be aboard when *Evasion* hit dirt. Either way, the ORCs would get to Llandudno roughly the same time as *Evasion* did.

A wordless response informed him the commandos were ready. His datafeeds showed them forming up by squads near the bay doors, checking their gear and sealing helmets. The crates had been daisy-chained together and linked to specific troopers who'd haul them out of the ship with themselves.

EB had never made an orbital or even high-altitude jump like the one the Cinnead commandos were planning. He was told it was one hell of a rush, but he didn't think he'd ever want to jump out of a perfectly functional spacecraft.

But then, he'd never thought he'd jump a ship into a planet, either.

"Hang on everybody," he announced throughout the ship. "Nova in five."

A silent countdown popped up automatically on his headware as he took a deep breath and held it.

Four.

Three.

Two.

One.

He exhaled and triggered the nova command in the same moment. The universe rippled again—and then punched him in the gut as parts of his reality tried to be in four places at once. The physical body blow warned him that he'd got *something* wrong—and the spots flashing across his vision as nausea tore through him were more than a warning!

His datafeed flashed with an alert as the cargo bay doors opened—and then *Evasion*'s proximity alarms went off and EB realized how badly he'd screwed it up.

"Contact close," he snapped, more to himself as anyone else. Spots were still flickering across his vision as he yanked *Evasion* to the side, the forty-kilocubic ship barely managing to swerve to avoid the kilometer-wide monitor *directly ahead of her.*

Vexer had overshot his nova when they'd first arrived, emerging inside Estutmost's upper atmosphere.

EB had made the opposite mistake and emerged on the wrong side of the Spacer blockade. And with a ten-minute cooldown on the drive, there was no way he was going to get out of this.

"Holy shit, they're *jumping*."

Reggie's shocked exclamation dragged EB's attention back to the cargo bay. The commandos had opened the bay the moment he'd completed the nova. They had to be able to tell that *Evasion* was too high up, but the ORCs were going anyway. Squad by squad, each squad trailing a chained-together link of crates, the commandos were jumping out the cargo bay doors.

A warning shot flickered through space past *Evasion* and EB threw the ship into a wild series of turns and flips. He couldn't get the freighter out...but he could make it look like he was *trying* until the commandos were out.

If they were ridiculous enough to make the jump, EB would pull out enough stops to let them try.

"Freighter, this is the monitor *Aldrin*," a gravely voice said over the speakers. "You have ten seconds to cut your engines, or we will stop firing to miss!"

For a seemingly eternal three or four seconds, EB looked at the command that would trigger *Evasion*'s multiphasic jammers. They were full combat-grade systems that would turn everything in orbit of

Estutmost into hashed garbage—but he was within two hundred kilo-meters of *Aldrin*.

Even his jammers couldn't make the Spacers miss.

He sharply gestured, touching a command no one else could see, and shut down *Evasion*'s Harrington coils. There was still a single twelve-trooper squad of commandos aboard, but they made a flying leap out the side of his ship as he brought her to a halt relative to *Aldrin*.

"Behave, Reggie," EB murmured on the internal network. "Everybody, stand down. We didn't make it through, and there's no point in causing ourselves more trouble. Return any weapons you're carrying to your quarters and report to the mess."

There was no audible response on the network, but he saw the charge numbers for his turrets start dropping as Reggie started the deactivation sequence. The gunner saw the same situation EB did.

They'd rolled the dice to try and make it through the blockade a second time—but without Vexer to run the numbers, EB had got it wrong.

He tapped a command to return *Aldrin*'s hails.

29

THE SPACERS WERE TAKING no chances. A gunship hung fifty kilometers behind *Evasion*, her turrets trained on the freighter. Eight sub-fighters, the wings from two monitors from what EB could tell, hung around his ship in an even sphere.

His nova drive was almost finished cooling down now, but he had no illusions. If he tried to nova, one of those ships would land a shot before he got away. Novaing with a plasma bolt in the effect field was…impressively destructive.

But he'd been ordered to a different monitor than the one that had ambushed him. The ship now filling his forward screens was bigger than *Aldrin*, and he guessed she was the flagship.

She also had a docking bay that could take *Evasion*, an open maw that swallowed his ship as he surrendered control to the bay controller.

Seconds ticked away, moment by moment, and then *Evasion* touched down under remote control.

"Remain where you are," the bay control officer told him. "Unseal your airlocks. A boarding party is on their way."

"Understood," EB replied crisply. He activated that command and leaned back in his chair to wait. His next steps were either already active or, well, not under his control.

According to his headware, it was just over three minutes before a pair of shipsuited women stepped into his bridge.

"Stand up; keep your hands where we can see them," one barked. "Name."

"Captain Evridiki Bardacki," he introduced himself. "This is my ship."

"Not anymore," the Spacer told him with a grim smile. "Turn around, hands behind your back."

EB obeyed. Cuffs snapped onto his wrists and then a firm hand gripped his shoulder.

"Let's move, *Captain*."

He obeyed. There was no point in being difficult about this. He was going to piss them off enough in a few minutes anyway.

He was marched through the already-empty mess hall, suggesting that his people had already been removed from the ship. His escorts didn't know their way around his ship and took a longer route to the exit ramp than they needed to—but he wasn't exactly going to play tour guide.

EB didn't blame the Spacers for their blockade and *definitely* didn't blame the grunts on the ground, so to speak, for enforcing it. He wasn't happy to have been caught up in it, not when his boyfriend and kid were on the planet, but he couldn't blame the women escorting him.

But he also wasn't going to go out of his way to make their lives easier. An attitude exemplified, he knew, by what happened the moment his escorts walked him out of *Evasion* and onto the exit ramp.

The airlock doors slammed shut behind them. EB's practiced ear could hear the sliding bolts of the security locks activated as *Evasion* went into full lockdown.

"I really hope you didn't have anyone else aboard," he murmured. "The ship doesn't handle my being removed by force very well."

"You son of a bitch!" one of the guards snapped.

"Peace, Leslie." The one who'd originally spoken cut her off. "We *don't* have anyone aboard—and I'm *guessing* the lockdown has a protocol for showing someone out?"

EB smirked silently. She wasn't wrong. If anyone had still been aboard ship, they would find exactly one door open out of whatever room they were in. That pattern would follow until they reached an external airlock.

He couldn't get back onto *Evasion* without the permission of his captors—but he could also make damn certain that the Spacers couldn't get onto her, either.

"I wouldn't count on that helping you much," the senior soldier told him. "We have very good software people."

EB said nothing. If the "very good" software people from a system lost in the Beyond were up to cracking the top military security protocols of a mid-Rim military anchored on better hardware than the Spacers had ever seen…well, at that point, they were geniuses enough that nothing he could do would stop them.

"Commodore is waiting," the noncom finally said with a growling sigh. "Leslie, bring 'im."

THE TWO SOLDIERS escorted EB into an observation gallery. Monitors, due to the nature of their construction, had far more available volume than any nova ship. Even so, the room seemed excessive for the single man standing in the middle of it, studying the screens surrounding him.

While the semicircular room attempted to appear like it had windows, EB hadn't passed through the right kind of narrow upward stairs to be on the surface of the monitor. They were still on the safe side of twenty or so meters of nickel-iron armor.

Holographic imagery of the blockade was superimposed over the view of the planet beneath them, allowing the Spacer commander to see the full scope of their command from this one space.

"Commodore Malone," the senior soldier announced. "We have Captain Bardacki for you."

"Thank you, Sergeant McMahon," the officer replied. "Leave us. Secure the door."

"Are you sure, ser?" McMahon asked.

"He's cuffed and unarmed, yes?"

"Yes, ser."

"Then leave us."

The two shipsuited soldiers withdrew, leaving EB alone with the commander of the blockade in his command center.

Malone examined him silently and EB returned the favor. The Spacer was a tall man, with the oddly elongated limbs of someone raised in low gravity. *Most* space stations and spaceships would maintain ninety-plus percent of a standard gravity, but you could save a small but measurable amount of energy and money by running at under fifty percent.

Children weren't supposed to be raised in facilities like that, but it happened often enough that EB recognized the signs in the Commodore. Malone's iron-gray hair and heavily lined face spoke to that having been a long time before, as did the metallic hand he raised to gesture for EB to approach.

The Spacer's right arm was not merely artificial but *obviously* artificial, EB realized. Even the Standard Colonial Database had the details to build functional and decently disguised cybernetics, so an obvious prosthetic was…either a choice or a sign of someone being *very* cheap.

Given that Malone wore the uniform of the Staid Chorporra na h-Estutmost's orbital security forces, he had to be one of the mutineers that had stolen said security force's *ships*—which said that either his employers hadn't seen fit to update his cybernetics or that he'd kept them as a statement of solidarity with the Spacers.

Either way should have been a warning sign.

"You command the freighter that ran our blockade?" Malone finally asked.

"*Evasion*," EB said quietly. "My name is Captain Evridiki Bardacki. I was hired to deliver a cargo to the Cinnead." He shrugged. "I have neither fired on nor otherwise engaged in hostilities against your people, Commodore Malone."

"You *did*, however, deliver a significant selection of armaments to the surface, despite the blockade. And that's putting aside the fact that we did, eventually, realize that you'd had your cargo bay doors open while we were detaining you."

EB said nothing.

"Did you realize that the *orbital* part of Orbital Recon Commando was quite literal, Captain?"

"No," he admitted. "I was expecting a high-altitude, low-open drop from later in the process. When the nova came in short, I was expecting them to surrender with us."

Malone snorted and pointed with a long metal finger.

They had an amazing view of the Dachaigh from there, EB realized. Malone was pointing at Llandudno, highlighted with several icons now.

"I don't know if a single company of ORCs will change anything, but it's going to be a pain for the Staid Chorporra," the Commodore said drily. "Less so than the tank brigades the Cinnead are assembling."

He shook his head.

"You do realize, Captain, that you may have single-handedly extended this war by six months to a year and likely caused at least a hundred thousand extra deaths?"

"War is hell, Commodore. I won't claim a lack of responsibility for it continuing, but I didn't start this war and I'm not giving the orders."

"And yet."

EB looked at the layout of the blockade and sighed. They were aboard *Armstong*, the newest and largest of the monitors, but the rest were deployed in a decently distributed shell. Mercenary gunships and local sub-fighters filled in the gaps. Outside of someone managing the low-atmosphere nova that Vexer had arranged, no one was getting in to Estutmost.

There likely weren't many nova ships left on the planet to get out, either, though that part was easier. Even EB had been able to plot that nova, after all.

As invited, EB stepped up to stand beside the Commodore as Malone studied the blockade himself. That close, it became clear that it wasn't just the man's right arm that was artificial. His leg was of a similar quality of exposed cybernetic, and part of the right side of his face was a far-higher-quality implant.

"Your ship and crew will be detained until further notice," Malone finally told him. "I'm informed that you've locked down your vessel to prevent us from accessing her. That does not, I must note, aid in any protestations of innocence."

"I'm not protesting innocence of any kind. Under normal circumstances, I would volunteer to pay a fine and leave the system. That is the normal response to a hired third party attempting to run the blockade, is it not?"

"Had you been captured on the way in the first time, perhaps," the Spacer said. "But you made damn fools of my people, Captain Bardacki. You extended a war I'm trying to shorten and have generally made my life a lot fucking harder."

"Shortening the war would have been a lot easier *before* you stole the Staid Chorporra's monitor fleet," EB said drily. "How many people died in the mutiny to seize these ships, *Commodore*?"

Only one entity in the Estutmost System could have funded, built, and operated twenty-two monitors. While EB knew at least one Estutmost-flagged nova warship was outside the system, the sublight warships were all definitely in Spacer hands—and they hadn't started there.

Malone grimaced.

"We'd *hoped* that a peaceful seizure of the orbitals would bring the Board and the Commission to the negotiating table, create a chance for improvements for everyone," he admitted. "We were wrong."

"And now you're stuck, I take it? Despite being in control of the orbitals, able to run supplies to either side and having the ultimate high ground?"

"Do not let the rank fool you, Captain. I am in command because my people follow me; my ability to impose control is limited." Malone was looking at the planet again. "As the Cinnead complain about the Tuathans, so the Spacers complain about the Cinnead. No faction in this system is innocent of trying to pressure and injure others.

"I could not convince my people to fight for the Board. Not now. But enough of them would not fight for the Cinnead that neutrality is our only option. A pox on both their houses, and they'll sort out their own problems in blood and fire.

"You've added to both, Captain Bardacki, and that is a nightmare I'd rather not have had to deal with. But here we are."

From where EB stood, Commodore Malone held *all* of the cards. He had the monitors, the gunships, the blockade. The same funds that were paying for mercenary gunships could easily hire mercenary tank brigades—harder to find than gunships, but they definitely existed.

If the Spacers *really* wanted to put an end to the war, all they had to do was pick a side.

Except that from what Malone told him, that was the one thing they *couldn't* do.

EB STOOD in silence for at least thirty seconds, watching the holographic icons move around the planet beneath them. The Galahad-led advance of the Tuathan assault column was clearly having trouble, even from this height. The mobile Cinnead forces were playing a successful game of cat and mouse to slow the government advance.

The current game wasn't going to change much. The Staid now had more soldiers and tanks in the Dachaigh a Deas than the Cinnead did. It would be a few more days before the column was in position to assault Dinas Fferm, but the mobile forces weren't going to slow them down.

The war would be decided on the outskirts of the Cinnead capital, when General Owens took his newly formed strike brigades into battle for the first time. Either the tanks and artillery EB had provided would be enough to carry the day for the city's defenders, or their destruction would force the Cinnead to surrender.

He sighed.

"You didn't have your people bring me to you to complain about us breaching your blockade," he told Malone. "What do you want?"

"In truth? I wanted to meet the man who was smart enough to manage to run my blockade both ways—and was dumb enough to come *back* after he got away," Malone replied. "Until we went back over the data and saw the ORCs dropping, I had no idea what the hell you were thinking.

"Whatever the Cinnead paid you for that drop, I hope it was worth it."

"I was heading to Llandudno anyway. My partner, my daughter and my ship's doctor were helping deal with the Tuathan bioweapon when the attack started. They're still in that city. I'm going to get them out."

Even EB was surprised by how determinedly that last statement came out. He was a prisoner now, trapped on Malone's monitor in handcuffs.

"Ah." Malone turned away from him. "That makes a few things fall into place, doesn't it? We do foolish things for love and family."

"The man who really ran your blockade is my boyfriend," EB admitted. "If *he'd* been navigating *Evasion*, we'd have made the nova the second time, too."

The Commodore chuckled.

"You still wouldn't have made it down. We were ready for you this time. You'd shown us your tail once too many times to get away with a *fourth* time."

"So you say."

The silence that stretched after that grew oppressive. Malone was clearly thinking *something*, but he wasn't sharing his thoughts with his prisoner—and EB couldn't exactly *leave*.

"I'm surprised to hear you refer to the virus as a bioweapon," he finally said. "Estutmost's native viruses are the only part of its biosphere that *have* adapted to Terran physiology. Unanticipated and unpredicted viral outbreaks are an unfortunate fact of life on the surface.

"I wouldn't have expected a starship captain to be quite so credulous of the Commission's propaganda."

"My doctor was in their hospital in Llandudno," EB reminded Malone. "*They* were the one who determined that it was a bioweapon. Stabilized artificial organism, specifically tailored to neutralize a defensive position with minimal true lethality.

"I trust anyone in this star system about as far as I can throw your flagship, Commodore, but I trust Dr. Lan Kozel with my life. More, I trusted him with my daughter's *brain* at a critical moment. If they tell me that the virus sweeping Llandudno is an artificial bioweapon…it's an artificial bioweapon."

"Huh."

Malone turned his back entirely to EB for a moment. His gaze was tracing the blockade, studying the monitors positioned around Estutmost.

"Are you familiar with the concept of *parole*, Captain Bardacki?"

EB blinked. That was not the question he was expecting to be asked.

"I was a fighter pilot once, a long way away and a long time ago, but that was covered in my officer's training, yeah."

"If you and your crew will give me parole, your promise not to attempt to escape, we can allow you with a reasonable degree of freedom of movement aboard *Armstrong*." Malone was still facing away, but his chuckle was clearly audible.

"When she was built, it was unclear for a while whether she'd be a monitor or our first true asteroid fortress. She spends enough of her time in orbit to basically be an asteroid fort, which means we actually have a civilian concourse aboard.

"You will be restricted to that concourse in the main, but we will provide comfortable quarters as matters proceed."

"For how long?" EB demanded.

"I don't know," Malone admitted. "I now have an extra concern, it seems, one I didn't think was actually likely. I don't *believe* you, Captain, that the virus was a bioweapon. But at the same time, I don't believe you have a reason to lie to me.

"And if the Staid Chorporra has turned the biotechnology that is this system's pride and hope into a *weapon*, then the terms of engagement of this war may have changed. I am not certain, yet, how to prove that one way or another.

"But you have no reason to lie to me," he repeated softly. "So, I am prepared to consider the possibility and investigate it. Therefore, I will extend a degree of courtesy I might not otherwise."

"I'm not leaving this system until I have my family," EB warned.

"And I'm not letting you go anywhere. But we can compromise on the terms of your detention, can we not?"

EB exhaled a sigh. It wasn't a good offer. At best, it made a long-term imprisonment aboard *Armstrong* more comfortable. But the alternative was cells for him and his crew.

"Fine," he finally said. "I promise I will not attempt to escape nor will I order my people to attempt to escape. But my family is on the surface, Commodore. I have to do *something*."

"There are arguments every way you want, Captain, with regards to what must be done about the surface. Truth be told, though, I suspect your family may be safest if you do *nothing*."

30

THE NEWS FEEDS across the city were clear: it was raining men.

Also, Trace figured, women and a few other gender presentations. Soldiers in specialty gear had dropped out of the sky without much warning, landing in scattered pockets across the city. Many had been shot down by the defenses erected by General Griffith's Second Division, but most made it to the ground.

Some of those troopers had made contact with the resistance. She knew *that* because she was sitting on the edge of Major Vaughn's command center, watching the Cinnead communication team arrange pickups for cargo.

It was harder for the resistance to make squads of commandos disappear, but from what Trace could hear, they were doing it anyway. No one on the ground had any idea how many troops had been dropped yet—or even *how*—but they were finding safehouses for some of them.

Others were apparently disappearing on their own, following plans that Trace suspected predated the rebellion.

"Who are these guys?" she asked K-5. The teenager was leaning against the wall next to her. *His* job in the room was security, but she was finding him a reassuring presence.

She'd run into the youth who'd stared at her again. His name was Fernand Calvin and he seemed nice enough. But her interactions with him felt ever so slightly off.

If nothing else, she supposed, he was still embarrassed about being caught openly staring at the chest of a girl six years his junior. She *hoped*, at least. She was still more than a bit squicked out by that.

"Which guys?" K-5 asked. Despite everything, he *still* hadn't actually given them his name—which suggested he had a far better sense of security and secrecy than a lot of people in the command center.

It was a good thing for the resistance, in Trace's uneducated opinion, that these people weren't allowed out. It felt like some of them would be putting *I work for the resistance command center* in their public information profiles.

"The ones dropping on the city," she told K with exaggerated patience. "Who else?"

He snorted.

"Right, you're not from around here. Those are ORCs: the Orbital Recon Commandos. The stars of half of our action movies and two-thirds of the recruiting videos for the Staid before the war.

"Feels like most guys I know wanted to either be pilots or ORCs growing up. But there's only a few hundred of them, and they only took the best from the security forces—and they defected as a unit right when the war started."

K sounded *very* pleased about that.

"Really helped make it clear which side was the right one, when the elite of the Staid security troops chose the other side."

"Are they going to make a difference?" Trace murmured.

Some of K's enthusiasm dissipated and he fell silent.

"Don't know. Major hasn't said, and she'd know. They brought guns and armor that we're squirreling away, but they're also a spark. We don't get to choose our moment now."

The ORCs had chosen the moment. There was fighting across the city, though none of it had turned into a major conflagration yet. Trace couldn't see a few dozen soldiers, however well equipped or trained, turning the balance of power in the city.

Hopefully, the commandos would manage to get into hiding before they caused the resistance *too* much damage—or, most importantly, from Trace's perspective, drew attention to the command center she was hiding in!

LAN REJOINED Trace and Vexer in their shared office-turned-apartment roughly an hour later, a small medical case in their hand.

"Both of you, sit down and roll up your sleeves," they ordered. "I don't think we've been exposed yet, so let's kick the chance before it even becomes a problem."

"You finished the vaccine?" Vexer asked as he and Trace followed orders.

"Ran the first two dozen doses of both the vaccine and the counter-viral," the doctor confirmed. "Hold still, Trace."

The hypospray hissed and Trace managed not to flinch too much. It was telling that she'd managed to make it that far before flinching, she realized—the first few times Lan had given her shots of any kind, she'd needed to hold someone's hand.

She'd been drugged a *lot* while she in the Siya U Hestí's hands. Even her cooperation and obedience had only bought her so much freedom or trust.

"You might feel a bit rough for the rest of the day," Lan warned as they turned to Vexer and applied a new hypospray. "That's part of why I'm back. I shot myself up with both the vaccine and the counter-viral, just in case."

They grimaced.

"I'm about eighty percent sure I got exposed at least twice, with everything going on. Countervirals will handle that, but I was already getting sick. Going to be a rough few hours for me."

"Then get your overqualified ass into bed," Vexer ordered. "We don't have anything we need to do or anywhere we need to be."

"I did need to get the vaccine producing before the Cinnead made any kind of push in town," Lan said as they took a seat on the bed. "Glad we had that rolling before the locals decided to drop soldiers from on high."

"They launched from *Evasion*," Vexer said quietly. "Vaughn told me."

Trace sat up straight and looked at him.

"Is Dad-E coming?" she asked.

"He was," Vexer said, but he shook his head sadly. "The nova cut short. They emerged in a higher orbit than planned. The ORCs managed to make their jump by sheer foolhardiness, but *Evasion* ended up under the blockade's guns.

"EB surrendered, Trace. Everyone's fine…but they're prisoners now. They're not coming to save us."

Trace wrapped her arms around herself as that hit home. She'd been counting on EB to come rescue her—for as long as she'd known him, he'd managed it every time it had mattered.

Now…he'd tried and failed. She wasn't sure what came next. Only that she was afraid.

Vexer was there before it hit too hard, wrapping his arms around her as she curled into a ball and holding her against him.

"EB's smart and persuasive," he reminded her. "If anyone can talk the blockaders into letting him go, it's EB—and he might be better off trying to rescue us with their support and permission than running the blockade."

"Or we're just all doomed," Trace murmured.

"War sucks," Lan said. They were lying back on the bed now, staring at the ceiling. "You haven't seen much of the city. I have. Both the Cinnead and the Staid tried to keep the fighting out of Llandudno, but there are still entire blocks that have been leveled.

"*And* the Tuathan security troopers are still rounding up suspected sympathizers and known Cinnead members, anyone they can find. The city is…"

"Llandudno is occupied by a hostile army," Vexer finished for him. "We're safe here. We have to wait and see what happens now, Trace."

31

"APPARENTLY, I should promise not to escape more often. This is nicer than my quarters on *Evasion*."

EB glared at Reggie, not entirely seriously. The weapons tech wasn't wrong, not really. The six members of *Evasion*'s crew aboard the monitor were sharing a pair of two-bedroom apartments in *Armstrong*'s "civilian concourse."

That concourse was a stretch of stores about the length of most city blocks, with a facing segment of hotel suites and small apartments meant for the store staff. All told, it probably took up about five or six thousand cubic meters of the monitor—a space no nova warship could sacrifice but that the kilometer-long asteroid warship likely didn't even notice was missing.

"This doesn't have to nova," Ginny pointed out. While the split between the two suites had ended up being men versus women, Ginny had joined EB and Reggie in their suite and was staring at the coffee table with them.

"They have space. *Evasion* doesn't. And there's a lot to be said for being in control of your own fate." EB wasn't doing much more than staring at the coffee table himself. The half-eaten sandwich sitting on the table was his—both Ginny and Reggie had finished their own meals.

He could barely force himself to eat. That was…unhealthy, but his last real bastion against the failure of leaving his people—his *family*—behind had been that he would go get them himself.

But he no longer had his ship. Without *Evasion*, he was just…one more man. His skills were useless without a starship. Without his skills, without a ship, without the things that gave him control, he couldn't do anything to save his lover or his daughter.

He had left them behind and he had failed them.

"I fucking hate being a prisoner, if that's what you mean," Reggie said quietly. "I've done real jail time, in a system without modern rehabilitation-based detention. Things could be a lot worse."

"Not sure how," EB growled, then swallowed anything further. His people didn't need to hear his fears, his angers.

"If we were locked in little solitary cells in the actual *brig* of this warship, we wouldn't be able to do anything for our people on the surface," Ginny told him. "Since we're being allowed some level of freedom and ability to talk to the crew, we can learn more about what's going on.

"The more we know, the more able we are to put together our plan."

"If *Evasion* was in the civilian docks, a skip down the corridor from here, we'd have a chance," EB replied. "But she's in the military hangars, on the other side of *four hundred meters* of restricted areas, security posts, patrols and sensors."

"Maybe, but this ship is badly undercrewed," Reggie said with a shrug. "Didn't you notice?"

EB stared at his gunner.

"What do you mean?"

"You may have been dragged off to meetings with important people, but *I* did spend time in those solitary cells Ginny just mentioned," Reggie pointed out. "Got hauled through a good chunk of the ship, and I've spent time on monitors in the past.

"Now, those were Rim monitors and had that much better tech, but you'd think they'd have had *less* crew than a monitor out here.

Instead…" He flicked his fingers thoughtfully in the air, the sign of someone accessing headware data.

"I have to wonder if this ship is supposed to be in commission at all," Ginny said into the silence. "I had a similar all-over-the-place journey here as Reggie did, EB. He's right. The ship is undercrewed. Chunks of her aren't properly finished. She's operational, but there were sections of the ship I was taken through that weren't fully closed up."

"If she's that undercrewed and things are that unfinished, I see options." Reggie flipped the file he'd been poking at to the other two. It was a rough map of the monitor, the parts of it Reggie had seen at least.

Almost half-consciously, EB started adding the corridors he'd seen —and saw Ginny start doing the same. His two crewmates had followed very similar tracks, but each bit of information gave them a bit more.

"If it's as rough as it looks, there may not be as many sensors or guards as I would think," he murmured. "On the other hand, we gave our word."

Not to escape, Ginny's voice said in his head. *Didn't say anything about getting back on* Evasion, *heading back to the surface to grab our people, and then surrendering again, did we?*

That is pushing *the definitions,* he replied silently.

There was a decent chance everything they said aloud was being recorded, but headware-to-headware should be secure.

"I wasn't saying we *should* do anything," Reggie said virtuously. He'd been included on the silent conversation and the attendant concerns about recording. "Only that it was something to think about.

"This is family we're talking about, after all. We're going back for them, boss. Sooner or later."

Let's see if we can manage that without actively pissing off our captors, shall we? Keep your eyes open…see what we learn. But no jumping the gun.

If we break our word and get caught, they won't trust us a second time.

PACING the length of the civilian concourse gave EB a chance to stretch his legs and let some of the spikier cobwebs fall out of his brain. There wasn't a great deal of decoration in the triple-width corridor that served as a promenade, and the stores were mostly practical things.

It looked and felt like it had been intended to be: the standard basic suite of stores on an asteroid battle station. Since most systems' first battle station acted as the counterweight for an orbital elevator with a civilian station attached, only so many amenities were needed.

But any permanent installation inevitably needed more amenities than a ship moving around. To EB's mind, *all* monitors counted as permanent installations, but the people who built them didn't always agree with him there.

The sixty-meter-long concourse had twelve stores and six restaurants. Clothes, specialty groceries, personals, electronics, burgers, Chinese-descendant cuisine…the usual array.

There was even a tiny jewelry store tucked away at one end. A glance at the window suggested that they specialized in small gifts for partners service personnel had been away from…and engagement rings.

That was a thought that fell back into those spikier cobwebs. EB and Vexer had been engaging in an on-and-off relationship for almost as long as Vexer had been aboard *Evasion*. More than friends with benefits, less than life partners, with occasional pauses.

Since…since EB had rejected Lady Breanna's offer to become one of her Cartel shippers, dragging the whole crew into the nightmare of running like crazy as the most powerful syndicate in this chunk of the galaxy tried to chase them down, it had become something more.

Adding Trace to the mix had only solidified it. EB didn't expect another of their pauses, but he couldn't put his finger on *why*. Having the teenager to look out for didn't *require* them to still be together romantically—it took a village to wrangle a highly intelligent and heavily traumatized teenage girl, or at least a starship crew!

But EB still felt that his relationship with Vexer had taken a new step, and he wasn't entirely sure when or how. If he wanted to be *sure*, he could ask…or could have, before he'd decided to leave the man he loved and the daughter he'd sworn to protect in a city being invaded.

He realized he'd been standing in the corridor, staring at the jewelry store for several minutes, and shook his head, laughing at himself.

The solution, after all, was to *ask* Vexer. Communication solved a lot of confusion, in his experience.

The question probably wasn't *Will you marry me*…but EB had to admit that the answer to *that* question would also solve a lot of confusion.

For the moment, though, he was supposed to be investigating guard positions and security checkpoints, not weaving sweaters from mental spiderwebs.

Turning away from the store, he returned to his pacing.

EB's headware was capable of replaying everything he was seeing later, and he took advantage of that. Images of the exits superimposed themselves on his vision as he walked away from them, allowing detailed examination. A translucent overlay of their rough map of the monitor appeared over his vision as he walked, marking the paths they knew would get them back to *Evasion*.

None of his people had been brought directly there. With three different routes mapped out by the crew's various journeys from ship to hotel, EB could localize roughly where the hangar with his ship was.

There was definitely a more-direct route, and his pacing let him identify which exit from the concourse led toward it. They'd go right past the jeweler and to a security gate that had a single gray-shipsuited soldier guarding it.

Security pickups were positioned around the door too, and EB suspected there were concealed stun fields as well. The transition from the small civilian section of the monitor to the rest of the warship was as decently secured as the locals could manage.

But while EB and his crew weren't allowed into the civilian dock next to the concourse, that meant there was *more* security on the internal division of the civil section of the ship. Three troopers and a pair of drones were guarding that entrance.

The four exits heading into the real warship had more built-in security…but fewer guards. Including the three guards on the dock entrance, there were only eight members of *Armstrong*'s crew providing security on the concourse.

And the door that he estimated would lead them most directly to their ship only had *one* guard.

The problem was sensors and automated systems…and depending on what EB could find in terms of access points, he could work with that.

He'd been the cyberwarfare specialist for his fighter squadron, after all, and he'd brought a *stack* of Rim military-grade software with him when he'd deserted.

32

TRACE WOKE up sharply at a sound she didn't recognize. Rolling over and grabbing a stunner, she saw that both Vexer and Lan had woken up as well—and then the sound repeated.

She was used to metal doors and headware alarms. Someone hammering on the composite door with their bare fist was out of her experience. Both Vexer and Lan had recognized it, and three stunners were trained on the door as Vexer rose.

"What is it?" he asked.

"Pack your shit," K-5 barked through the door. "Center's compromised. We are *moving*."

Trace swallowed a curse and immediately started shoving her stuff into her backpack.

Vexer crossed the room to the door instead and pulled it open. The teenaged resistance fighter stood outside, dressed in a long casual jacket that currently failed to conceal the blaster carbine he was carrying.

"What do you mean, *compromised*?"

"What does it sound like, Dolezal? *Somebody*'s surveillance drone breached the perimeter. We can't take any chances, so we're relocating everybody."

Past K-5, Trace could see movement as the electronics and other equipment were being packed up.

"What about the clinic?" Lan asked, striding forward to join Vexer.

Trace was finished packing—she'd limited how much she'd taken out of the backpack in the first place—and she joined the adults by the door.

"Packing up to move them as well," K-5 said grimly.

"Some of those people should *not* be moved," Lan snapped.

"It's that or leave them for Griffith's people. What can we do?"

"Fuck. Trace, Vexer, I need to go check on the wounded," the doctor told them. "Hell, K, you're with me too. We're going to go help with the clinic move."

"Major said I'm your watchman and guide," the teenager said. "I'm not *supposed* to take you to the clinic but…you're the doctor."

"Yes. I am. So, let's grab our shit and move, because the only chance some of those poor people have is for the doctors to ride herd on them the whole way."

FOR SOME REASON, Trace had thought "the clinic" that Lan had been helping out in was an actual clinic or ward of some kind. Instead, it was the same kind of "this was built for a cubicle farm" open space as Vaughn's command center on a lower floor in the building.

Most of the equipment was packed up into crates by the time they arrived, but there were several sets arranged around the worst cases. Two women in surgical gear were hovering over those beds, trying to rig up something Trace couldn't see.

"Mel, Sara," Lan greeted the two women as he joined them. "You're overthinking it. We need the blood-stabilizer units and the oxygen. Everything else can be suspended for up to three hours without long-term damage.

"Do we know where we're taking them?"

Trace sighed in relief, turning away to see where she could help. Lan definitely had the doctors and the wounded in hand.

"Over here, Trace," K-5 called her. The teenager was helping another pair of resistance fighters to load crates of medical equipment onto antigrav pallets.

She joined in. The crates were heavy enough to *need* the pallets. Two people at a time could lift one crate—and a single person could lift and guide a pallet of four crates.

"Thanks," K said as they got the last crate on. "This is a mess. We thought the building was secure."

The local was older than Trace, but he managed to feel very young and afraid to her. She reached out and squeezed his shoulder.

"But there's a plan, right?"

"Yeah," K confirmed, glancing at the other two fighters. Following his gaze, Trace felt a chill run down her spine.

K-5 was eighteen and still probably too young to be involved in this mess. The other two resistance fighters, both with blaster carbines slung over their backs to mark them as *fighters*, were even younger than him.

They were older than Trace, but she wouldn't have pegged either of the girls at over seventeen. Old enough that one of them was looking at K-5 in a rather non-comradely way, but too young to be involved in an armed conflict.

"You two get the pallets moving downstairs," K instructed them. "There's a truck waiting in the loading bay."

"On it, Kieran."

He shook his head at the girls, but his smile suggested that the girl's interest was far from unrequited.

Trace was younger than any of them, but she was still taken aback by their age. They were all too young for this.

"Let's go check with your doc," Kieran told her. "They'll need hands and everyone else is busy moving gear or watching for the Second Division's move."

"Kieran?" Trace asked with an arched eyebrow.

He snorted.

"Kieran McNamara, Lance-Corporal, LRD-Five-Five-Niner-K," he recited. "That's all you get to interrogate me for, kiddo."

"You're one to call anyone *kiddo*," Trace pointed out as she fell in beside him.

Kieran was silent for a few seconds.

"Mom died on the Line," he said quietly. "Dad is somewhere in the plains in the mechanized infantry. Major Vaughn's my aunt, but I *am* a fully enlisted and trained Cinnead Militiaman."

"And those kids?" Trace asked, gesturing back toward the girls loading the antigrav pallets into the cargo elevator.

"Volunteers. Most of our cadre of real troops is here, but we don't have enough hands."

And the *adults* who were willing to fight for the Cinnead were already in the Militia, Trace guessed.

"ANTIGRAV PALLET UNDER THE EQUIPMENT. Power cell will last for two hours," Lan instructed Trace and Kieran. "I hope where we're taking these people isn't that far away."

"It's closer than that," Kieran confirmed as he slid the pallet into place. "Tie this to the one under the bed?"

"Will that fit in whatever we have for transport?"

"Should. Cargo elevator is a bigger problem, but I think it'll squeeze."

"Do it," Lan ordered.

Trace had located the connection points. The antigrav pallets were designed to link together, and connecting the bed to the pallet with the equipment kept everything together—and using the antigrav pallets *should* keep the bed stable.

Almost as good as not moving the patient at all, she presumed. If nothing else, Trace figured that Lan knew what they were doing.

She was also very carefully *not* looking at the woman in the bed. The patient had lost both legs to an artillery shell during the assault on the city—and *then* had the bioweapon finish incubating.

Nothing about the patient looked good to Trace, but she believed Lan when the doctor said the woman would be fine. So long as she wasn't jarred too badly while they moved her.

"Cargo elevator takes us down to the loading bay," Kieran told them. "There are two trucks waiting down there. The drivers know where they're going."

"And we don't?" Vexer asked, the navigator sliding another set of antigrav pallets up to the remaining ward bed.

"No. Division of information and operational security," the older teenager reeled off. "I know, just in case, but we're keeping the information held tight."

"Fair enough," Lan said before Vexer could say a word. "Trace, you're with me. I don't like moving Em Bogomolova at all, which means I'm going to stick with her the whole way."

Nodding, Trace programmed the pallets' controls to follow her commands.

"I'll meet you in the loading bay," Kieran promised. "One more patient, one more doctor and then we're on our way."

THE LOADING BAY was a hive of activity, with the two trucks for the medical equipment only part of it. A fleet of a dozen vans, some commercial and some consumer, was lined up along one side, to receive the electronics equipment from the command center—and from the looks of it, there'd been more to start with.

The doors on one van slammed closed as Trace and her adults moved their patient out of the cargo elevator, and the vehicle took off almost instantly.

"Dr. Kozel," a voice projected. "We've got an ambulance waiting over here for Bogomolova."

Trace turned to see Fernand Calvin approaching, waving them over. At least in this chaos, the awkwardness of their previous interactions was missing. His focus was very much on Lan, though, which might have been intentional.

"That'll help," Lan said. "I thought we were bringing her on the truck."

"We weren't sure we'd have the ambulance," Calvin told them. "She just made it in. But Bogomolova is the worst off, right?"

"That's why I'm with her," Lan confirmed. "Driver knows where we're going?"

"*I'm* driving," the soldier admitted. "Paramedics abandoned it in an alley. I have to drop it back off when we're done, but we have it for about an hour."

"I was hoping for EMTs, but I guess Vexer and Trace will do. Come on."

Trace wasn't sure she would make a good paramedic herself, but she'd try. Whatever was needed.

First, they pulled the antigrav pallets up to the back of the ambulance. There was fancy equipment for loading in stretchers, but since they didn't *have* a stretcher, moving Bogomolova into the ambulance's bed was…difficult.

Trace found herself holding cables and tubing as Vexer and Lan slowly and carefully moved the unconscious woman between beds. Once she was situated, Lan gestured Trace over.

"The ambulance has its own equipment, so we need to hook her up in here," they told her. "Hold the tubes up, and I'll take them one by one and hook them in. Sound good?"

Trace nodded, doing her best to keep everything separate to make it easier on the doctor.

It was a swift process, though. It *had* to be, she suspected, or the patient would suffer.

"Okay. Everything is hooked up to the ambulance. Leave the gear to go on the other truck," Lan ordered. "Then get in, both of you."

The doctor looked at Fernand Calvin.

"Drive slowly, kid," they ordered. "Even with the ambulance's shocks, we need to avoid every bump we can."

"I know," Calvin promised. "I'll get us there safely, I promise."

"Good. Her life is riding on it."

33

THE AMBULANCE WAS out of the loading bay and halfway down the first street before Trace realized they'd been supposed to meet Kieran still. The teenage militiaman had said he was supposed to be their guide and watcher for this trip.

There might have been a missed connection—especially since Calvin had said they hadn't expected to have an ambulance—but that still seemed…worrying.

"Trace, I need you," Lan snapped.

Her attention locked on to the doctor.

"What do you need?" she asked swiftly.

"That panel next you to is the oxygen monitor and control," they told her. "I need you to up her oxygen flow by ten percent. I don't like her breathing."

It took Trace half a second to study the panel in front of her and find the control for that. Increasing the flow as instructed, she saw the main metric on the screen slowly begin to rise.

"The countervirals aren't doing as much as they should," Lan said aloud. "Her injury has weakened her entire system, and without a proper ward and regen system…"

They shook their head.

"She's going to make it, but the combination of the damn bioweapon and her injuries is rough. I really wish we hadn't had to move her."

Trace glanced at the injured woman, then looked away. There was fresh blood on the sheets covering her legs.

"Her legs," Vexer said.

"I see it," Lan replied. "Vexer, the cabinet by your left should have units of plasma. Trace, keep your eye on her blood oxygen levels. If it drops below eighty-five, increase the O-two flow again. If her blood pressure drops below eighty over fifty, tell me right away. Understand?"

She nodded shakily as the doctor got to work. Watching the monitor meant she *wasn't* watching the patient—which, given that the last thing she *did* see was Lan pulling the sheet off Bogomolova's legs to get at the amputation scars, was probably a good thing.

"Got the plasma," Vexer declared. "I know how to give it."

"Okay, do it. I need to re-suture this *crap*."

Trace could only be very glad that her dad was *Evasion*'s backup medic. The iron scent of blood in the vehicle was bad enough for her. If she had to actually *look* at Bogomolova while Lan worked, she suspected she'd become absolutely useless.

"THE BLEEDING HAS STOPPED," Lan finally said. "Heart rate stable, blood pressure stable, breathing stable."

They stripped off the gloves they'd been wearing and leaned back against the ambulance wall, studying their patient.

"Thank you, Trace, Vexer," they said. "We just saved her life. Again. Whichever Staid drone pilot got lucky can rot in whatever hell they believe in, as far as I'm concerned."

"I hope wherever we're heading is as well equipped," the navigator noted. "I don't know much about running a resistance, but I'm *guessing* that losing their command center is going to be a pain unless they have an equally equipped backup."

From the urgency the resistance crew had shown while loading electronics into vehicles, Trace wasn't going to bet on it. Anything they couldn't take with them probably wasn't going to be there at the other end.

Hoping to get a sense of whether the occupiers had moved yet, she tried to link into the news feeds…and then froze as she failed to connect.

"Does either of you have signal?" she murmured. "I'm not getting a *no signal* warning, but I can't connect to anything outside the ambulance."

"That's not right," Vexer said. "Let me—"

Trace could connect with Vexer, she realized a moment later. And Lan. She could even detect the network from Bogomolova's headware, though the unconscious woman couldn't give her permission to connect.

But nothing outside the back of the ambulance existed. There was a network of *some* kind, enough to fool her hardware into thinking it had signal and prevent it from throwing up a warning, but that was it.

"We're being blocked," Lan said slowly. "I can't even raise the driver. What in void?"

"We've been on the road for over twenty minutes. Didn't he say he had to return the ambulance inside an hour?" Trace asked.

"He did," Lan agreed. "An act that is likely now impossible. We appear to be trapped."

Trace was already poking at the rear doors, but she was unsurprised when they turned out to be locked from the outside. Somehow, she doubted that was a normal feature of an ambulance.

"What do we do?" she asked.

"We keep Em Bogomolova alive, and we wait to see what happens. All we have on us are stunners, we have no means of escaping the ambulance until Fernand lets us out—and if I leave Em Bogomolova, she will die."

"How far are we going?" Trace wondered alive.

"We will find out soon enough."

IT WAS another ten minutes before the ambulance finally came to a halt. The rear doors remained determinedly closed, though, and Vexer hammered on the front divider.

"Hey, what's going on?" the navigator demanded.

No one answered and Trace shivered. Her stunner was in her hand, but she had no idea what she was going to do with it.

"We need a proper medical suite sooner rather than later," Lan said.

Trace followed Vexer's example and hammered on the back doors.

"Hey!" she shouted. "Calvin, what are you doing?"

As she went to hammer a second time, the doors suddenly swung sharply open. She barely managed to keep herself from falling forward out of the vehicle—and into the hard-faced man pointing a stunner at her.

"Everybody out of the vehicle," he barked.

"My patient can't move and I'm not moving without her," Lan growled.

"Not my problem," the stranger growled. "Move, or I make her nobody's problem."

"That wasn't the deal," Calvin's voice snapped from out of view.

"Then get the idiots out of the damn van before I start stunning people."

"We're coming," Trace promised, slowly stepping out of the van, her hands spread wide.

Another stranger neatly plucked the stunner from her hands before she even saw them. A tall woman with a cybernetic eye, they swept the obvious prosthetic up and down Trace, clearly scanning for weapons.

"She's clean."

"Move her over, check the other two." The first stranger gestured for the two men to exit the ambulance. "Weapons on the ground, or I *will* stun you."

Lan and Vexer slowly stepped out of the vehicle, the doctor death-glaring at the stranger.

"What the void is going on?" Lan demanded.

"You're coming with me," the stranger replied. "That's all you need to know."

"And if I refuse?"

"We stun you, and you come with me. Either way, you're coming with me."

Trace found Calvin hovering against the walls of what looked like an industrial garage.

"What in void and starfire is this, Fernand?" she snapped.

"What was necessary," he told her. "Save the city, save the planet. You aren't shit to me, so we cut a deal."

"Move," the strange woman ordered. "Your deal was with the boss. *She'll* decide if you've kept it."

34

IT TOOK EB longer than he really wanted to admit to find an access point into the monitor's internal systems. Someone with proper authorizations could have done everything he needed to do from a wireless link to the monitor's networks, but since he had no such authorization, he needed a hard link.

Unfortunately, Estutmost's monitor designers had kept the civilian concourse quite thoroughly separated from the warship systems. He managed to breach the hotel network from their suite, but that didn't serve him at all.

In the end, he ended up removing a wall panel in the back of a utility closet in the staff section of the Chinese restaurant. He'd sneaked in while going to the bathroom and had barely managed to avoid notice.

But his map said that this closet was next to what his experience said *had* to be a data-processing trunk for the civilian hangar—and once the panel was off, it confirmed his hope. He couldn't squeeze into the space, but the fiberoptic cable bundles were definitely there.

A few minutes of poking at those cables and establishing links, and he'd even made sure they were the *right* ones. It was going to take time to link to the security controls for the civil concourse, but once he'd done that, he could leave preprogrammed software commands that would respond to wireless signals and shut down most of the systems at the gate.

He'd have to move quickly once they were in place, though. The software crawlers running in the system were *good*, and he didn't think they'd miss his code for long. *He* could avoid detection, but any software he left in the monitor's network would get caught and wiped.

If EB were capable of coding the worms from scratch, he could probably adjust the ones he had to avoid detection. But the truth was that he used a suite of prebuilt tools provided by Apollo Intelligence years before.

He could use them and use them well, but more than basic modifications or assembly from component parts was beyond him. Still… hardware could allow what software wouldn't. If he installed a receiver on the data trunk, he could load data in through that later.

He was poking through the utility closet's contents, hoping to find something that would serve, when the door suddenly swung open, and he found himself staring into the bright light of an under-barrel flashlight.

A long-suffering sigh greeted him.

"Captain Bardacki," Sergeant McMahon said. "The boss wants to talk to you. Now."

"Ah. I, uh…got lost looking for the bathroom?" he suggested, his tone as innocent as possible.

"I'LL ADMIT, Captain, I expected you to keep your word. I'm disappointed."

Nothing had visibly changed in Commodore Malone's observation deck office. EB wasn't even sure if the Spacer had moved from where he'd been standing when they last spoke.

Presumably, there was an actual command center somewhere where the Commodore kept a staff. The observation deck made for a useful thinking and planning space, but it wasn't well designed for Malone's support team to be positioned around him.

"It is splitting a particularly fine hair, I know," EB admitted as he stood behind the Commodore, "but we did not break our parole. We were investigating *how* we *could*, but even my intrusion where Sergeant McMahon found me was purely information-gathering."

"A fine hair indeed." Malone turned to look down at EB. "I wish you hadn't split it. My next steps may well be shaped by your claims, and now I do not know if I can trust you at all."

"If it was your daughter trapped in Llandudno, what would you do?" EB snapped. "I'm not your enemy, and I have no reason to lie to you outside of one very specific purpose."

"And what do you think would happen if you stole your ship and got down to Llandudno? The city is occupied by an entire division of the Board's troops. If General Griffith had your family, you'd already know. The Board would be *delighted* to trade them for information on what you delivered the Cinnead and where."

"Wouldn't help them much. They already know Dinas Fferm is the heart of their opposition. Either the city falls or this war drags on."

"Frankly, Captain, I hate both of these options."

Malone was still studying EB like a raptor looking at a particularly tasty running morsel.

"Everything I have done has to been to minimize the impact of this war. I don't need you to tell me I've *failed* at that," Malone said drily, holding up his hand before EB could say anything. "I had hoped that when my ships and I mutinied against the Board and declared our neutrality, it would be enough to force peace talks.

"Instead, neither Board nor Commission have been willing to talk since the beginning."

EB was beginning to realize he had been dragged up here to be vented at, not punished for trying to escape. He'd just added his near-breach of parole to the things he was going to be vented at about.

"You have the ultimate high ground," he pointed out. "You have the monitors, the gunships, the asteroid mines... You could end this war in an hour."

"The Snowden Range is geologically unstable," Malone noted conversationally, turning back to the big holodisplay and waving a new layer onto it. Now the continental plates were overlaid on the map, and EB grimaced as he saw the thick lines under the mountain range dividing the Dachaig.

"It's a volcanic range, one we have traditionally kept a close eye on and managed for geothermal power. That factor is *useful* to us—the magma under the Snowdens provided sixty-two percent of Dachaigh a Deas and Dachaigh a Tuath's power needs.

"But our calculations suggest that even a handful of relatively minor kinetic strikes along the mountain slopes could trigger a super-volcanic event. Had we, for example, destroyed the Cinnead's Snowden Line from orbit, we would likely have triggered a planetwide dust storm that would have ruined crops for years."

EB wasn't a geologist, but he could see the problem. The fault line where one plate went under the other was a clear weak spot, and hitting it with orbital weapons would be…messy.

"Putting aside the political hesitation in the Spacer factions, the delicate balance we maintain up here and their unwillingness to commit to one side or another, we lack the ability to intervene in a measured fashion.

"Orbital strikes are not a subtle tool, Captain, and we have no soldiers."

"But you stole the Staid's entire fleet."

Malone chuckled grimly.

"Almost. I missed the flagship. My boss is out there somewhere, trying to marshal the resources to breach the blockade for the Board." He shrugged. "We had one corvette, one gunship. Hell of a nova fleet, huh?

"But the other security forces Commodore got out with the corvette. I got twenty-two monitors and the gunship. I figure I win."

"Estutmost doesn't."

"The Board ordered us to bombard the Snowden Line."

Malone's soft words hung in the observation deck for several seconds.

"That's when we mutinied. We made common cause with the Spacer factions afterward, but the security force mutineers are their own group. We don't want to fight the Board, Captain. We were loyal soldiers once, even if half of us are Spacer-born."

"So, you let the war drag on and kill more?"

EB knew there wasn't much point to the conversation. He was needling the Spacer commander, which was probably *against* his best interests.

"I have roughly three-quarters of the crews of nineteen monitors," Malone told him, turning away to gesture at the big display. "Spread out across twenty-two monitors, to make up for personnel who died or were detained in the mutiny and the fact that *Armstrong* only had a skeleton crew to begin with.

"The Spacers put up the money to hire the mercenary gunships and enough personnel to get the ships operational, but that gives them say in what I do. Many of them hate the Cinnead as much as the Board.

"And here you walked into the middle of it, Captain Bardacki, with the hand grenade of an accusation of bioweapons."

"You'll forgive my limited sympathy for your factions," EB said drily. "Get my family and crew out of Llandudno, and I'll happily sympathize with your issues." He snorted. "Hell, at that point, Lan could explain why it was definitely a bioweapon."

The room was silent again for at least a dozen seconds, then Malone chuckled bitterly.

"Whatever proof they had, they didn't manage to forward to the Commission," he told EB. "The Board, of course, denies any such thing. They have informed me and the other Spacer leaders that Morrigan Biologicals remains bound by the codes of principles and ethics laid out by the founders of our world.

"Their *phrasing* makes me nervous," Malone admitted. "If Morrigan is still bound by the bioethics codes we built into our use of customized biologicals, that doesn't mean they haven't created a sepa-rate entity.

"Of course, Morrigan Biologicals has a full monopoly on our biotechnology—because they *are* supposed to be bound by that code of ethics. But, of course, the Staid Chorporra controls Morrigan."

"I know the Commission accepted Lan's conclusions."

"We are a planet and a star system whose very survival in the medium and long term depends on a level of biotechnology extraordinarily rare this far out in the Beyond. We are *thoroughly* familiar with the risks and dangers of biotech.

"That makes the concept of turning the minds and machines that build the Dagda to the manufacture of *weapons* utter anathema to us as a culture. Even the hint of it is a weapon the Cinnead can use against the Board—the Commission would be fools not to lean in to the accusation."

"But the only proof you have is my word of what my doctor said."

"And you're making me doubt if I can trust you."

Malone stepped away, a gesture zooming the display in on the plains of the Dachaigh a Deas.

"As we speak, the security forces are getting closer and closer to Dinas Fferm," he told EB. "I assume that somewhere in Dinas Fferm, the Cinnead are preparing new forces based on the tanks and artillery you provided.

"In a few days at most, the war will come to a crisis. If the Spacers are to affect the conflict, we must make a decision in the near future. A pox on both their houses only takes us so far."

"Neutrality will not protect mutineers if the Board wins," EB murmured.

"Perhaps, perhaps not. It's not like you truly have a side, is it, Captain?"

"No. I just want to get my family and get out."

35

IT WASN'T the first time in her young life that Trace had been cuffed. That didn't make it any better—quite the opposite, in fact. She focused on controlling her breathing as the strangers escorted the three of them through what appeared to be a converted warehouse.

If she hadn't already known that this *wasn't* the resistance's command center, she might have been easily fooled into thinking they'd been relocated to Major Vaughn's new base. In many ways, the converted warehouse looked *more* like a military command center than the resistance base they'd been evacuated from.

"My patient needs medical supervision," Lan was still insisting as they were marched through the building.

"Someone will check on them," their escort repeated.

The back-and-forth had been repeated at least four times since they'd left the ambulance and Trace had an ugly pit in her stomach. She wasn't entirely sure where they were or who their new captors were, but she suspected that the ambulance wasn't getting back to Calvin's friend…and that Bogomolova might be in real trouble.

Their escorts definitely weren't soldiers. They were armed and she was reasonably sure she'd spotted concealed body armor, but they wore regular street clothes with baggy jackets to cover their gear.

There was a pattern to how they moved, how they spoke…one that was terrifyingly familiar. Between the cuffs and the fear crawling through her stomach, her control of her breathing was getting shaky.

A set of double doors swung open, and they were escorted into a sumptuously decorated large office that was as out of place in the faux military information center around as it would have been in the original warehouse.

Centered in the room was a large wooden desk, easily the size of most *beds* Trace had seen. Seated behind the desk with her hands steepled together as she watched the prisoners marched in was a tall woman with the front of her head shaved and the long black hair at the back braided into a queue.

A woman that Trace recognized from her picture and file. She'd never met the woman—she'd never been to Estutmost before, after all—but the Siya u Hestî database she'd had stuffed in her head had included recognition files on every Level Eight, the planetary leaders of the Cartel.

Kunthea Chey was the senior member of the Siya u Hestî Cartel on Estutmost. She was a drug baron, a human trafficker—a slaver and a murderer and the last person on the planet Trace would have wanted to *meet*, let alone be taken prisoner by.

"Sit down."

"I must object," Lan snapped. "A patient under my care is in desperate need of care and you have dragged me away from her."

"You are not in a position to make demands here, Dr. Kozel," Chey said calmly. "Sit."

Trace and Vexer stayed upright, flanking Lan, as they glared at the crime lord. One of the guards started to draw a stun baton, but Chey held up a hand.

"It would do a disservice to our proposed alliances and purposes for a member of the resistance to die in our care," she observed. "Make sure one of the nurses takes care of the patient."

Trace glanced sideways at Fernand Calvin. Whatever the teenager's involvement in this was, he wasn't comfortable with Bogomolova dying for it—and he didn't feel like his position was strong enough to insist.

There was clear relief in his eyes at Chey's order.

"Now, *please* sit down," she repeated.

Trace followed Lan's lead, taking a seat in one of the three chairs in front of the desk.

"Em Calvin, our business is complete," the crime lord told the teenager.

"You haven't done—"

"I will," Chey said sharply. "Guns, intelligence, sabotage. Major Vaughn will receive it all. You have my word.

"Now go. Ada, see him out. Seal the office door behind you, in case our *guests* get clever."

The remaining guard escorted Fernand Calvin out of the office, leaving Trace and her adults alone with the ruler of a planet's underworld.

"If any of those inevitably clever ideas are roosting in your heads, I suggest you ask young Tracy about me," Chey told Vexer and Lan. "I believe your database includes at least some detail on my augmentations?"

Trace blinked, accessing the data.

"Commando-grade biological improvements," she read aloud. "Bone marrow density modifications, additional adrenaline glands, adrenaline reformulation, tendon-tissue catalyzing…"

She glanced sideways at Lan.

"I don't know what half of this *means*," she admitted.

"That's she's faster than any of us and can probably break us with her pinky finger," Lan replied. "She's Siya u Hestî?"

"Level Eight Kunthea Chey," Trace confirmed. "Files say the contact points are at Galahad Station."

"I haven't been up to Galahad in years, but yes, the dead drops for making contact with me are on the orbital," Chey agreed. "Which brings us to the whole purpose of this conversation."

"Other than kidnapping, threats and potentially killing my patient?" Lan asked.

"Dr. Kozel, let me be blunt. Your primary value to me at this moment is as a lever on Tracy Finley. Some of what I've heard about your work for the resistance raises other potential uses, but frankly, I have very little concern over how this war shakes out."

Lan shut up and Trace shivered. Somehow, Chey using her birth last name instead of her new one sent new chills down her spine all on its own…and there was plenty else going on to chill the soul.

"You traded weapons for me?" she demanded.

"More than weapons, but yes. Fernand Calvin has been one of my people for a while now. Like several of my young guns, he requested and was granted a leave from my service to fight for the Cinnead.

"But he'd seen the bounty orders for you and recognized you. He realized that I might be able and willing to help his new cause if he delivered you into my hands. A discussion was had, an arrangement made.

"I will provide the Cinnead resistance with weapons and intelligence, and arrange for certain critical infrastructure to fail at key moments."

She shrugged.

"You were not cheap to me, girl, so I hope you are prepared to cooperate."

"I have no interest in giving *anything* to any of the Shadow and Bone," Trace snapped, using the English translation of Siya u Hestî with pointed intent.

Chey softly cracked her knuckles and leaned back in her seat.

"You seem to be under the impression that you have a choice in the matter. The question, bluntly, is not whether I will get that database; it is how much difficulty we both go through along the way.

"My preference is that we come to an agreement. The information will be cleaner if you provide a copy of the database, and your adoptive father has proven himself to be quite destructive to those who harm you.

"You do not benefit from the database only being in your head. I am prepared to recognize the value of the information you have and compensate appropriately. I would also guarantee your security here in Llandudno until such time as the war is over and you can be safely extracted."

Trace remained silent, glaring at the crime boss. Everything about being back in the Siya u Hestî's control was wrong. She had no weapons, no escape, no clever plans. Months of freedom and a hopeful future had just vanished into ash and dust...but she wasn't going to give a Siya u Hestî Level Eight the keys to rebuild the Cartel.

"And how many other young girls would find themselves trapped in lies and rapes?"

She *felt* Vexer wince next to her, her dad unable to reach over and comfort her. She swallowed hard, drawing on the two adults flanking her.

She might be trapped, but she was *not* alone.

"You, of all people, should know the path that leads there," Chey told her. "Whether the Siya u Hestî is reborn under my command or another's—or even not reborn at all—will not save fools from the consequences of their choices."

The woman behind the desk shrugged dramatically.

"But it doesn't matter what you want, Em Tracy. You do not need to cooperate for me to get the information I need. I am prepared to recognize value and compensate for it—but I am also prepared to have my people cut the silicon out of your brain and break it down piece by piece until we have what we need.

"Lady Breanna's control-freak tendencies have left us in a difficult situation, and your escape threw an ugly wrench into the communication-protocol updates. I need the information in your head to make contact with the rest of the Cartel and rebuild what you have attempted to destroy.

"The region is better served by an intact Siya u Hestî trying to do business than it is by a dozen fragmented Cartels making war on each other for territory and wealth. *You* are better served by cooperating with me."

Trace had no idea what the right answer was. She wanted to *shoot* Chey, but she was unarmed. She was handcuffed. She had no leverage except what Chey was willing to give her.

I have a plan, Lan's voice suddenly said in her head. *Play along. Keep her talking.*

"I..." Trace trailed off. "Maybe."

She let that hang in the air.

"But I want off Estutmost. *Now*, not when the war is over. I want my other dad and our ship freed from the Spacers. Manage that, and I'll give you your database."

Trace figured that was an impossible ask. She also realized that she might well *take* that deal, if Chey could manage it.

"That's...not a small task," the crime lord told her. "Either part of it. I *think* I could get the three of you off-world, but to break Captain Bardacki free from the Spacers...mmm..."

"The nature of the blockade's command structure means I have less influence than I would like. That is more than I can afford, little one. I can see the three of you safely delivered to Nigahog with sufficient funds to live in comfort until Captain Bardacki is free to join you, but that is the best that I can do."

Negotiating was...fraught when the other side's alternative to an agreement was to kill you and get almost everything they wanted. Trace wasn't experienced at negotiations in the first place, and here she was trying to argue for her life—and play for time.

"My father's fate is hardly a concern we can put off," Trace said. "If the Spacers seize *Evasion*..."

"My sources tell me that he's already rendered that impossible, to their frustration." Chey smirked. "I have never met Captain Bardacki, but from everything I have heard, I'm impressed. I can see why Lady Breanna wanted to recruit him and acquire his ship.

"For my own part, I have no desire to end up on the wrong side of the good Captain. A deal is better for us all, child. But seeing you and your companions safely delivered to Nigahog is already a high price to pay for what you can provide. It is my fina—"

The explosion that shook the entire building came without warning. Part of the wall behind Chey shivered into debris, poorly installed drywall falling to the floor.

"What the *hell*?" she snapped. "Ada!"

The woman with the cybernetic eye had already opened the door and charged back in.

"The Second Division is *here*. Aircar IFVs just took out the AA launcher on the roof and landed troops. APCs and IFVs are in the streets around us. We're surrounded!"

"What the hell is Griffith *doing*?" Chey demanded, then shook her head. "Doesn't matter. Activate the defenses; secure the perimeter. Get our people up on the roof and make *their* people dead."

"On it."

Two more guards appeared in the room at a wordless command as Ada disappeared—and a holographic representation of the area appeared above Chey's desk.

"Get them to a safe cell," Chey ordered, gesturing at Trace and her companions. "Then move to Sector Six. We'll have positions sorted out for everyone by then."

Trace couldn't read most military iconography. Thanks to the database in her head, however, she could read *Siya u Hestî* iconography. The hologram showed the area for at least five kilometers in every direction from the warehouse, in enough detail for Trace to be able to place their location compared to the rest of Llandudno.

Icons in different shades of green were positioned through the surrounding buildings. Bright green lights marking human personnel with active tactical networks were appearing across the map as the Siya u Hestî prepared to fight.

Whatever sensors the system had access to were rapidly updating, providing the position of the approaching Board troops. They really did have the warehouse surrounded—and there were at least thirty troops on the roof.

Trace had been on the other side of the war up until this moment, but she didn't think she'd ever been happier to see *anyone* than she was to see the Tuathan soldiers at that moment.

A blinking light appeared above the hologram as one of the guards pulled Trace to her feet, and Chey activated the message.

"Em Chey," General Griffith's uniformed image said calmly. "I've been waiting for you to fuck up. I'd also been looking for Bardacki's crew. And now, conveniently, several tasks align at once.

"Surrender yourself, your people and the crew from *Evasion*, and I will guarantee your life, despite the penalties due for your many crimes."

Chey killed the call with a sharp gesture, then looked up at Trace and her escorts.

"It appears you are popular, Em Tracy. Get her to safety," she barked.

Before the gangsters could move in response to Chey's order, *Lan* moved. Trace had almost forgotten about their promise of a plan—and she suspected that whatever Lan's plan had been, the Tuathan's attack had thrown it into disarray.

But plan or no plan, Lan had ended up within reach of one of the armed guards. They promptly demonstrated that they'd picked the lock on their handcuffs at some point in the interview by stealing the guard's stunner.

The weapon crackled in the silence of the office, and the guard crumpled away from his prisoner.

For her own part, Trace dove for the floor as Lan stunned the guard pulling her along. More stunners crackled—and then a blaster cracked as Chey took cover behind her desk.

Lan had been using one of the guards as a human shield, and the crime lord put three rapid blaster bolts into her own minion. Trace started crawling for cover behind a wall as Lan returned fire, the sound down to *one* stunner and Chey's blaster.

This wasn't Trace's first firefight any more than it was the first time she'd been cuffed and she was trying to keep track of everything. All of the immediate gang members except Chey were down, stunned unconscious. *Vexer* was also down, stunned by one of the gangsters.

Lan was tucked behind a wall of Chey's own office, taking advantage of the fact that the crime boss had armored her own space to protect themselves as she kept shooting at them.

Chey was *fast*. Each time Trace saw Lan try to do more than fire blindly around the corner, a blaster bolt clipped the corner to discourage them. She doubted that the wall was going to hold up to blaster fire for long, either.

She wasn't an ex-spy like Lan. She couldn't pick her handcuffs with a paperclip or whatever they'd done. Whatever Trace was going to do, she needed to do with her hands cuffed behind her—and if she didn't do *anything*, she was going to watch her doctor get shot dead in front of her.

The answer literally rolled into her leg a second later, an elongated egg shape that had detached from the belt of the guard holding her. She stared down at the weapon in fascinated horror for a few seconds, then grabbed it.

She worked through the controls by feel. Whichever gangster had acquired the grenade had gone for old-fashioned. No digital igniters, no headware detonation commands. Just a ring to pull to release a pin.

Trace had no idea what kind of grenade it was. It was just the grenade she had, which made it the best kind for the situation.

Contorting herself around on the floor, she managed to get the grenade wedged against the wall and *mostly* lined up with the office door. A blaster bolt flickered over her head as she did—and another series of explosions rocked the building as the attack continued.

Lan's stunner buzzed again, followed by a curse of pain. That was it: Trace was out of time.

Taking a deep breath, she yanked the pin out of the grenade and awkwardly tossed it into the office. She heard it bounce and roll, a clattering sound that wasn't nearly intimidating enough.

From the sudden cessation of blaster fire, Chey realized exactly what had happened. There was a moment of utter silence in the room and its surroundings.

"Fuck."

The curse was replaced almost instantly by a thunderous roar and a wave of heat as the plasma grenade detonated in a pulse of compressed fusion. Trace was thrown back to the ground by the shockwave, and she heard Lan grunt in pain.

"Lan, you okay?" she asked.

"Alive. A bit burnt, a bit shot, but alive. You?"

"I think I just killed someone," Trace whispered as the shock came crashing in on her. She'd stunned a few people before, but she'd just blown up Chey's office with the woman inside.

Lan was there before the thought finished percolating, helping her to her feet and letting her lean on them as they both surveyed the wreck that *had* been a crime lord's office.

The grenade had clearly rolled under the massive wooden desk. That had helped preserve some of the room—but it hadn't helped preserve the desk itself or Chey. The desk had been converted into flaming debris that had shredded the walls. The shockwave and fire had finished what the debris had started, and the armored shell of the office was now obvious.

Chey herself was unrecognizable, but Trace made herself look at the dead woman. She'd been badly burnt, had wooden shrapnel tear through her body, and then been thrown against the back wall by the grenade.

"Stop looking at her, Trace," Lan told her, their hand heavy on her shoulder. "You saved my life. And we'd never have made it out of here as it was. Come on."

They gently turned her away from the wrecked office. Trace was sufficiently in shock that she didn't even realize they were picking her cuffs until her hands were suddenly released.

"Let's grab Vexer and get out of the middle of this mess," the doctor said. "We need a plan and fast, but I'm *starting* by getting away from Griffith's main target!"

36

MORE EXPLOSIONS SHOOK the building as Lan led Trace into a section of offices that looked far more appropriate for a warehouse than Chey's had. These were utilitarian and a bit run-down, with cheap furniture and cheaper holoprojectors.

They'd also clearly been in use until the attack had started, with logistics and shipping-management programs still open on the holo-projectors. The cargo being moved might have been guns, drugs and kidnapped innocents, but Trace suspected the tools used to manage it were about the same as a regular warehouse.

Lan lowered Vexer into one of the chairs with a sigh and a grimace. Trace looked at the two adults and shivered. Vexer was still stunned. Lan was trying to pretend they were all right, but...

"You got shot," she finally said aloud. "Chey hit you."

"Not quite," Lan told her. "Chey blasted enough of the wall that I got hit by debris."

They pulled their jacket aside to show their lower abdomen. A dozen small wounds were spread across their right side. None of them looked severe, but all of them were bleeding.

"For *fuck's* sake, *you're the doctor*," Trace snapped. "Treat that!"

"I was a bit concerned about keeping you and Vexer alive."

Still, they started dismantling their jacket to create an impromptu bandage. The *only* things they had were a couple of stolen stunners. No medkit, no gear.

Trace shook her head at the doctor and linked into the Siya u Hestî network. The codes and protocols she had were for a guest user, but it was enough for her to locate the medkit in the office section.

She grabbed it and handed it to Lan, who gave her a pained nod of thanks.

"You're in bad shape," she told them.

"I know. I'll live—but carrying Vexer here was too much. I can't take him farther, and he's out for at least another hour."

Trace looked at her father and grimaced. Her tall and dark younger father might have been lanky instead of heavily built, but he was still beyond even a fit thirteen-year-old girl's ability to carry.

"So, we're stuck," she murmured.

"And this building is under attack. I don't know about you, but I'm not enthused with ending up *anybody's* prisoners."

Trace nodded, watching uncomfortably as Lan shivered under the plastiskin spray bandage they were applying. The doctor was wavering. Her dad was unconscious.

Somehow, it was going to be up to *her* to get them out of this. The starting answer…was the networks around them.

She had the network access intended for someone visiting Estutmost's Siya u Hestî facilities. But the logistics people in this office had left their programs running, which should…

"I'm into their network," she told Lan. "Dad-E's been teaching me some stuff, though this was mostly user panic working in our favor. Hold on one second."

Trace waved her hand experimentally in the air, testing the layout of the controls and seeing if she could find what she was looking for. Emergency communication networks—there!

The logistics programs vanished and were replaced by a similar holographic map to the one Chey had used to start the defense. It was less detailed, mostly only showing Trace where the defenders were.

"That's funny," she muttered. "There were a *lot* more icons on Chey's map."

There were about a hundred people on the emergency network. She had the audio turned off, but their links still told her where they were. Mostly, the Cartel troops were either on the top floors of the warehouse, presumably fighting back the paratrooper landing, or digging in on the perimeter to hold off the incoming Tuathan troops.

The map in Chey's office, though, had included other icons—what Trace was reasonably sure were automated defenses and similar systems. Systems that weren't available from the emergency communication network available to the regular Cartel members.

EB had done more than *teach her a few things*. One of the advantages of the extra silicon the Siya u Hestî had shoved in her head, now that she had full control of it, was that she had far more storage space available in her headware than most people.

The high-density holographic storage used for cybernetics installed in people's skulls wasn't known for running out of room, but there were limits. The library of hacking software that EB had brought with him from the Rim was easily stored in *Evasion*'s computers, but even he only had a few key utilities loaded normally.

And since Trace had more storage space than she knew what to do with, she *also* had those "key utilities." She fed them the information she had—Chey's name, the data she'd recorded while Chey had been logging in with them in the room, the logins and codes from the main database—and unleashed them through the access accounts the logistics team had left open.

"What...what are you doing?" Lan asked, their tone fainter than she liked.

"Trying to make sure I know what's going on around us. I think I've got enough of the pieces for Dad-E's software to get me the same visibility that Chey had—read access to the sensor feeds and such."

"That'll help," Lan agreed. "Once Vexer is awake, we'll want to sneak out. But with two different groups trying to catch us..."

"The more information, the better."

The first round of utilities returned. They'd failed to penetrate anything, but their attempts had provided more information. A lot of that data came in the form of compressed data kernels that *Trace* couldn't read—but the utilities could.

One of the things she could take away from the programs herself was that no one was running active overwatch on the computer system. That let her do things slightly differently, and she spent ten seconds updating the options and command sequences on her utilities, then started them again.

"That should be enough," she told Lan. "Either Dad-E's programs will get us into Chey's account before Dad-V wakes up, or we do something else."

She had no idea what *something else* would entail. She was hoping Lan did—but from the exhausted look the doctor turned on her, that might be a frail hope indeed.

Waiting wasn't good for Trace's calm, either. Once she was no longer *doing*, she started *remembering*. Remembering Chey's burnt and battered corpse, pinned to the wall by debris where she'd died.

Where Trace Bardacki had killed her.

Regardless of what deals Chey had been trying to make with Trace, the woman had been a murderer, a kidnapper, a slaver…at the very least a rapist by proxy. Trace could easily make the argument that Kunthea Chey had deserved to die significantly more horribly than she had.

But Trace had been the one to throw that grenade. The one to kill the woman.

There was blood and ash on her hands, and she wasn't sure it would ever wash off.

She was staring at the smeared streaks on her fingers when a soft chime announced the utilities needed her attention. Only half paying attention, she accepted whatever they were telling her.

The holographic display vanished, and Trace swallowed a curse as she focused on the here and now. Whatever account she was logged into now didn't have access to the same emergency communication network she'd been using for the data.

She wished she'd paid a bit more attention. Forcing herself to focus on the operation system, she started searching for the right utilities…

An ash-streaked finger stole her concentration for a second. There might have been blood in the ash, she wasn't entirely sure, but her hands were definitely dark with *something*.

Shaking her head, she focused past the finger and tapped a command in the air, reactivating the holoprojector.

This time, it was *exactly* what she'd seen in Chey's office. A quick check confirmed Trace's initial surprised assessment—Chey had logged in from scratch with them in the office, providing her headware with *just* enough extra information for the utilities to break into the Level Eight's accounts on the building network.

Trace now had full access, and she stared grimly at the three-dimensional map of the city block. There were at least sixty vehicles in a perimeter established half a kilometer back from the warehouse. A dozen more were making a direct push from the northern edge of the perimeter, a full company of mechanized infantry making the first probing attack.

The aerial attack had failed, she observed. There were no more red icons on the roof of the warehouse—though the sensors were suggesting that the schematics were no longer an entirely accurate representation of the roof.

The explosions had made quite the mess. The Siya u Hestî controlled the entire building, but the process had been messy.

The exterior blockade was the worst part from Trace's perspective. There was an entire *regiment* encircling the building, over a thousand Tuathan soldiers. She wasn't on the Siya u Hestî's side there, but she had been counting on them acting as a distraction.

Her icons now told her that the gangers were in prebuilt positions with heavy weapons. Some of those systems were still showing as locked out—and she realized that there were message icons flashing on the display as well.

She reached out and activated one.

"This is position North-Bravo," a voice said swiftly and shakily. "Our secondary weapons positions remain locked out. We need authorization to activate the turrets, or we are badly outgunned.

"Someone has to have the damn key codes!"

There were no key codes, Trace realized. Or if there were, they were a backup system for if something happened to Chey—one that wasn't available to anyone alive—because the program she'd *thought* was a surveillance utility was a tactical control network.

She searched for North-Bravo and located a command-and-control center, roughly the size of a closet she figured, in a building a hundred meters north of the main Siya u Hestî warehouse. From there, the network flagged a links to a dozen remote-controlled weapons.

North-Bravo had weapons on site, enough to delay the advance if the Cartel soldiers opened fire with them, but their main firepower was those turrets. Turrets they couldn't activate on their own.

A soft tap in the air, on a button no one else could see, released those turrets to control of the Siya u Hestî defenders. Washed-out green icons on the map lit up brightly, and Trace considered the situation.

"You have the key codes, don't you?" Lan murmured. They were sitting on the edge of a desk, studying the holographic map. They looked a bit less peaky than they had before, but they were still definitely at the end of their rope.

"I can release all of the exterior positions' remote-controlled weapons," Trace confirmed after a few more seconds' poking. "But…"

She winced as new information codes flickered up above North-Bravo. The Tuathan advance had been almost on top of the Cartel position, she realized, and the battle was well and truly joined.

The red icons of vehicles flashed and disappeared as the weapons Trace had given the gangsters were unleashed.

"People will die if I do," she whispered. "People *are* dying…"

"And you can't change that," Lan told her. "I doubt the Siya u Hestî are going to surrender calmly. There's a war going on. Whether we like it or not, we ended up on the Cinnead's side. Turn on those weapons, and you're giving Major Vaughn's people an edge. An opportunity.

"Don't…and we end up Griffith's prisoners." They shook their head. "I don't know what the Staid Chorporra's military governor wants with us, but I imagine that he wants leverage on EB. A freighter that already ran the blockade once…they'll assume we can do it again."

"But Dad was captured," Trace protested.

"I doubt that will improve our situation once we're in the Board's hands," Lan said grimly. "Our side was chosen for us. For our own safety, Trace, we have to act *against* the Staid Chorporra."

Trace looked away from them for a long handful of seconds, watching the icons on the three-dimensional map shift as the Tuathan scout company slammed into the single position engaging them.

The soldiers had the numbers, but the gangers had the advantage of position and the remote-controlled weapons. Still, the infantry company moved forward and the defenders' icons flickered and went out.

Exhaling a long sigh, Trace released the rest of the outer northern perimeter. North-Alpha and North-Charlie engaged moments later, weapons flashing green as they caught the advancing company in enfilade fire.

For a few seconds, she thought she was going to have to release the remote weapons position by position, but then she finally found the *Release all* command, giving every exterior position control of their weapons.

They were going to need them, she realized. One company had been driven back, but the Tuathan soldiers now knew what they were dealing with.

"They probably thought Griffith was nuts when he had them muster an entire regiment to go after a crime syndicate's base," Lan said. "But if this was the Siya u Hestî's planetary HQ, they pulled out all of the stops to defend it."

Trace left that thought hanging as she dug deeper into what the inner layers of defenses were. Somewhere in this mess, she figured Chey had to have an escape route hidden away.

The second layer of defenses was filling out as she checked through the system. The Cartel soldiers who'd defended the roof were moving out, taking up positions in command centers and fortified bunkers.

Whoever had operated in the warehouses around the Siya u Hestî base had either been spectacularly oblivious or under Chey's thumb—and Trace would bet on the latter. Every structure around the building they were in had been reinforced, with weapons positions added to cover the approaches to the Cartel headquarters at the center of the district.

"An entire district acting as a fortified trap," Trace whispered. "And Griffith is sending his troops right into it."

"He's assuming that Chey only has a hundred or so troops. Force multipliers are a thing, but he has a *division*, and she has a couple of platoons of thugs."

Trace kept poking, trying to find the escape route. It took her a minute to process what she *did* find...even checking the legend in Chey's system against her database, she wasn't entirely sure what she was looking at.

"Lan," she finally said, focusing the map on the icons she'd been confused by. "What's an AMP?"

"AMP?" they asked. "In this context... They didn't. They couldn't have."

There were six of what appeared to be...bunkers or garages of some kind labeled as AMP deployment sites. Her database confirmed that meaning for the icons, but she was still digging into just what an AMP *was*.

"Autonomous mobile platform?" she read off—and then finally accessed the schematics and fell silent.

"Combat drones with artificial stupid intelligences and minimal remote control," Lan told her. "I'd say they're illegal on every goddamn planet, but so is human trafficking. How many?"

Trace was counting.

"Twenty in each bunker," she told him. "If they're the ones in my database...twelve-ton antigrav units with quadruple assault cannons and either an antitank or antiaircraft launcher."

"You have control."

It wasn't a question but she nodded anyway.

"I'm not sure how much control," she warned. "I can definitely activate them, but...I can't read the details of the programming I can access, Lan. I don't even know where to start."

Lan stepped into the big hologram, linking into it with their own headware as she opened it up. A test command from them activated the interior line of defenses in response to a call from the Cartel soldiers spreading around the base.

Trace lacked the knowledge to judge the efficiency of the defenses or of the Tuathan encirclement. Between defender and attacker, she was *very* sure she, Vexer and Lan were trapped.

"What do we do?" she whispered.

"I don't know," they admitted. "Have you found an exit yet?"

Lan's thoughts on Chey's potential plans followed Trace's own, but she was drawing a blank.

"Either it's well hidden or she didn't even include it on her private maps. We're stuck here."

"So, we wait—at least for Vexer to wake up. And we see how the attack proceeds."

At that moment, there *wasn't* an attack. The government troops had encircled the district, with a surprisingly good guess as to where the Cartel's defensive line was. But Trace figured that Lan was right, too.

General Griffith was assessing the result of his first probing attack and deciding what the next steps were. He might not have set out to wipe out the Siya u Hestî on Estutmost, but now that he'd started, he was going to have to finish the job.

Trace was grimly aware that the three of them were at least part of the prize Griffith was expecting to get out of this operation. And at the end of the day, *she* now had the button that would unleash over a hundred heavily armed and highly illegal autonomous combat drones.

37

EB WAS MORE than done dueling Commodore Malone with words, but the Spacer commander still stood there silently, watching him, as if patience would somehow break EB into admitting that he had a side in the war raging on the surface.

"Your choices shape a world, and you only choose what you're paid for, I suppose," Malone finally said.

"I make sure I'm not committing evil, as a rule, but freighters don't fly for free. I don't know what you want from me, Commodore. You've made your own choices that have a far larger effect on this war than I ever could."

"What I *want*, Captain, is your promise to keep your parole," the Commodore said sharply. "And before you ask, I have a team of techs sealing up that data trunk now. You won't have that access again."

EB sighed.

"Frankly, Commodore, I *was* considering stealing the ship, returning to the surface and then surrendering again to honor my parole. Which feels *damn* stupid, but it would at least have got my kid and boyfriend out of a city filled with troops that will see them as the enemy."

"General Griffith has been given very specific orders with regards to your crew," Malone noted, turning away to survey the hologram of the planet. "If nothing else, the Board would very much like to know exactly what was delivered to Dinas Fferm."

"What, so they can decide whether to nuke it?"

"I *believe* that my old comrades recognize both that the blockading fleet will shoot down any attempt to deploy HVMs or nuclear weapons against the city—and that even the *attempt* will end any neutrality on our part.

"We are not monsters, Captain Bardacki. Nor are the Board."

"But you set up this blockade to allow the government to win while keeping your mutineers and the Spacers happy with hating the Board," EB guessed aloud.

"The displeasure amongst the spaceborne residents of the Estutmost System with both the Staid's Board and the Cinnead's Commission cannot be understated. Like the Cinnead, the miners and gas divers have faced heavy quotas and strict price controls—since, officially, the Staid Chorporra owns the entire system and all of its resources.

"But the Cinnead has responded to their own quotas and price controls on sales to the Staid by raising the prices they charge the Spacers. While we have rigged up kelp and algae farms to provide a basic level of self-sufficiency, no one is going to pretend that algae protein bars do more than fill the stomach.

"Better food grows more and more expensive off-world, even with the limited imports we've been able to source. But the Spacers are enjoying having the whip hand of the blockade. For once, they are not forgotten and ignored."

"You didn't answer my actual point," EB noted.

Malone chuckled bitterly.

"I am seventy-three standard years old, Captain Bardacki," he noted. "I have spent my entire life in space—and *fifty-five years* in the service of the Staid Chorporra na h-Estutmost. That is half as long as the Estutmost System has been settled.

"I believed in our system. I served the Board loyally and helped build our defensive fleet to its modern state—from a single monitor and an old nova corvette to a monitor flotilla able to stand off any power of the Beyond.

"I cannot lightly throw aside half a century of loyalty and service. So, yes, even as I defied the Board's foolhardy order to destroy their enemies, I still favored them over the Cinnead. Our system *worked*, after all."

"And now?" EB asked softly.

"And now I cannot quite bring myself to utterly deny the possibility that my friends and comrades will turn weapons of mass destruction on Dinas Fferm. I cannot ignore the evidence that they turned the technological birthright of our culture into a weapon—and if it was deployed at all in this war, the Board has been preparing bioweapons for some time."

"You said I had no evidence."

"Nothing solid. But the opinion of an off-world doctor...even secondhand, that has weight." Malone wasn't looking at EB. He was still staring at the hologram of his planet.

"There is no formal leadership of the Spacers. A few corporate executives, a few town leaders, a handful of well-spoken and -regarded captains...and me. We form a rough and informal council that commands and funds this blockade. We were divided on who to support and whether to support anyone at all, and the blockade was the simplest answer."

EB remained silent. He wasn't sure why Commodore Malone had decided that EB was going to be his sounding board, but he was getting tired of it.

The power to end the war was in Malone's hands. Even the *threat* of orbital strikes could end the conflict.

"And now the Council wavers," Malone whispered. "Now *I* waver, Captain, and it's your damn fault. All you had to do was stay out of our system and leave us to our own affairs."

"I didn't drop a bioweapon in Llandudno," EB objected. "I didn't launch an armed rebellion on your planet, either. The Cinnead paid for weapons to come in from out-system. Someone was going to carry them, Commodore. *I* was professional about it.

"I will promise to keep our parole, Commodore. You caught us before we actually broke it, so we can split the hairs and behave going forward. I'll take that headache off you, but I can't promise I won't take any clear opportunities to rescue my family."

EB looked past the Commodore to the holographic planet with its holographic blockade. Llandudno was highlighted on the display, as were the icons that represented the main Board assault force pushing toward Dinas Fferm.

The assault column was in the middle of the plains. Malone's complaint about orbital strikes having collateral damage had never applied less. If the Spacers chose a side before the attack column reached Dinas Fferm…

"I can't tell you what to do about your war, Commodore. That's *your* world and your problem. I haven't seen anything I like from your government, but I'll freely admit that the Cinnead was *far* too ready for this conflict for me to be comfortable with them, either."

"I don't think anyone here can blame them for that," Malone admitted.

"Either way, unless there is some way that I can actually help you, may I return to my people?"

Malone didn't answer, staring at a new set of icons appearing above Llandudno. A sharp hand gesture zoomed the entire display in until suddenly EB was looking at a bird's-eye view of the agrarian port city.

At this level, individual vehicles and such weren't visible, but the icons splayed across the map made it clear that Malone's monitors were using their sensors to good effect. EB suspected that the Cinnead would have paid good money for the kind of overhead images and data he was looking at.

His gaze, however, was drawn to the same spot that Malone was looking at. An industrial warehousing district set well back from the docks was now encircled by bronze icons that EB guessed represented Staid Chorporra security units.

Inside that circle were flickering purple icons, marking unknown combat units.

"What in stars and rockshit?" Malone murmured. "What are you *doing*, Valentine?"

EB stayed silent, trying to get a mental handle on what he was seeing. It looked like at least a regiment's worth of troops was laying siege to a random chunk of warehouses—but those unknown combat units suggested that there was something there.

Apparently, Malone was on a first-name basis with the commander of the occupying garrison. That wasn't a surprise, though it added weight to EB's suspicion that the Commodore had never truly stepped away from his original side.

"Christian, I need an update on what Second Division is doing in Llandudno," Malone said into the air, ignoring EB. He paused, listening to the voice in his head, then swore. "That's not what I... But *what?*"

A new set of icons, scarlet red, flashed up on the other side of the city, and a voice now spoke audibly in the room.

"They'd divided the Cinnead prisoners by a threat ranking, and Griffith just ordered the execution of all level-five prisoners," the voice —Christian, EB guessed?—declared.

"We *think* he's trying to either provoke the resistance into acting or free up troops from the regiment he's got securing the prison camps."

"How many prisoners is that?" Malone asked.

"Level five is...about one percent of the prisoners. Maybe sixty people, but they're the ones with the training to potentially organize or lead a breakout."

Provoking the resistance or not, there was no way anyone could get to the prison camps in time to prevent those executions. Not unless the guard units dragged their feet *hard*.

Also...

"They locked up *six thousand people* just for being Cinnead?" he demanded.

Malone glanced sharply back at him. The Commodore apparently *hadn't* forgotten he was there; he'd just been distracted.

The analyst on the other side of the call clearly heard EB, though.

"Over sixty-two hundred as of our last review," Christian reported. "They've arrested anyone with a membership card for the Cinnead, anyone with family ties to the key clans, anyone who's worked on a Cinnead farm or with a Cinnead business..."

"And now they're shooting them," EB finished. He gave Malone a level look. *This* was the side that the man was trying to be able to support.

War was hell, but humanity had decided on the rough rules of it a long time ago. Rounding up civilians on minimal suspicion was stretching those rules. *Shooting* said civilians because it made your security problems easier was well past them.

So were bioweapons, in a way that even nukes and kinetic strikes weren't. Even biostabilized virii were only so reliable in containment and lack of mutation. The Staid Chorporra was apparently pulling out all of the stops.

"I don't like that, but it wasn't my question," Malone said quietly. "The warehousing district. What the hell is going on?"

"We're not entirely sure, but we *think* they found a Siya u Hestî base and moved on it," the analyst replied. "The tech is too entrenched and too expensive to be a resistance arrangement. A Cartel transshipment center could justify that, but only the Siya u Hestî could afford this level of automated defenses.

"Griffith has ordered two more regiments in to support the one maintaining the perimeter. The first company they sent in got caught between automated defenses and shredded. We don't know how many people or weapons systems are inside the zone, so we're guessing that Griffith doesn't either."

Three regiments was a full quarter of the troops in Llandudno, EB realized as he studied the icons on the display. Five thousand troops, give or take.

What did Griffith think was *in* that set of warehouses?

"McMahon," the Commodore called sharply. "Please see the captain back to his quarters."

He leveled a stony gaze on EB, a sharp gesture presumably cutting off all the com channels.

"I think you've awoken my guilty conscience enough for one day," he said drily. "Whatever happens in Llandudno, it looks like your family isn't in the middle of it, at least.

"Unless they signed on with the Siya u Hestî recently."

EB stared at the armored vehicles crossing the city and the heavily armed perimeter. His people wouldn't have *voluntarily* ended up at a Siya u Hestî base, but he hadn't even realized Lady Breanna's Cartel had a major presence in Llandudno—Trace's files put their main presence in this system on one of the orbitals, after all.

The Siya u Hestî had screwed with his little family a lot over the last year. Somehow, he wasn't prepared to bet that they *weren't* causing him more trouble right now.

But there was nothing he could do about it now. Parole or no parole, he was a prisoner—and that meant he was going with Sergeant McMahon.

38

"I WOULD GIVE a great deal to never experience stunner hangover again."

Vexer's declaration that he was awake earned him a hug from Trace. She'd known he was just unconscious, but it was still scary to see one of her fathers slumped on the floor like that.

"We all would," Lan agreed. "Sorry, Vexer, but I wasn't able to carry you as far as we'd like. I'm…a bit beat up myself."

Trace helped Vexer to a sitting position, allowing him to survey the room, with Lan and the hologram easily in his view. Lan had shed their jacket, which made the rough bandages and blood spots on their torso more visible.

"You look like shit, doc."

"Our friend Chey was shooting at *me* with a blaster," Lan pointed out. "This is just shrapnel, but I'm not moving fast or carrying anything heavy."

"I *feel* like shit," Vexer observed.

"Stunner hangover, as you said. You're awake faster than I expected."

Lan gestured for Vexer to come over to them.

"I need to check you out," they told him. "But I'm not walking if I don't have to."

Trace couldn't conceal her flash of concern, whipping around to stare at the doctor as they confirmed her fear that they were doing worse than they were pretending.

"I'll *live*, Trace," Lan assured her. "But unless you find a *vehicle* escape route, I'm not going anywhere quickly."

"I remember something about a bloody army," Vexer said, kneeling next to Lan as the doctor starting palpating muscles to examine them.

"Government troops had surrounded the district. They launched an aerial attack that the Cartel drove off, and they've sent in a couple of probing attacks on the ground that were fought off by the automatic weapons grid."

Vexer groaned as Lan found the spot where the stunner had hit him.

"So, this place is fortified to hell," he guessed.

"Yeah," Trace told him. "We have some level of control from here; I…I managed to hack Chey's account. But it's not telling me any way out."

"Control of the *weapons grid*?" her dad asked, wincing as Lan poked at another sensitive spot.

"I don't think I can take direct control of anything, but I have the unlock keys to release weapons to the perimeter bunkers. Which I've done."

"So, the Cartel has all of their guns and is dug in against the Tuathans. Wonderful. Any idea how this is going to end?"

"The sensors we have only extend so far," Lan noted. "But it looks like the occupation force is assembling a new assault. A real one, not a probing attack. They've got twenty thousand soldiers. The Cartel has a few hundred at most…and who knows what they're fighting for at this point."

"Where did Chey end up?"

Trace looked away, a spike of horrific memory catching her as she tried not to hyperventilate.

"Dead," Lan said quietly. "Trace threw a grenade into her office."

"Couldn't have happened to a nicer person. You okay, Trace?"

She looked up at Vexer and met his concerned gaze for a moment before she shook her head.

"I don't think so, Dad," she whispered. "But what can we do? We have to survive."

Lan gestured that Vexer was free to go and he crossed to Trace, kneeling down next to her and wrapping her in a tight embrace.

"I'm sorry," he murmured. "That's not something you ever should have had to do. Might have saved our lives, but it still hurts."

She leaned into his hug and realized she was crying. She *knew* Chey didn't deserve her tears, but…she wasn't really crying for Kunthea Chey.

"Perimeter is opening on the south side," Lan warned them. "Here comes the assault wave."

Still clinging to her father, Trace turned to examine the hologram as new icons flickered up. The Tuathan assault was opening with an infantry advance—a power-armored one, she realized, reading the icons.

A full company of two hundred troops in power armor led the way, with four more companies without power armor behind them. Two dozen vehicles moved in a few seconds later, moving down the streets in carefully arranged echelons of four.

The advance was at a careful walking pace, even the armored soldiers keeping to cover and moving slowly. After thirty seconds, Trace realized that a second path was opening through the perimeter on the east side—and another regiment-scale assault began to move through it.

"Griffith really thinks these people are armed to the teeth," Vexer said. "That's got to be—"

The first southern positions opened fire. Trace couldn't tell immediately which weapons systems were firing, but she was able to identify it in a few seconds. They'd started with mortar rounds and followed up with remote-controlled aerial drones, keeping to indirect weapons that didn't expose the location of the bunkers.

Red dots began to flicker as the information from the sensors became less reliable.

"Where are we even getting this data?" Vexer asked, whatever he'd meant to say forgotten.

"It's being automatically synthesized from optical pickups throughout the entire region, plus what looks like a dozen electromagnetic receivers on the rooftops," Lan said instantly. "I had to look myself."

"Which is why we're losing detail?" Trace was poking to see if there was anything she could do to clean it up, but it looked like she had every sensor feeding into the display.

"Explosions throw up dust, heat and sound," the doctor agreed. "Blocks every sensor in existence, to one degree or another. So long as they're shooting, we'll get less data here."

The eastern assault came in first, and Trace shivered as icons flickered and went out. People were dying and there was nothing she could do—she had more sympathy for the Tuathan soldiers than for the Siya u Hestî fighters, but she didn't want to end up a prisoner again.

She didn't want anyone to die, but she had no idea what she could do *except* enable the defenders.

"Southern assault is falling back," Lan noted. "That seems odd."

Before Trace could ask what, they discovered that Second Division *did* still have artillery left. The hundred-and-twenty-millimeter magnetic tubes the Tuathans had assaulted the city with had suffered under *Evasion*'s guns, but at least one remained.

The southern launch positions for the aerial drones were the first target, shells hammering into it from the sky with explosive force. A steady metronome followed, a shell every ten seconds as the single artillery gun worked over the southern defensive positions.

From the center, Trace could assess the effectiveness of the barrage with surprising ease—and was surprised by how *ineffective* it was.

"Half of the mortars are still online," she murmured. "Drone launchers are gone, but the vehicles already took out all of the drones."

The southern advance had lost over half of their vehicles in the process, but they'd neutralized the southern posts' UAV contingents. Blowing up the launch sites was…irrelevant, after that.

The eastern advance was still pushing forward as the shells pounded the southern defenses. That meant they ran into the next layer of defenses as remote-controlled rocket launchers, assault cannon and lasers tore into the front company.

Again, the map lost its detail as combat was joined—but Trace could see weapons positions going dark in a slow arc that moved toward the central-eastern position.

The bunker had weapons of its own, though, and the defenders set to using them with a will as the assault path reached range of them. The map sanitized the violence, Trace knew, but that made it all the more sudden when everything linked through that bunker suddenly went dark on the display.

"They hit the bunker with something heavy and blew the network connection," Lan guessed. "But there's still two more bunkers on that side, right?"

And the violence wasn't slowing. Some of the weapons controlled by the dead bunker were taken over by the other positions. Others were destroyed. A second bunker went dark just as the assault on the south resumed, though, opening a major gap in the Siya u Hestí's defenses.

Trace couldn't tell how much that gap had cost the Second Division…but the southern assault had paused and refocused on the most eastern position, attempting to open the gap wider.

More artillery shells hammered the buildings along the streets, and the holographic map bleeped at her to once again advise that its map was no longer matching the reality the cameras were showing.

Searching for an update function let Trace distract herself from the violence and death taking place only a few hundred meters from where she sat. Once she found it, the holographic map adjusted, buildings updating to show at least some of the damage they'd taken.

Several of the warehouses were just gone. Artillery strikes on the structures had taken out key pieces and collapsed entire buildings. Others had been reinforced to hold weapon positions and were still intact despite those weapons being destroyed.

With four bunkers gone, the government assault seemed to pause. The infantry icons were pulling back toward the southeast corner, while the vehicles swept streets for mines. They were still in range of indirect fire from the other positions, but the artillery cannon was now focusing on counter-fire.

Any mortar that fired received at least one shell in reply. Most received several, still at that steady metronome of a round every ten seconds.

"They've got to run out of ammunition eventually," Vexer murmured.

"If they have one mag-tube left but have the ammunition for the *sixteen* they attacked Llandudno with…I wouldn't count on it anytime soon," Lan observed. "This is going to be ugly. There's still another entire layer of defenses."

"And the AMPs." Trace was staring at the garages again. She had the activation codes…but she didn't want to push the button that would kill hundreds more people.

"The what?" Vexer asked.

"Autonomous mobile platforms. Artificial stupids strapped to light tanks and given targeting parameters," the doctor said grimly. "Trace has the button to release them. And I think we may just have to."

Trace wasn't entirely certain what would happen if she activated a hundred and twenty autonomous combat robots. She *was* sure that a lot of people would die—and it would be her fault.

There were already too many nights where she woke up with nightmares of the other trafficking victims on Breanna's station. The ones that had control chips implanted into their headware and had been sent out to fight the bounty hunters.

She knew they'd been innocents—but equipped with anti-stun shielding and lethal weapons, their control chips had left the boarding teams no choice but to kill them. Those deaths were on Lady Breanna's head, Trace knew that…but her nightmares didn't.

If she let killer robots loose to destroy her enemies, she'd be adding to the nightmares. But she could see the Tuathan troops forming up an assault group across from the gap they'd opened in the defenses.

The Cartel soldiers were falling back to the inner defensive line. The outer bunkers were now rigged as booby traps—a problem for later, Trace suspected.

There were more messages piling up. The perimeter teams didn't know Chey was dead, Trace realized. She wasn't entirely sure *what* they were fighting for, but she wasn't sure they'd have fought on if they'd known their boss was gone.

"I don't think I can," she whispered. "They're already out there fighting for *nothing*. I...hate the Siya u Hestî, but I don't want to deceive them to their deaths—and I *don't* hate the Tuathans."

Vexer put his hand on her shoulder and squeezed.

"Can you give me control of the drones?" he asked softly.

"I know you're just going to turn them on," she pointed out. "That doesn't absolve me of responsibility."

"I hate to be manipulative, but there is a factor in here that I don't believe you've considered," Lan interjected. "Can you bring up that logistics panel that was up when we came in here?"

That took a good thirty seconds. Trace's current access had the same information but different tools to access it. Chey, after all, needed *information* on the logistics and cargo status of the warehouse. She didn't need to be changing or working with that information.

The advantage, of course, was that Chey's view into the warehouse's status was high-level enough to make the information Lan was looking for immediately obvious.

"Seventy-three prisoners," Trace said, staring at the number. Before Lan could do anything, she'd clicked through for a detailed summary.

Names, photos, measurements...both the amount and type of information readily available to the head trafficker on her victims was disturbing. The oldest of the prisoners was a thirty-year-old woman who, while gorgeous to Trace's eyes, was flagged for her skills as an artificial stupid programmer.

The youngest were a pair of twelve-year-old twin boys, and the limited flags on *their* file left Trace seeing red.

She waved the listing of human misery aside and turned her gaze back to the main holographic map. The Tuathans had consolidated the remnants of two regiments and brought up a third, preparing for an advance that would probably punch through the remaining defenses.

"They're after us," she whispered. "But how careful are they going to be? What's going to happen to those people?"

"Let's not do Staid Chorporra's security force the disservice of *assuming* being rescued by them will be a bad thing," Vexer pointed out. "But...they're vulnerable. If the defenders fall back to the final positions on *this* building..."

Artillery strikes on the fortified positions on the Cartel warehouse could easily kill the prisoners. Worse, Trace knew damn well that the Siya u Hestî would freely threaten their hostages to buy themselves time.

The best way to make sure those prisoners were safe was to make sure that *Evasion*'s crew controlled the warehouse.

She brought up a new command menu and highlighted a location on the map.

"This is the central defense center for the main warehouse," she told her adults. "From there, we can take control of the remote systems protecting this building, even keeping the Siya u Hestî out."

"What are you thinking?" Vexer asked, looking at the now brightly glowing room on the map.

"We send the AMPs out to meet the Tuathans. And *we* take control of the warehouse, free and protect the prisoners ourselves while we try to find the way out that *we* know has to be here," she said.

"Can you move?"

Lan grimaced at her question but raised themselves to their feet and nodded.

"So long as I'm not carrying much. Vexer will have to deal with anyone in the command center."

"Two people," Trace warned. "They already have full control of the warehouse weapons, but there's a delegation protocol for exterior positions. I can't disable it from here. I need to be at the command center."

"But you can do everything else?" Vexer asked.

"Chey had a *lot* of control built into her network access, but some things require the physical hardware. We could probably do everything we need from her office, but I blew it up."

"Command center it is. What else?"

"This."

A big red virtual button materialized in the air in front of Trace. She was the only one who could see it, but its presence loomed in the room for half a second before she pressed it with her palm.

"AMPs released," she whispered. "May my nightmares forgive me."

39

THE CIVIL SECTION of the monitor at least had access to news feeds. The Spacers were running their own news media on the war. EB suspected that *nobody* on the surface was happy to have the surprisingly objective news reports on the conflict available to everyone.

"Reports from Llandudno prior to the city's fall confirm the widespread presence of a respiratory contagion that disabled the defenders at what many analysts are suggesting was a suspiciously optimal timing for the offensive by Tuathan forces," the news anchor declared.

Estutmost was sufficiently backward and Beyond that EB was reasonably sure the attractive woman in the hologram playing over the coffee table was real. Most worlds would use a mix of digital simulacra and people, but the simulacra he'd seen there came up short compared to live footage of humans.

"In agreement with that suspicion, the Commission of the Cinnead has formally accused the Board of Directors of deploying a bioweapon in the contested city," the anchor continued. "While the Commission has not provided any evidence supporting this claim, other than the obvious circumstantial evidence, they also note that the doctors who were working with the disease are currently under Board occupation.

"While this station refuses to speculate, we do find ourselves obliged to note that no soldiers of the security force's Second Division have fallen ill during their occupation of the city—and that a vaccine against the virus was made available within two days of Llandudno's fall.

"We suggest that our viewers draw their own conclusions, but the situation does seem suspicious at the very least."

"Do you have to watch this *every single moment*?" Ginny asked as she stepped into the living room EB and Reggie shared. "Didn't you get enough of that when you got hauled on the carpet by the Commodore?"

"I'm not even sure I was being hauled on the carpet so much as he wanted to vent at someone who wasn't involved in his political shit-show."

EB muted the news feed as it moved to an overhead view of the plains of Dachaigh a Deas. Icons showed the known positions of the various forces in the ongoing mobile battle across the farmlands.

Any hope for a Tuathan blitzkrieg had died at least two days earlier. The Cinnead troops had forged their knowledge of the open plains and their local support into a powerful weapon, one that had turned the entire advance into a slog through deadly molasses.

A journey that could have taken twelve hours was currently at five days, and the assault column was still almost a hundred kilometers short of Dinas Fferm.

"I'm trying to keep myself informed of what's going on," EB told Ginny. "It's hard. I'm used to having a lot more direct control of my information. And, well, everything else."

"Well, we seem to have decided we're keeping our parole." She dropped onto the couch. "Any idea if we'll get the ship back at some point?"

"When the war is over, we'll be fined and released. That's the usual spiel, anyway. They could, theoretically, fine and release us right now —or seize the ship, for that matter—but since they *haven't*…"

"I wish them luck getting through the security lock," Reggie noted morosely. "Except, well, I don't. I *like* my bunk and my turrets."

"Pretty sure those are *my* turrets." EB glanced back at the newsfeed hologram. "I want my ship back, but I also want my family and my doctor. *Fuck*."

"Nobody could have known things were going to get this messy," Ginny reminded him. "Owens said she'd get them out. She tried pretty damn hard, from what I know."

"Yeah, and our people up and vanished to protect themselves. And now there's a goddamn war going on *in* Llandudno, and I can't shake the feeling that any mess involving the Siya u Hestî probably involved us somehow."

"All we can do is wait," Reggie said, still staring down at his coffee. "Have I mentioned, boss, that I hate waiting and I hate being imprisoned? Even if this is much nicer than any other prison I've ever been in."

"I don't think anyone is aboard *Evasion* because they wanted to end up in prison. But until this war is over..."

EB shook his head, pausing as the newsfeed suddenly flashed up with a *BREAKING NEWS* alert.

Reggie turned the sound back on before he did, to a loud sigh from Ginny.

"We have live updates from the city of Llandudno, where a policing operation in the dock district by the Second Division appears to have grown wildly out of control. At last count, *seven* of the Second Division's sixteen regiments had redeployed to the docks district.

"It is unclear what is going on or what has changed, but new orders appear to be relocating multiple *other* regiments to the docks district in response to an emergency call. We will bring you the la..."

The anchor proved her humanity by being shocked to silence as new updates began to hit her own personal feed. A moment later, a map of Llandudno appeared in front of her, with glowing icons.

"Breaking news, unknown forces—presumed to be Cinnead resistance—have attacked the primary detention facility being used to hold suspected dissidents in Llandudno. More news coming in... Forces unknown have sabotaged both the North and South Orme bridges, removing the ability to travel north-south across the estuary.

"Forces unknown also appeared to have ambushed Second Division's Hotel Regiment in the streets. Open warfare is now being waged on the streets of Llandudno."

The anchor was trying to catch up, clearly looking for the right words to say as an entire city descended into fire and chaos in front of her eyes.

"We strongly recommend that any of our viewers in the city of Llandudno now remain indoors until the immediate conflict has subsided. We are receiving additional reports of multiple resistance strikes across the city, while the Second Division appears to be moving their forces to the docks district to deal with their policing operation.

"Llandudno appears to have descended into a three-way war. We *strongly* recommend avoiding the city if you can or sheltering in place if you cannot."

EB swallowed hard, an acid feeling in the pit of his stomach as the news feeds gleamed with faux fire icons. The Second Division had moved to neutralize the Cartel…and the resistance had taken advantage of their distraction.

He hoped they'd managed to take the penitentiary *before* the executions took place. It looked like General Griffith had detained the wrong six thousand souls in the end—and, in doing so, had probably handed the resistance six thousand willing recruits.

"Our kid is in the middle of that," Ginny whispered.

"What do we do?"

Reggie had finally looked up from his coffee cup, but his question was no less morose for actually looking at EB.

"I don't know," EB admitted. "We don't have any levers, people. We don't have access to our ship. We don't have allies. We have money and that's it."

"Mercenary gunships are usually bribable."

EB snorted, considering it. Five of the six nova gunships reinforcing the blockade were mercenaries. So far, he'd been impressed with the competence and professionalism of mercenaries in this chunk of the Beyond—but that same professionalism meant they wouldn't be as bribable.

So, hiring those gunships to do something against their contract would be expensive. EB could probably muster the funds from the vault on *Evasion*…that he couldn't currently access.

"We can't afford them," he admitted. "I'm really not sure what we can do. Wait. And pray, if any of us are of the inclination."

He wasn't, but he was sure there was *some* religion among his crew. It wasn't a question that was polite to ask.

Before anyone could respond to his hopeless statement, there was a sharp knock on the door. It slid open in response to a security override before any of them could move, and Sergeant McMahon once again appeared in EB's new living room.

This time, she was wearing body armor over her shipsuit and had a stunner in her hands. A pair of troopers stood behind her, weapons at the ready.

"Captain Bardacki," she snapped. "You're coming with me. Now."

"What's going on?" EB asked, careful to keep his hands visible. He really didn't need to add *getting stunned* to the day's list of headaches.

"The Commodore just figured out the poison pill you dropped off in Llandudno."

EB had *no* idea what she was talking about…but also had no inclination to argue with heavily armed soldiers.

THE SPACER SOLDIERS very nearly dragged EB into the room, his steps barely keeping up with their grip as they marched him into a space he hadn't seen before.

It only took him a few seconds to realize he was on *Armstrong*'s flag bridge. A central dais held Commodore Malone, surrounded by tactical displays of the entire system. Sunken working spaces around the dais held analysts and communications officers, busily working to keep the blockade operating.

EB found himself marched along the walkway to the central dais, completely ignored by the crew supporting Malone's command. Given his escorts' body language, he was half-surprised he hadn't been manacled along the way.

"Captain," Malone greeted him coldly. The Commodore had his

back to EB, looking at what appeared to be yet another map of Llandudno.

"It's only been, what, three hours since we last spoke?" EB replied. "I certainly haven't done anything since then."

"No. Our concern is what you did *before* we ever captured you. I am impressed, Captain, and furious. Impressed at how quickly you offloaded in Llandudno...and furious that I believed your talk of conscience."

"I...don't understand, Commodore."

"Did you think we wouldn't notice, Captain?" Malone asked. "Did you think we would blame someone else? For a man who speaks of conscience, I did not think *you* would be the one to have delivered autonomous war machines to my world."

EB was struck silent for a few seconds, then he slowly stepped forward and away from his escorts to look at what Malone was seeing.

"We delivered three containers of Galahad-Deuce heavy tanks and enough equipment for about three companies of medium infantry to Llandudno," he told Malone slowly as he saw the scans of the docks district.

"Every tank I delivered to Llandudno participated in Commissar Owens' suicide charge to cover the evacuation transports. I'm quite certain the guns and armor I delivered are in the hands of the resistance fighters making the Staid Chorporra's life hell right now...but I did not deliver artificial stupid war machines.

"But since you're accusing me of it, I'm guessing someone did?"

"The Staid's attempt to seize part of the docks district ran into heavy fixed defenses—and now someone has unleashed a fleet of off-world autonomous combat drones against that attack. Valentine, to his credit, has recognized the threat and is scrambling to concentrate his forces against them."

Every few decades, *somebody* built autonomous combat drones. It rarely ended neutrally, let alone well. Robot spaceships, especially, had a tendency to turn on the multiphasic jammers that shredded communications and never turn them off.

Ground- and air-combat drones generally had some limited autonomy but operated under direct control from humans. Ones that didn't tended to become trouble. True AI couldn't fit in anything useful as a nova ship, let alone a tank, which meant only artificial stupid algorithms could be loaded into combat drones.

And those algorithms literally *could not* be perfect. Collateral damage was an inevitable consequence. While EB personally suspected that most militaries had *some* autonomous drones in their inventory, they were regarded in the same light as weapons of mass destruction.

"I did not deliver robotic tanks to Estutmost, let alone to Llandudno," EB repeated as he looked over the maps. There were dozens of the things. Maybe a hundred or more—and the robots had already thrown Second Division's assault on the docks back in disarray.

Combined with the resistance's move, Llandudno's occupying garrison was in shambles. Even *EB* could tell that Griffith was abandoning everything in a desperate attempt to concentrate his forces.

But unless someone could turn the autonomous tanks *off*, the Tuathan containment effort appeared to have already failed.

"You expect me to believe that?" Malone asked. "You delivered weapons to Estutmost. You landed in Llandudno. And now a poison pill of killer robots has been unleashed."

"Except your *poison pill* emerged from the Siya u Hestî base," EB pointed out. "And I know you don't know my history...but believe me, Commodore Malone, I would rather nuke the Cartel from orbit than do them the tiniest favor.

"But the Cartel also has the resources to provide themselves with a last-ditch defense to secure their facilities. Those tanks, Commodore, were here before this war ever started."

"Ser!" One of the analysts had turned toward the dais. "Status update on the Staid Chorporra First Army. We intercepted new orders being transmitted—they're turning around!"

"Heading back to Llandudno," Malone said grimly. "Because their entire logistics pipeline runs through that city, and they're on the edge of losing control of it—either to the resistance or to the damn robots."

EB wasn't familiar with ground operations, but he doubted that the Tuathans were going to be able to turn a multi-division column around particularly quickly. It would take them hours...but on the other hand, the retreat to Llandudno would go faster than the advance on Dinas Fferm.

The Staid army would be back in Llandudno in a day, maybe two. If the resistance took control, they wouldn't have enough time to refortify the city before they were under attack again.

"What do we do, Commodore?" someone asked. EB didn't see who.

"Why would the mission parameters change now?" Malone replied. "We aren't getting involved in the war on the surface."

EB was being ignored now. More reports were coming up from the analysts around them, new data flickering up on the holographic maps surrounding the dais. Llandudno was a chaotic nightmare. It *looked* like the resistance was winning—with the Tuathan troops caught between a well-prepared campaign of ambush and sabotage on the one hand and the Siya u Hestí's defenses on the other.

"The Cinnead will sortie," he murmured.

"What?" Malone wheeled on him, fire flashing in the Commodore's eyes.

"The Cinnead has, what, eight brigades in Dinas Fferm and another three or four causing havoc in the plains?" EB gestured to the map. "But they know the resistance can't hold Llandudno on their own.

"So, they'll sortie everything they've got to chase the First Army across the Dachaigh a Deas and pin them against whatever defenses the resistance can muster. Both armies are about to be in the field, Commodore, in the clearest positions for safe orbital strikes you will see in this entire war."

"We are not getting involved," Malone snapped.

"No one wins from this war continuing," EB told him, stepping closer and lowering his voice. "You know that. The Board has the resources on-planet. So long as you stop Nigahog and others supplying the Cinnead, they'll eventually grind the Cinnead down— or their control of the terraforming systems will force them to surrender.

"One of them controls the crop seed but the other controls the ground's ability to support crops. Your blockade is going to leave people on the surface *starving* if this goes on. The last chance for a quick victory just died when the Siya u Hestî *fucked* General Griffith—and old loyalties aside, Commodore…

"Can you really side with the people who deployed bioweapons and rounded up every civilian even remotely associated with the Cinnead—and then started executing them based on potential threat rather than any action or guilt?"

"A pox on all their fucking houses," Malone snapped, loud enough that EB suspected everyone heard him. "I cannot support the Board, no. I won't destroy them, either. I have friends in that fucking army. We all do."

The flag bridge was silent, and EB realized that every eye and ear was now focused on the dais. Malone's people wouldn't challenge him. They were torn themselves. Some almost certainly shared his desire to be loyal to the state they had served their entire careers. Others hated the Cinnead for jacking up food prices—and others still hated the Board for bringing it to this point.

A pox on both their houses really did sum up the Spacers' attitude, EB suspected.

"Then make them stop."

The only sound in the monitor's command center was the whir of fans and the buzz of computers as everyone seemed to stare at EB.

"You have the high ground," EB told Malone. "You have *all* the fucking cards. You're sitting up here on your high horse and your bullshit moral stance that you manufactured to justify doing nothing. But *you* have created a situation where the only way this war ends is in starvation and misery for thousands upon thousands of innocents.

"Right now, one army is in a position where you could wipe them out with a single command. The other is probably going to join them. So, *demonstrate* that. You don't need to hurt anyone. You just need to prove that they can't actually fight a war of maneuver across Dachaigh a Deas without your permission.

"And that they don't fucking have it. You don't want the Board to win this war. You don't like the Cinnead, for your own reasons. But you have the ability to make them stop, Commodore. You can force them to the negotiating table and demand a seat for the Spacers.

"You've trapped yourselves in the pattern you built when the fight was stalemated in the Snowdens and you *couldn't* do anything. But now you have the ability to control the situation. You have the upper hand. *Use it*.

"Or sit up here bitching about the problems you helped create while doing nothing."

He gave an exaggerated spread-palms shrug.

"I'm just a prisoner whose ship you've detained. What do I know? My bias is that I want my family back—and that'll be easiest when this war is over!"

Silence answered him, then Malone looked away from him. The Commodore's hand gestures suggested he was running through something in his headware as he studied the map of the continent.

"You're an asshole, Bardacki," he finally said.

"I promised not to escape, not to refrain from pissing you off."

"I should phrase my requests more carefully in future." Now icons were dropping onto the holographic map as Malone interfaced whatever he was working on into the system.

"Christian, Harrison," he barked. "I want full sensor sweeps of this region. Send in a sub-fighter sweep if you have it, but I need to know, with one hundred percent certainty, that there isn't anyone in this zone."

The highlighted section was directly on First Army's path back to Llandudno.

"Toews, begin a targeting setup. I want to put six heavy plasma blasts from Armstrong into the center of that zone over a ten-second period. I want it big, bright, flashy—and I want you to cross-reference with Christian and Harrison to make sure it's harmless.

"We're going to be noisy and we're going to make a point, but there will be *no* collateral damage.

"Our off-world friend is right. Our friends, comrades, colleagues, acquaintances and enemies have arranged to give us a chance to tell them to sit down and shut up.

"I think we'd be breaking our promises if we didn't take it."

40

VEXER LED the way into the command center, stunning both of the Siya u Hestî gangers operating the last line of defense before Trace or Lan even saw them.

"Do your thing, I guess," he told Trace as she came in. He had the two older Cartel operatives tied up in a corner to keep them out of the way. "I'm going to move these gents somewhere else. Lan?"

"I see a proper medkit, so I believe I am going to be busy for a few minutes, and then I am going to *not move* for an extended period."

The doctor looked a lot paler than they had when the group had left the warehouse office. Trace wrapped an arm around them before they could say a word, helping them to a seat in the small room with the dozens of surveillance feeds.

"Sit, I'll grab it," she instructed.

The "command center" was more accurately a security room. It had holoprojectors throughout, but they were mainly showing the surveillance feeds from the exterior of the warehouse. The two men running it had been watching the building, including keeping an eye on the prisoners to make sure no one escaped.

Trace managed not to stop and glare at the image of the portion of the warehouse converted to cells as she grabbed the medkit. Prefabricated cages, the type made for *zoos*, had been lined up in rows to create a crude prison, with only limited cloth hangings for privacy.

Anger drove her to move faster. Once she'd opened the kit and passed it to Lan, she took a seat at one of the other three chairs in the room and linked her stolen account to the security systems.

Chey's credentials opened up the entire system to Trace. What she hadn't had before was the direct access to the security hardware for the main building. She loaded several of the programs EB had given her into that hardware, expanding her control and locking anyone else out.

"Secondary security centers were uncrewed," she told Vexer and Lan. The doctor was paying more attention to the synthskin dispenser they were spraying across their skin, but her father was just outside the door.

"So, those two were the last," he concluded. "That helps."

"I'm locking out everywhere except here anyway. We have control of the building defenses, if everything else goes to hell."

"Which puts us between those prisoners and *anyone* coming after them—assuming those defenses aren't locked out from firing on Chey's own people?"

"Somehow, I doubt it." Trace took a few seconds to check. "No lockouts at all. No auto-targeting modes. Someone has to assign targets manually."

Most of the guns had enough automatic functions to track and engage a target on their own, but someone had to tell them to fire. They were the *normal* kind of semi-autonomous weapon system.

Unlike the AMPs that Trace had unleashed on the city.

She'd tried to ignore the elephant in the world, but now that she'd secured their current position, she had to see what was going on.

Even *she* had to feel that the drone tanks were poorly designed. The system she had access to could only give the broadest of orders, which she felt was *asking* for them to go rogue.

"I'm starting to suspect that a potential loss of control on the AMPs is a feature, not a failing," she muttered.

"They're terror weapons," Lan replied. "Nobody uses artificial stupid combat platforms for efficiency. These are intended to create a panic, cover the evacuation of the facility so the Cartel can go back into hiding."

"I activated the default orders, which are apparently to sweep and destroy all combat vehicles in the city," Trace noted as she pulled up the feeds from the tanks. So far, at least, the AMPs were still sending information back to the Siya u Hestî network.

They'd breached the perimeter around the warehouse, she realized, and the Tuathan troops were falling back in disarray. Their first-order objective seemed to be in hand, but that left Trace with a new problem.

"We're getting lots of coms requests from the bunkers," she told the adults. "And…one just cut the line. And another."

Trace could *see* the wave effect as one bunker after another realized their central position was compromised. They went dark on her screens, even as the sensor network insisted they were still intact and operational.

"We're losing control of the exterior defenses," she murmured. "Not that we really had it in the first place. Um. What happens now?"

Vexer put a hand on her shoulder and squeezed reassuringly.

"If we're lucky, they decline to throw good money after bad and disappear into the city. If we're not…"

"They're going to try to take the warehouse back from us," Lan said, their voice weak. "They may even know where the secret escape routes are, which we don't. They probably can't use them to attack us, but…"

"They may not need to," Trace warned. "The warehouse doesn't have that many weapons pods. With just the three of us, they're going to overrun us."

"Right." Vexer was staring at the displays with her. "Can we turn the AMPs on them?"

Trace shivered.

"I don't think so. I think they have enough IFF gear to protect the Cartel troopers. We need more hands."

Her gaze turned back to the video feed showing the holding area for the Cartel's kidnap victims.

"Fortunately, I think I know where to find them."

MOVING through the warehouse was *creepy*. Part of that, Trace suspected, was that she was *intimately* familiar with the kind of horrors a human-trafficking operation inflicted on its victims. Part of it was that the place was completely empty and silent despite the war going on outside.

No one and nothing barred her and Vexer's way to the holding cells. She had to hope that Lan was feeling well enough to run the warehouse security for the moment—none of the Siya u Hestî fighters had left their bunkers yet when she'd last looked.

Vexer certainly hadn't been about to let her wander around the traffickers' warehouse alone. She was having enough shivers and dark memories to make her *very* grateful for her father's presence, even as she channeled pure rage and spite to carry on.

She suspected she was going to pay for today in her nightmares for years, but she needed to get through it all first. She regretted loosing the AMPs on the Staid Chorporra security forces, but she found herself shockingly short of sympathy for the Siya u Hestî's gangers.

They all knew what they'd served. She didn't know how anyone could have walked into the prison cells in that warehouse and not known that they had sold their soul to evil.

It didn't look any better in person than it had through the cameras. The people in the cells were sitting on the floor, actively trying *not* to look at Trace and Vexer as they entered the room.

She suspected they thought she was another victim, and anger burned through her.

"Good evening, everyone," she declared loudly. As she spoke, she was checking into the systems in the room. As she'd feared, the cages were on a partially segregated network, requiring someone to be in the room to unlock them.

As she'd *hoped*, Chey's access was sufficient to do so. A soft ripple of locks clicking open ran through the room, and she smiled as she suddenly had everyone's attention.

"My name is Tracy Bardacki, and not that long ago, I was a prisoner of the Siya u Hestî like you," she told them. "Thanks to that, I have a *small* grudge against them and have managed to get myself in some trouble.

"Right now, the Siya u Hestî have abandoned this warehouse to try to push back government troops trying to overtake them. Unfortunately, they have succeeded and are now realizing that my companions have seized control of this building and its defenses."

Doors were sliding open, and the prisoners were looking hesitantly at her.

"You are free," she told them. "I'm not going to demand repayment for that. I'll warn you that I don't know any safe ways out of here. The Siya u Hestî have us surrounded. The Tuathan occupying army has them...mostly surrounded. The Cinnead fighters in the city have the Tuathans confused and disoriented.

"This city in a state of chaos. Our best hope is to secure this warehouse and protect ourselves—and we have managed to take control of the defenses and hope to use them for that purpose.

"But there are three of us."

Trace spread her hands wide.

"You are free to run on your own, if you want. You are free to tear through this building for clothes and food and medicine to take care of yourselves; I don't care. But if you want to take a shot at the monsters who locked us all up and were going to make us into objects and slaves...

"Well, we need hands to run the defenses and people to stand off the people who put us in here."

A tall woman stepped out of the closest cell. Trace recognized her from the imagery, though the picture in the file of the oldest prisoner had included fewer bruises and more hair. Someone had shaved her head and she'd picked up a black eye in the process, but the spark of fury in her eyes was *very* familiar to Trace.

"I'm Amelie Harris," she introduced herself. "And I don't know *how* you pulled this off, kid, but if you need hands to shoot these *fuckers,* I'm in."

Others stepped forward to volunteer. Not everyone, not by a long shot, but Trace hadn't expected that. She wasn't sure *she'd* have signed on for a fight in their place, after all.

"All right." Vexer stepped up beside her. "Those of you who are with us, we're going to take you all to the main security center and then see how we can best split up.

"Everyone else, I only ask that you keep in touch with us and stay safe," he continued. "We believe there is an exit out of the docks district from somewhere in this building, but we haven't found it. We haven't had time.

"If you want to search for it, we would be grateful. But the main thing we need from you is to keep your heads down and *stay safe*," he repeated. "The last thing we want is to have freed you to get you hurt."

HARRIS WAS BARELY HALF a step behind Trace as they reentered the security center. The tall programmer was in a seat before Trace had finished checking on Lan, linking her headware into the systems and then coughing in surprise.

"What access *is* this?" she asked.

"Security admin," Trace replied. "I have Chey's account but only from my own headware."

Lan looked even paler now, but the bleeding seemed to have stopped. They smiled up at her.

"I'm going to be okay," they assured her. "But I pushed too hard and I'm paying for it."

They waved a hand at the displays.

"The Siya u Hestî have cut us out and established a secondary network. They're cutting us out of sensor clusters one by one, but I think that's manual."

"The system is built such that they'll need to do that with hardware access," Harris said, her fingers deep in the holograms as she manipulated the datastream with an easy grace Trace could only envy.

"They made me help with the coding," the older woman observed grimly. "They had decent-enough programmers to make sure I didn't do anything dangerous, and they were...testing to see if they *could* control me."

She shook her head.

"So long as they have physical access and we don't, we'll lose whatever external access we have. If they know what they're doing, they can literally unplug the original network and plug in a new one."

"We can see them coming with the sensors they can't reach, but we'll lose our view of the wider city," Lan said.

"That's not quite true." Trace was checking the feeds in her own headware, because she *thought*… There. "Adding a new set of feeds."

The holographic map expanded to cover more of the city, small zones of updated information centered on moving green icons: the AMPs.

"You're still getting data from those?" Vexer asked.

"They're still talking to me so far." Trace couldn't link the controls for the robotic tanks to the main displays, but she could run the sensor data.

She was really looking at them for the first time. They'd gone even farther than she'd expected. The Tuathan army was retreating, and the AMPs were spreading out through the city in a search-and-destroy pattern.

"Can we use them against the Cartel?"

"No." Trace shook her head at her dad's question. "We already looked at it. They have IFF programs to keep them firing on their own people. I…"

She didn't trust the artificial stupids running the AMPs not to start classifying civilian vehicles as hostile combatants. Her education had included specific examples of robotic starships and war machines making all kinds of classification errors.

Fully autonomous combat robots were a civilization-wide nightmare, one that Kunthea Chey had made real as a final defense—and one that Trace Bardacki had unleashed.

"I'm ordering them to fall back on the docks district in a defensive perimeter," she finally finished. "The government army is wrecked, and it doesn't serve anyone to have the AMPs running wild in the city."

Harris was looking at the map with a clear sinking expression.

None of their other volunteers were following the discussion, but the programmer had clearly caught up.

"They had combat robots."

"Yeah. We used them to drive off the government army, but now the Cartel isn't busy keeping the Tuathans away, so they've realized we've compromised their central hub."

"Hence needing extra hands," Harris realized aloud. "Okay. How do we help?"

"You, I suspect, help best by sitting right here and helping Trace run the whole setup," Lan said softly. They weren't even sitting up straight, just slumped in their chair. "The rest of you, I worked out which four secondary security rooms are going to serve us best.

"We need about three people in each; I'll forward you maps."

Trace tuned out the conversation, her focus now on giving orders to the autonomous tanks. Chey had built in a series of preset orders to make command of the units easier. It was possible that, given time and actual coding, she could give the AMPs orders to engage the remaining Cartel forces and protect the warehouse.

But the canned orders she had access to could only order them to fall back and defend the district itself. She could hope that would intimidate the Siya u Hestî fighters into surrendering, but that was a small and frail hope.

"Harris, I'm going to copy you some of the information I have on the preset orders Chey had for these things," she told the programmer, extracting as much of the code as she could into a package she flipped the woman. "I don't know if we'll get anything useful out of it, but if we can convince the tanks to attack the Siya u Hestî, we'll be as secure as anyone can be."

"I'll take a look," Harris promised. "I'm familiar with the code used for targeting antimissile defenses and such, if only because the Siya u Hestî made me learn."

Trace had a damn good idea of what kind of sick *incentives* the Siya u Hestî would apply to get an attractive woman to learn skills they wanted.

"It'll have to be enough. Either way, we are going to make these monsters hurt. I promise."

41

THE FIRST ATTACK was a stark reminder of the fact that while the Siya u Hestî had military weapons and well-designed defensive installations, they were criminals, not soldiers—and that most of their number weren't even criminal enforcers.

Most of the Cartel "fighters" now surrounding Trace and her companions were people like the logistics team whose office they'd first used. They were basically office workers who worked for the evilest industry in the galaxy.

Chey had sent them all out to operate the defenses, and they'd all, Trace assumed, had some training in that vein. But they weren't actually *soldiers*.

The attack opened with an attempt to ram one of the side doors open with a civilian ground car—which was hit by an assault cannon blast six meters short of the wall and flung away in multiple pieces— followed by a dozen gangers on foot.

There was no power armor in evidence, and without it they never stood a chance. Trace forced herself to look away from the video feed and focus on her interface for the robotic tanks.

She didn't need to see *more* people die today. Her sympathy for anyone who knowingly and voluntarily worked for the Siya u Hestî was almost nonexistent, but death was a very final punishment.

Death allowed no room for redemption, absolution or justice.

"They won't try that again," Harris said in a satisfied tone. The local *hadn't* looked away from the massacre at the doors. "I don't think they've got the bodies to actually cause trouble."

"Now if only they'd surrender. Or just…go away," Trace muttered. "This city has already seen enough death and horror for anyone."

"Fuck the Siya u Hestî," Harris said bitterly. "They can charge into a wall of fire and burn forever, for all I care. They've earned it, all of them."

"I think Trace is as much concerned about what it'll do to us as to them." Vexer squeezed Trace's shoulder again. As a reassurance, it was lacking a lot, and he'd been repeating it a lot in this mess…but it helped.

"I'll worry about my soul later," the woman said. "Right now, I'm going to *delight* in watching the *fuckers* who kidnapped and raped me *burn*."

"Fair." Trace still wasn't going to watch people die. Her nightmares had been bad enough *before* today.

"Wait. What the hell is that?"

There was a new icon in her link to the AMPs tactical network. Pulling it up and identifying it only took her a couple of seconds, and she swallowed a curse.

"Someone in the bunkers has a set of security codes for the AMPs," she told the others. "They're trying to take control of the tanks. My codes are higher-authority, but…"

A flashing alert suddenly interrupted her controls. Whoever was trying to take control of the robots away from her knew more about their software than she did, and they'd activated a security routine.

"I'm locked out," she hissed. "Looks like they've got a routine to identify compromise control vectors, but…I'm attempting to override."

Trace *really* doubted that Kunthea Chey had set up a system that let her subordinates take control of the robots away from her. But the truth was that the control channel she was using *was* compromised, and it was possible that the artificial stupid subroutine was smart enough to make that distinction.

In which case she was in real trouble.

The main holographic map shrank sharply as the telemetry feed failed, and Trace glared at her control link... then shivered as she realized what she'd done.

"They blocked me out," she admitted. "But...I think I blocked them out, too."

"So, who's in control?"

"The stupids. They've flagged *everybody* as compromised and locked out all external commands." Trace grimaced, looking at the limited data they had. "I *think* they're still running defensive orders, but they're going to shoot at *anything* that comes near them."

And *that* was why nobody built combat robots. Though she suspected that most people didn't count on thirteen-year-old *idiots* giving the wrong orders!

"NEWS REPORTS throughout the city have confirmed that the Staid Chorporra's Second Division appears to be in full retreat," the news anchor declared. "Reports from the Dachaigh a Deas, however, have confirmed that the Staid's First Army is now en route back to Llandudno.

"Worrying reports out of the docks district, however, suggest that an unknown third party is now engaging both retreating Staid forces and Cinnead forces attempting to secure the district. We have no information on these unknowns at the moment.

"We reiterate our recommendation: if you can possibly avoid it, stay off the streets. So far, all combatants appear to be respecting the safety of noncombatants, but have no way to be certain that will remain the case.

"Keep your heads down and stay safe. This is Llandudno News."

The newsfeed continued, but Trace cut the audio so she didn't have to listen to it.

"We've lost all off-site feeds and we have no access to the AMPs,"

Harris told everyone. "The Siya u Hestî now have those sensors, but they don't have the AMPs. We won't see them coming…but they'll see if we try to run."

"Wasn't planning on running," Vexer said. "Not unless we've found that sneaky getaway."

"A few people looking for it, but no luck yet," the rescuee told them. "So, we hold until the Siya u Hestî are dead or give up."

"Except for the slight problem of rogue AS tanks now tearing into *everybody*," Trace pointed out. "Which is…my fault."

"We don't know *what* they're doing. The last orders you gave them was to secure the docks district in a defensive perimeter. They should still follow those orders, even with no control authority anymore."

"They're just going to shoot *everyone*," Trace told Harris. "Except *maybe* the Siya u Hestî, assuming the IFF protocols hold up."

"Probably at least partially connected to the control code," the programmer told her. "Plus, with the security routines sweeping for compromised control nodes, the *idiots* probably gave the stupids the ability to override IFF systems."

Trace wilted a few more degrees. The drones she'd unleashed were truly rogue now, and she wasn't quite sure what they were going to do. Major artificial stupids were notorious for following orders in ways that didn't quite make sense from a human perspective—the paperclip optimizer problem, some of her courses had called it.

That was why people didn't *build* things like the AMPs. Part of her couldn't believe that Chey had been that stupid.

Trace was far too able, sadly, to believe that *Trace* had been stupid enough to turn them loose. It had seemed like a great idea, and they'd done exactly what she'd activated them to do.

"I should have turned the damn things off, not ordered them back," she muttered. "Shut them down wherever they were."

"That would almost certainly have triggered the routines sweeping for compromised command nodes," Harris pointed out. "Shutting down drones in the field is the first thing an enemy would try."

Trace was tearing through Chey's information on the AMPs. She'd discovered that the Siya u Hestî had acquired around a thousand of the killer robots, assigned in packets of twenty drones to assorted facilities scattered across a dozen star systems.

None of the notes from her database or Chey's files told her how to shut the things down. There was an explicit assumption in some of the files that deploying the AMPs was an area-denial tool. While there was a chance that they could be recalled, the Siya u Hestî had assumed that they were unleashing the tanks and then abandoning whatever base they'd been in.

Crime cartel bosses were disturbingly willing to cut their losses and let someone *else* bear the cost of cleaning up after them. By the plan Trace found, the plan would have been to release the tanks and then for Chey and a few other key personnel to evacuate by some kind of getaway vehicle while the city burned.

"Well, that actually helps," Trace said. "Chey's getaway is an atmospheric fast mover, somewhere near the top of the facility. Can we pass that on to the volunteers searching?

"May not be able to extract everybody, but we might get *some* people out."

Like Lan. She did not like the way the doctor was looking. They seemed a bit stronger now, but she still wanted them in the hands of a doctor with proper gear. Not treating themselves with a medkit.

"We can; that will help," Harris agreed. "Doesn't deal with our being on the inside of, what, a three-layer siege?"

"Five, I think?" Trace corrected. "We're inside the Siya u Hestî, who are inside the tanks, who are inside the Tuathans, who are inside the Resistance…who are facing an assault by the *rest* of the government army."

"I see you made *many* friends before I met you," the rescuee noted. "And I still like you better than my cell. Ideas?"

"Running out of anything except fight," Vexer admitted. "What's the Sun Tzu? 'In difficult ground, press on. In encircled ground, devise stratagems. In death ground, fight'?"

"So, is this encircled ground or death ground?" Trace said. "Should we be planning to fight to the death or to find something clever?"

"I'm not a fan of fighting to the death, but we *should* be able to hold off the Siya u Hestî until things stabilize in the rest of the city."

"And is that before or *after* the hostile army shows up to retake the city from the resistance?" Trace asked grimly. "This is a fucking mess, Dad."

"Not arguing that. But I'm afraid this *is* death ground," Vexer said. "We hold until someone comes to get us."

Trace shook her head, turning away to focus into her headware and try to find *something* that could help…and then stopped as she saw an addendum to the technical schematics of the AMPs.

She'd missed it at first because she'd been relying on the copy of the schematics from the database in her own head, the one she'd been supposed to deliver to one of Chey's fellow Level Eights.

The local copy of the schematics had a second file attached, a note from Chey to herself along with an additional set of schematics.

Breanna is a fool. The failsafe my people added should help—not least to protect us if our "Lady" decides to turn these robots on us.

The schematics… Trace expanded them in her own view and then almost swallowed her tongue.

"Kunthea Chey was a paranoid monster," she said aloud.

"Trace?"

"She figured the AMPs were set up so that Lady Breanna could activate them remotely and turn them on her own people if they disobeyed," Trace told her father. "So, she arranged for her own failsafe to be installed on all of the units here, despite the anti-tamper systems."

"What kind of failsafe?" Harris interrupted.

"Bombs." Trace was already plugging in the additional frequency information in the file. She was rigging up the software as she went, but she had the pieces. "I have confirmed links to ninety-three units. Any reason I *shouldn't*?"

"Blow them all to hell, Trace," her father told her. "They've done what we needed."

42

EB WASN'T ENTIRELY sure what his role in the affair taking shape around him was at this point. He'd been summoned in front of Commodore Malone to answer for bringing killer robots, but he'd apparently successfully defused *that* charge.

And he'd managed to convince Malone to finally take action. But while that didn't require him to do anything, he was also very clearly stuck in *Armstrong*'s command center as the plan for forcing everyone to stand down took shape.

The targeting scheme was ready in a few minutes, but Malone was waiting for something. EB wasn't sure what, but the Spacer Commodore was staring at the displays.

"Ser, reports from Dinas Fferm," an analyst finally reported. "A six-brigade column has formed up and is moving out. Scans suggest a significant number of Galahads and Katyushas."

Malone turned a level gaze on EB at that, but the captain just shrugged.

"What? You knew I delivered those to them. I didn't give you *numbers*, but that's no surprise."

"Fair." The Commodore shook his head. "Do we have numbers, Christian?"

"Forty thousand–plus soldiers, looks like around two hundred combat vehicles including the Galahads. Infantry numbers are lower than First Army, but if they rendezvous with the mobile forces that were harassing the First, the numbers will be about even."

"So, if we do nothing, there's a decent chance they pin the First Army against Llandudno and wreck them as a fighting force," Malone concluded.

"At which point the Board builds up in the Snowdens, the stalemate continues and the war drags on until one side or the other starves," EB murmured.

"You already made your point, Captain. No, I was waiting for Owens to sortie. What are our timelines, Christian?"

"Staid Chorporra First Army is ten hours from Llandudno, assuming no interruptions or major logistics problems. Cinnead assault force is about six hours behind them, plus whatever it takes to rendezvous with the mobile brigades."

Malone nodded silently, standing straight-backed in the center of the room as he looked at all of the displays.

"Any updates from Llandudno?" he asked.

"Last report is that Griffith himself has abandoned the city with his command detachment. He's extracted two regiments intact. The rest are either tied up in street fighting or just…gone. Defeated or scattered."

"And those robots?"

"They pushed the Tuathans out of the docks district and chased them for a bit, then fell back into the warehouse district. We're not entirely sure what's going on there, but we have detected hints of further fighting *not* including the robots."

"Someone is playing games and I'm not sure I like it."

At this point, EB was starting to feel grimly certain his family was *in* that damn district. It was enough chaos for Vexer, Lan and Trace to be creating it. And if the district had been controlled by the Siya u Hestî…his family would be more than willing to make a giant mess of it.

"Wait, ser!"

Malone turned to look at the analyst.

"We've got new signatures from Llandudno docks...multiple explosions, across the district perimeter. We're still resolving, but..."

"But what?" he demanded.

The analyst stared at their feed for a few moments more, then swallowed and turned to face their boss.

"At least ninety of the robot tanks just self-destructed. Internal explosions. Suicide charges."

"Huh." EB glanced at the displays. "Someone was actually thinking about the risks of using the damn things. Handy."

"Very," Malone agreed, his tone dry. "That does remove the last complicating factor, doesn't it?"

No one answered him.

"Toews," he addressed the gunnery officer. "You have those targeting patterns?"

"I do, ser."

"They are clear?"

"We've checked, checked again, triple-checked and triple-checked again," Toews said firmly. "There is no one inside the target zone, but it's directly on First Army's approach to Llandudno."

"Thank you. You may fire."

Such a simple statement to mark the complete change of the Spacers' position in the war. *Armstrong* didn't even move. The monitor didn't *need* to. Three turrets, already aligned for the firing pattern, fired.

Six heavy plasma bolts, each sufficient to gut a nova battlecruiser, blazed through space and hit Estutmost's atmosphere. They would lose power and cohesion in the air, but they still hit the surface with the force of a sub-megaton-range nuclear weapon.

Six of them created a short-lived but intense firestorm visible on the scans from orbit, and a chill silence descended over *Armstong*'s officers.

"I want a wideband transmission covering the entire planet," Malone ordered. "But make sure both Dinas Fferm and the First Army can hear it."

"Ready, ser."

Malone nodded and leveled a stern face at a pickup EB couldn't pick out.

"Forces of the Cinnead and the Staid Chorporra. I am Commodore Andrew Malone, formerly the second-in-command of the Staid Chorporra's space security forces and now the commanding officer of the blockade securing Estutmost against foreign interference."

He paused for a moment.

"The Spacers have little love for anyone on the surface," he continued. "Some of us swore our service to the Staid Chorporra, but the Board I once believed had the best interests of our world at heart has dragged our world's hopes and dreams through muck and blood.

"Bioweapons. Executions. Rounding up civilians." He shook his head. "It must end."

He gestured toward the screen behind him.

"Both the Staid and Cinnead armies are now in the fields of Dachaigh a Deas," he noted. "That has moved both forces well away from civilian populations and rendered them engageable with orbital bombardment with minimum collateral damage.

"I have run out of patience with this war, and I have the high ground. Both armies will stop where they are, right now. You will set up camps and recognize that you under the guns of the blockade.

"We do not wish to end this war in fire and devastation, but we have the ability to do so. I *request* that both the Commission of the Cinnead and the Board of the Staid Chorporra send representatives into orbit inside the next forty-eight hours.

"The Spacers have remained neutral in this fight, laying a pox on both your houses. Now, to prevent further loss of life, it appears that we must become the adult in the room. We will host talks and mediation to end this war."

That hung in the air for at least ten seconds, everything still transmitting, and Malone glared at the pickup.

"And if you are tempted to try a different course, then know that if it appears that only one side wants peace...that will very much help us decide which side of this war we're on!"

THERE WAS a general sense of waiting aboard *Armstrong* for the next few minutes. No one was sure just how anyone on the surface was going to react to Malone's ultimatum.

"Ser! First Army is stopping," an analyst reported.

The main display suddenly focused and zoomed in on the government assault column as it began the slow and careful process of stopping a dozen-plus kilometers of military forces. Vehicles moved to form a defensive perimeter; infantry began dismounting and pulling camp equipment from their transport vehicles.

The First Army was very clearly beginning to set up camp in the middle of the day. The only reason EB could see for them doing that was in obedience to Malone's commands.

"Transmission from First Army, General Cormac Monahan directly contacting us."

"Put him through," Malone ordered.

Monahan's holographic image materialized in front of the Commodore, a broad-shouldered man with a long red braid hanging in front of his shoulder.

"Andrew."

"Cormac."

The two military commanders glared at each other in silence.

"The Board will make the final call, Andrew," the Tuathan general finally said. "But I've halted First Army on my authority. I have no interest in being vaporized from space."

"I appreciate that, Cormac. I really don't want to vaporize you from space…but this has to stop. Our leaders need to *talk* and find an answer, not get other people killed."

"Easy for you to say, up in orbit and separate from everything."

"Maybe," Malone conceded. "But some days, I think that mutinying made me the only military officer in this system sufficiently detached from this mess to be neutral.

"So, it apparently falls to me to be the fucking adult in the room. Get Griffith's people out of Llandudno so the fighting can stop, and get the Board to send people to the peace talks."

"And if the Board decides not to play along?"

"It's already over, Cormac. I have the high ground."

The Tuathan General snorted.

"You were always an asshole, Andrew Malone. I really hope the Board doesn't make you kill me."

"So do I. Look to your people, Cormac Monahan."

The channel closed and Malone sighed.

"I'm his daughter's godfather," the Spacer said calmly. "But there's no way he didn't know about the bioweapon, which means I have to rethink a lot of things about my life."

No one said anything in response to that. Reports were coming in from more analysts, marking the Cinnead mobile brigades putting distance between themselves and the Tuathan camp.

"The Cinnead force has halted twenty kilometers outside Dinas Fferm," someone reported. "They're setting up camp as well. No communications."

"No, we won't hear from them. Owens hates my guts," Malone noted. "He'll do the right thing, but he's not going to give me the satisfaction of telling me that to my face."

The Commodore put his hands behind his back and surveyed the display.

"Situation in Llandudno?" he asked.

"Griffith's forces are either out of the city, surrendered or contained in defensive positions. The Cinnead appear to have pulled back from the last. The shooting has stopped."

"Then it's over. It's actually over."

EB figured the Spacers could have ended it days earlier, if not weeks or months, if they'd actually recognized their power and *used* it. Instead, a lot more people had died to get to this point, and his family had been trapped in a hostile city.

But at least it was over.

Silence slowly spread through the command center, the analysts looking at screens that were showing halted brigades and dug-in battalions...but no fighting.

"Well," EB said, stepping up close to Malone. "Not bad. Now you just have to get them to find an answer that dissatisfies everyone equally."

"The kind of answer we could have found without killing fifty thousand people."

"Yes."

EB knew his answer was harsh, but it was also true. He wasn't going to sugarcoat things for Malone.

"Permission to take my ship and get my damn family back, Commodore?" he asked after thirty seconds of silence.

He figured his odds were only fifty-fifty even at this point, but he *had* to ask.

For a few seconds, he wasn't even sure Malone had heard him, but then the Spacer raised a hand.

"Two conditions," Malone told him. "First, you come back here after. I'll take your word for it, but I want you to return to *Armstrong* once you've picked them up.

"Secondly, I'll need you to wait at least thirty minutes while we put together a task force to accompany you. You're going right to that Siya u Hestî base, aren't you?"

"Yes."

"Then I want you to transport whatever task force I manage to put together down with you. I want to make absolutely certain that all of those goddamn robot tanks are dead. I know someone triggered their suicide function, but killer robots have a *reputation* when it comes to those."

"They do," EB conceded. "I can live with those conditions, Commodore. I've told you already that I'm prepared to pay a fine for breaching the blockade."

They both knew that he'd been paid far more for the mission than Malone was likely to be able to justify fining him—especially now that he'd sounding-boarded his way into helping the man impose peace on his star system.

"Then you have my permission. The task force will join you on your ship in thirty minutes. Be ready to transport them."

"I will."

Thirty minutes gave him time for a quick stop in *Armstrong*'s civil concourse, too. His people could meet him at the ship, but there was something he needed to pick up.

43

ONE OF THE surveillance feeds flashed as a blaster emplacement opened fire. Trace couldn't see who the gunner was shooting at, but that didn't mean there wasn't anyone there.

The Siya u Hestî hadn't tried another rush yet. They were probing, sneaking around the edges and seeing how the freed prisoners reacted. Another car had tried to ram a door, but that one had been remote-controlled.

"You'd think they'd have run away by now," she muttered. "What's in this place that's worth dying for?"

"The evidence that will hang every last one of them," Vexer said. "We didn't give Chey a chance to wipe her records. We have more than enough evidence to identify and jail every member of the Siya u Hestî out there.

"Given that they can't flee the planet, destroying that evidence is the only chance they've got."

Trace figured the gangers could change their identities more easily than they could storm the warehouse, but they seemed to disagree with her.

"We found the fast mover," Harris interrupted. "I don't know how much use it's going to be."

She tossed an image of the aircraft onto the main holodisplay, and even Trace saw her point. It was tiny, with maybe enough room for three people.

"It's just a personal escape craft; we can't move any real number of people out of here with it."

Trace glanced over at Lan and considered making someone take the doctor to, well, *another* doctor. They were asleep now and she kept checking to make sure they were breathing.

"If we had somewhere to take them, we could medevac wounded," Vexer suggested, clearly following the same thought process as Trace. "But we have no idea what's going on in the city, let alone the countryside."

The news feeds they were getting were…almost as confused as Trace's companions. A lot of stuff around Estutmost seemed to have just *stopped*, but no information was being publicly released by the Cinnead or the Board.

"We could…I don't know, *call* Llandudno General?"

Vexer chuckled.

"Maybe. We've got pretty limited network access. There's been enough damage across the city that I'm worried everyone is overwhelmed with casualties too."

With their sensors lost and the AMPs self-destructed, Trace had no visibility more than about a hundred meters from the "liberated" warehouse. The cameras could pick up things down the open streets, but that didn't give her that much information.

She was feeling blind and trapped. The news was chaotic and confused, and no one seemed to know they were there. The only thing keeping her from feeling *alone* and trapped was that Vexer was sitting right next to her, a solid presence radiating calm and parental support.

For having parenthood unexpectedly thrust upon them, both Vexer and EB did pretty well at it in Trace's opinion. The bar was low, given that her comparison was benign neglect from wealthy foster parents, but they cleared it anyway.

"Are they going to be okay?" she murmured to Vexer, still looking at Lan.

"Yes." He smiled at her as she looked at him sharply. "I'm trained as a medic, Trace. I'm checking them regularly. The bleeding has stopped and we've got pressure on the wounds. They're woozy and weak from blood loss; that's all.

"They need rest and food, but they're going to be fine. So are we."

Trace nodded, taking a shaky breath.

"Yeah. We seem to have things in ha—"

Heat and light flared across all of the cameras as a ship appeared in the sky. Trace stared at the camera in shock and surprise—and, after a few seconds, delight.

"That's *Evasion*."

"He made it," Vexer agreed. "But what is…"

The horseshoe part of *Evasion*'s hull swung down into a street, opening enough to disgorge power-armored soldiers. Four by four, they leapt from the starship to the streets and began to spread out, clearly looking for something.

"I don't know and I don't care," Trace told her dad. "Dad-E is here. That's…that's everything!"

BY THE TIME *Evasion* actually landed—a far more complicated process than getting close enough for troops in power armor to jump—Trace and Vexer were outside. Harris was with them, helping Lan walk as they approached their home.

The ship was small enough to fit in a thoroughfare designed to have six trucks going side by side, but it still looked cramped away from proper landing facilities. Trace had watched the landing, and she knew enough to be impressed by the shiphandling skill shown.

"Show-off," Vexer muttered. "I'm a better navigator than him, but he has to show off that he's a better pilot sometimes. I guess."

Trace concealed her amusement. She didn't try to conceal her relief as the ramp extended from the operations hull, and she spotted Ginny and EB leaving the ship.

Reggie was right behind them—or, at least, his power armor was. The gunner owned one of the handful of sets of the armor aboard

Evasion and leaned heavily in to his role as the ship's muscle when he felt it was necessary.

Trace managed to exert self-control for the seconds it took EB to come about halfway down the ramp, then gave up on any semblance of composure. She bolted up the ramp and basically threw herself into her other father's arms.

EB let his breath out in a shocked *oof*, but his arms were around her and holding her tightly as she found herself sobbing into his shoulder.

"We're back together now," he told her. "All of us. I'm sorry I ever left."

"I'm sure it made sense at the time," Lan replied, the doctor looking up at their boss. "It's been a rough few days down here. This is Harris, by the way. She was a Siya u Hestî prisoner that Trace released who decided to stick around and help."

"Em Harris," EB said, nodding slightly to the woman. "From the look of my doctor's face, they're going to fall down if you let them go. Can I get you to take them to their infirmary? I think we'll all be happier if they have access to their medical equipment."

"I can do that."

Ginny stepped forward to guide the woman and Lan back into the ship, leaving Trace and EB and Vexer alone on the ground next to *Evasion*.

"Hey, you," Vexer said quietly. "Trace has had the worst of it, but she's also probably the reason we're all alive. Our daughter did damn well by us."

"I'm guessing she's the one who turned on the combat robots?" EB asked, still holding Trace as she leaned into his shoulder.

She nodded silently.

"And the one who blew them up," Vexer told him. "Guessing that's what the Spacer troopers are for?"

"They wanted to make *very* sure no rogue robots survived on the planet they like."

"They were more rogue than you might think. Trace and one of the Siya u Hestî officers had an override fight that everybody lost. No one was in control of the robots—but Trace found a separate failsafe to take them out."

EB exhaled a sigh and squeezed Trace. She took the silent message and stepped away from him, wiping her eyes as she let her dads embrace.

"I should never have left," EB told them. "But I had some time away from you both to think things through and realize I'm a twit."

He pressed a finger to Vexer's lips before the navigator could say a word.

"You know, I know," he said with a chuckle. "But I think we've made it this far in each other's back pockets, picked up a teenager for ourselves, and I realized I want to make sure you don't go anywhere."

Trace realized what was going on several seconds before Vexer did, she thought, not least because she saw EB take the jewelry box out of his back pocket.

"Vena Dolezal, will you marry me?"

44

A SENSE of normalcy was returning to Estutmost's spaceways. The monitor blockade still existed, but even from *Evasion*'s bridge, EB could see the change in pattern inherent to their current role.

Ships were being inspected to make sure they weren't carrying weapons, but the blockade was no longer complete. Cargo was going in, cargo was coming out.

Not as much of the latter as normal, he figured, but the locals hadn't talked things out solidly enough to get the terraforming bacteria and the crop seeds in the same place yet.

But the conversation was happening. *Armstrong* was now playing host to hundreds of diplomats and negotiators from all three major factions, with the mutineer monitor crews acting as a somewhat neutral fourth faction.

At that moment, EB was leaning back in his chair, flicking through a list of wedding locations in the surrounding star systems. He didn't think that getting married in Estutmost was going to happen, and he had come to the conclusion that he *didn't* want to just get married in *Evasion*'s mess.

There was a very nice mountaintop in Blowry that was currently at the top of his list. There was one other place that would have been giving it a run for his money, except that he'd known that he wasn't going to Icem even before he'd looked at the Black Oak Island Sanctuary.

Black Oak wasn't merely on Trace's homeworld; it was her hometown. She'd grown up in the terraformed bio preserve, and her foster family had lived there. The bio preserve had been the center of the plague that had devastated her generation's parents, hence the expectation that a politician like Sarah Vortani would *have* a foster.

Part of EB very much wanted to meet the Vortanis and give them several pieces of his mind over how they'd treated Trace. The rest of him was well aware that there would be some…interesting legal questions over whether his Nigahog adoption of Trace would hold up in a system where she was legally in someone else's custody.

He figured that the clear and complete disaster the Vortanis had made of raising Trace and the fact that the teenager had ended up trafficked off-world would cover his ass—but he also knew that Sarah Vortani was a member of the planetary parliament.

Power and privilege could often override logic, reason and law.

Not only did Black Oak have the extra weight of being Trace's first home, it *also* had an absolutely gorgeous headland with a Greek-style amphitheater looking out over the sea. Everything about the place appealed to him…except that he didn't want risk any problems with his custody of Trace.

Confirmation bias was a very real thing, though, and thinking about Icem meant he spotted the Icemi courier entering the system before she transmitted. Mailbag couriers served a lot of systems out here, but it was a significantly more ad hoc thing than the multi-system corporate postal services that started to appear in the Rim and were omnipresent in the Fringe and inward toward Sol.

What he *wasn't* expecting, however, was for a transmission to come to *Evasion* from the mailship. There was a back-and-forth confirmation sequence that was entirely automatic, and then a data package downloaded.

EB didn't know *anyone* in Icem who would be trying to reach him. Except, he supposed, potentially the Vortanis if enough information had made its way to them.

Nervously, he activated the message. There was no video attachment, just a data package and a message.

We need to talk. In person. There is unresolved business between us.

Attached are reservations at a restaurant in Icem High Home Station. Be there.

He stared at the message for a long time, then checked the attachment. As promised, it was digital "tickets" for three people to join a reservation at the Glorious Dragoon Restaurant on Icem's main orbital.

And Evridiki Bardacki could think of only one group of people who would want to meet him in Icem, secretively or not.

"Well. Shit."

ABOUT THE AUTHOR

Glynn Stewart is the author of *Starship's Mage*, a bestselling science fiction and fantasy series where faster-than-light travel is possible–but only because of magic. His other works include science fiction series *Duchy of Terra, Castle Federation* and *Vigilante,* as well as the urban fantasy series *ONSET* and *Changeling Blood*.

Writing managed to liberate Glynn from a bleak future as an accountant. With his personality and hope for a high-tech future intact, he lives in Southern Ontario with his partner, their cats, and an unstoppable writing habit.

CREDITS

The following people were involved in making this book:
    Copyeditor: Richard Shealy
    Cover art: Elias Stern
    Typo Hunter Team
    Faolan's Pen Publishing team: Jack, Kate, and Robin.

facebook.com/glynnstewartauthor

SCATTERED STARS

Scattered Stars: Conviction
Conviction
Deception
Equilibrium
Fortitude
Huntress
Prodigal *(upcoming)*

Scattered Stars: Evasion
Evasion
Discretion
Absolution *(upcoming)*

PEACEKEEPERS OF SOL

Raven's Peace
The Peacekeeper Initiative
Raven's Course
Drifter's Folly
Remnant Faction *(upcoming)*

EXILE

Exile
Refuge
Crusade
Ashen Stars: An Exile Novella

CASTLE FEDERATION

Space Carrier Avalon
Stellar Fox
Battle Group Avalon
Q-Ship Chameleon
Rimward Stars
Operation Medusa
A Question of Faith: A Castle Federation Novella

Dakotan Confederacy
Admiral's Oath
To Stand Defiant *(upcoming)*

VIGILANTE
(WITH TERRY MIXON)
Heart of Vengeance
Oath of Vengeance

**Bound By Stars: A Vigilante Series
(With Terry Mixon)**
Bound By Law
Bound by Honor
Bound by Blood

TEER AND KARD
Wardtown
Blood Ward

CHANGELING BLOOD
Changeling's Fealty
Hunter's Oath
Noble's Honor
Fae, Flames & Fedoras: A Changeling Blood Novella

ONSET
ONSET: To Serve and Protect
ONSET: My Enemy's Enemy
ONSET: Blood of the Innocent
ONSET: Stay of Execution
Murder by Magic: An ONSET Novella

STAND ALONE NOVELS & NOVELLAS
Children of Prophecy
City in the Sky
Excalibur Lost: A Space Opera Novella
Balefire: A Dark Fantasy Novella